THE MAGIC THAT REMAINS

"What *is* this?" Dee's eyes widened, pupils dark, full of the same overpowering need as Cenrick. "What's happening to me?"

He swallowed. "I don't know. Maybe you'd better just drive."

"Drive? I can't. I can't concentrate on the road. All of a sudden, all I can think about is how large you are." She took a deep, shuddering breath. "How tightly corded your muscles. You're...you're *beautiful,* Cenrick of Rune, Fae prince. And I want you."

MISSING MAGIC

KAREN WHIDDON

LOVE SPELL   NEW YORK CITY

LOVE SPELL®

November 2006

Published by

Dorchester Publishing Co., Inc.
200 Madison Avenue
New York, NY 10016

ISBN 0-505-52642-5

The name "Love Spell" and its logo are trademarks of Dorchester Publishing Co., Inc.

Printed in the United States of America.

Visit us on the web at www.dorchesterpub.com.

To all my family,
because they love having books dedicated to them.
Mom, Dad, Scott, Shawn, Sharon, Alex, and Stephanie.

To my husband, Lonnie, because he's the best.

And lastly, special thanks
to my critique partner, Anna Adams.
She reads a lot of dreck and helps me
turn it into something readable.

MISSING MAGIC

PROLOGUE

The summons came with the dawn, at that precise moment when the sun burst bloodred over the horizon. *Come with me.* Prince Cenrick of Rune sat up in his bed, rubbing his eyes and biting back a curse. He'd been up late, having struggled to complete his interpretation of an ancient runic text. He'd managed three hours sleep, at best.

Come with me.

The voice belonged to Kyslandra, King Roark's messenger, a sylph. As his eyes adjusted to the dim light, Cenrick saw her hovering in the air above his bed. Drifting on a nonexistent breeze, she dissipated and reformed, riding some unknown otherworldly currents. Watching him, her eyes glowed scarlet in the darkness, changing to sapphire, then emerald, then gold.

"Give me a minute," he told her, tossing back the gossamer sheet and reaching for his robe.

She hissed in disapproval at the delay, but she waited while he dragged the robe over his head. Still

1

groggy, he winked at her, then made his way to the crystal sink and splashed icy water on his face.

Come with me. This time, irritation laced her whisper.

"I'm ready," he said. Though he—and everyone else in the castle—knew the way to the king's chambers, he judged it best not to annoy Kyslandra further. She'd been known to vent her ire in an earsplitting wail that turned the blood to ice. That was the last thing he needed after less than three hours of sleep. No thanks.

Trudging the deserted hallways with the sylph drifting on ahead, he tried to think of what he'd possibly done to cause this early-morning summons. He came up blank. When they finally reached the massive obsidian crystal doors of the king's bedchamber, Cenrick reached for the silver handle and the sylph vanished in a puff of energy.

"Come in," a voice rang out. King Roark sounded tired, more exhausted than Cenrick had ever heard.

Entering and closing the door behind him, ducking his head to avoid the door frame as he always did, Cenrick was startled to see the Mage of Rune was also present. Mort looked wide awake, his lined face uncharacteristically worried. Tinth, his pet hawk—some said his familiar—perched on one shoulder.

Tension, worry and unease made the atmosphere heavy. Though only early autumn, the morning air carried enough chill for the room's occupants to have lit a fire in the crystal hearth.

"Father?" Cenrick froze, an awful thought striking him. "What's wrong? Is it Alrick? Has something happened to my brother?" Ever since his twin had bested a powerful mage from the future and decided to permanently live among humans with his wife, Carly, and soon-to-be-born son, Cenrick had worried. Alrick hadn't traveled to earth as often as Cenrick. Preferring to remain in Rune and live by the old ways, Alrick hadn't known nearly as much about humans or their customs as Cenrick.

King Roark stroked his beard. Though his years numbered well over three hundred, he still retained the handsome visage of younger man. He wore the snowy white facial hair only for effect. The same went for the diamond studs sparkling in his ears.

"No, no. Of course not." He squinted at his son. "Your brother is fine. You've gone across the veil often enough to know what it's like. I don't understand what you fear."

Rune was vastly different than the human world. In the many occasions Cenrick had visited, he'd seen enough of the vicious and vile side of human nature to know exactly what some men were capable of. Even against Fae. He would never understand why so many of his kind wanted to live there.

Exhaling, he tried to focus. "If not Alrick, then what?"

Mort the Mage touched his arm. "It's Talmick, your third cousin. He's in trouble again."

"Talmick? I thought he was past all that." Looking from one to the other, Cenrick wondered at the two older men's solemn faces. In the past, Talmick's scrapes had been minor. But then, Fae tended to judge less harshly than humans. "How serious is this?"

"Very serious."

"Father, I know I haven't seen Mick in a couple of years, but you know how close we were as children. While I'll admit he is a bit mischievous, he means no harm. Like most of our kind, he merely likes to have a bit of fun among humans."

Instead of lightening, King Roark's frown deepened. "That's what makes this so horrible. This is not one of his usual pranks."

Cenrick crossed his arms. "Last I heard, ever since he met someone, he's settled down."

"So I'd believed." King Roark sighed. "I've summoned him, ordered him to return to Rune from the human world, but he ignores me."

"What's he done this time?"

"If Mick is not the cause of this . . ." For a moment, Mort the Mage appeared at a loss for words. "If Mick is not the cause of this, then he is in great danger. Several Fae, all of them Mick's friends, have recently returned to Rune from the human realm. They've been"—he swallowed—"damaged."

"Damaged? I don't understand."

"They are soulless." Taking up where the mage left off, King Roark twisted his hands together. "Only their bodies returned. That which made them Fae is gone. Their personality, intellect, spirit—all vanished."

"What of their magic?"

"That too has disappeared."

"How?"

"We don't know. The Oracle has tried to discover the answer, and failed."

The Oracle failed? Cenrick wasn't aware such a thing could happen. She was the most powerful being in Rune.

Cenrick straightened. "What do you want me to do?"

"You must travel to the human world and find out what's going on," Mort said. "A scholar such as you is needed now." Tinth screeched in agreement.

"However," King Roark warned, stepping forward, worry darkening his gaze, "you must not place yourself in direct danger. As of yet, the Oracle has not been able to heal the others."

Horrified, Cenrick gulped. "You're saying there's a possibility these Fae might remain . . . husks?"

Neither the king nor the mage answered. Not good.

Cenrick looked from one man to the other. "And Mick?"

"We think it best if you do not let him know of your arrival, at least until you've ascertained more about the situation."

"I understand."

The king nodded. "Go with Mort. He will prepare you for the journey across the veil."

CHAPTER ONE

Murphy's Law? Dee Bishop wrapped her hands around a steaming mug of coffee and took a deep sip, welcoming the heat that seared her mouth and throat. They ought to rename it Bishop's Law after her. The way her life had been going lately, that would be particularly apt.

She squinted as the cuckoo clock—her latest garage sale find—chimed six times. As in six o'clock. In the morning. Who in their right mind was up on a Saturday morning at such an ungodly hour? She ought to be curled up in her bed still asleep.

But sleep didn't come easily these days. Not since she'd been called into the police chief's office a week ago and placed on suspension. She now had the dubious distinction of being the first female officer on the South Worth Police Department to be investigated for misconduct. Her, the most law-abiding cop she knew!

Facing Police Chief Ferguson while he outlined the charges against her had been one of the hardest things she'd ever done. Even though they were patently false—of course they were false—she could feel her hard won respectability seeping away like sand from a broken hourglass. And the disappointment in her mentor's gray eyes had been more than she could bear, making her feel like the awkward teenager she'd once been, pretending not to care as yet another foster family declined to adopt her.

Back straight, head held high, face expressionless, she'd marched from her office to her desk, retrieved her service revolver and turned it in. They hadn't asked for her badge. Not yet. That would only come if they turned the investigation over to a grand jury and she was indicted. It wasn't fair! As one of the city's few female officers, she'd always been careful to do everything by the book. But now everything was in jeopardy.

Worse yet, someone from the department had leaked the story to the press. Dee had made both the five o'clock news and the front page of the newspaper. Being the first female officer hired in South Worth had been a big deal in this good-ole-boy town; her disgrace was an even bigger story. Still, as she had while growing up, she'd refused to cry.

Things had got worse. That night, when she'd sought out her fiancé Peter for solace, he'd unceremoniously dumped her. He'd claimed the cloud hanging over her had nothing to do with his decision, but she'd known he was lying. A respectable accountant, Peter had never been entirely comfortable with Dee's lack of family or history. Her suspension was apparently more than he could handle.

Still, she'd shed no tears, even if her nickname around the South Worth Police Department, "Lucky," now seemed more of a cruel joke.

Just when it seemed she'd hit rock bottom, the other shoe had dropped. Dropped? No, *stomped* on her. The one person she could always count on, her best friend and the brother of her heart, Mick Morsi, had told her to stay away. Over the phone, no less. He hadn't even had the courtesy to brush her off to her face. That was when tears had finally filled her eyes, and she'd stammered her disbelief.

Had the world gone totally insane? She pinched herself, certain she had to be dreaming. Mick had always been there for her. Always. It was inconceivable that he wasn't there now when she needed him the most.

They'd met as kids, orphans farmed out to Trixon's Childrens Home, and immediately become fast friends. Mick had taken on the role of her protector, defending the younger, smaller Dee from various predators, both adult and child; and when he'd decided he wanted to make protecting children his fulltime occupation, Dee had followed him into the police force.

Mick had been on a mission, and he'd had a dream. Dee had tried to share it, and they'd made a pact as officers: If they could save just one child, prevent one little girl or boy from enduring the unspeakable horrors they themselves had endured, everything they'd gone through would be worth it.

Now all of that was threatened, and Dee didn't even know why or how.

Mick bailing on her was the final straw. She knew Mick, and he wasn't like that. Something had to be wrong. Something so terrible that Mick didn't want her to know. And so, with empty days looming before her, Dee had decided to make it her mission to learn what the problem was, no matter the cost. After all, she and Mick had always said there wasn't any trouble that the two of them couldn't handle.

Again, she called Jack, Mick's significant other, even though he hadn't answered the phone on any of her previous attempts. This time he picked up on the third ring.

"Dee?" His normally ebullient voice sounded hoarse and congested. "Did Mick ask you to call me?"

"No, but he's *why* I'm calling."

"Do you know where he is?" The anxiety in Jack's tone told her he didn't.

"I'm looking for him." She explained, "I may have to go look for him tonight when he's spinning records."

"He quit that job," Jack said, shocking her. "He's really changed, Dee. I'm worried."

"I'm worried too."

"He's—" A fit of coughing interrupted him, leaving him gasping for air.

"Are you all right?"

"I've been better," he admitted. "But we don't need to talk about me. I was hoping you could shed some light on what's up with Mick. Other than taking me to my doctor's appointments, I haven't seen much of him lately. It's like he's . . . pulling away."

Her heart sank. "It's Saturday. He always stays at your place on weekends."

"Not anymore." The raw anguish in his voice broke her heart. "Though he's promised to stop by tonight for dinner."

Another coughing spell made her wince.

"I'll come by soon, I promise. I've got to go."

"All right. Back to bed for me." He hung up.

Since the conversation had startled her and she didn't know what else to do, she got in her car and drove around for hours looking for Mick. She checked all of his favorite hangouts with no success. Finally she grabbed a late lunch at Vittoro's Italian Restaurant and headed home. As she was pulling into her parking lot, a glimmer of a plan occurred to her. She knew just what she'd do.

That night, as soon as the moon rose, she headed over to Mick's place, knowing he wouldn't be home. She still had his key since he hadn't asked for it back yet. After parking several houses down, she strolled casually up the sidewalk toward his place. As a cop, she knew she'd arouse less suspicion if she acted as though she had every right to be there.

From the street, the place appeared deserted. Not a single light illuminated any of the windows.

Dee laughed under her breath. You'd think as a cop, Mick would at least have a security system. But, no. It had been a running argument between them for years. Now Mick's distaste for alarms of all kinds would make her job as snoop a lot easier.

She slipped around the side of the house. A light came on above the garage. Motion sensors. Those were new. She froze, holding her breath. No movement from inside.

10

Exhaling in a loud puff of relief, she rolled her tense neck, trying to relax.

Amazing, she, who normally spent her life on the right side of the law, was entering Mick's house uninvited. How ironic that now, after she'd been unjustly accused of all sorts of illegal activity, she actually was doing something illegal.

Well, sort of illegal.

Mick had always told her she was welcome to drop by anytime. Previously she'd enjoyed carte blanche at his place. And so she patted her pocket and told herself it wasn't really breaking and entering if she had a key. Even if she had to dodge motion-sensing lights and scurry like a criminal through the shadows.

Another light flashed on. Cursing under her breath, Dee froze. When had Mick installed these spotlights on the side of the house? Last time she'd been out here, only a week or so ago, he'd had just the usual front and back porch lights, nothing more.

The bulb went off, plunging her back into darkness. She decided to move outside the perimeter of the sensor to keep it from flaring to life again, so she skirted the edge of the unfenced yard, her heartbeat loud in her ears. From now on she'd be more careful.

From now on? As if she were planning on searching Mick's house on a regular basis. She didn't even know what she was looking to find, other than why he of all people had also turned against her. The scent of the neighbor's freshly cut lawn brought back memories of cookouts and Sunday afternoon walk-fests. Together, the two orphans had formed the family luck had denied them. That bolstered her courage. Family always stuck together, didn't they?

Quietly Dee let herself through the back door, wincing as the motion sensor flashed on. Heart pounding, she waited until the light clicked back off; then she took deep breaths, trying to steady her nerves. No matter what anyone else might say, she wasn't a criminal.

Once her eyes adjusted to the dim light in Mick's kitchen, she steeled herself to methodically search the house. She knew it as well as her own. But what kind of clues she was seeking? Anything out of the ordinary, she supposed. If she found something suggesting Mick had been taken over by pod people from outer space, she wouldn't be surprised. Not with the way her life had been going. Not with the way Mick was acting.

She found nothing of the sort. The kitchen was neat as a pin, giving no hints. Neither did the den or the dining room. Out of habit Dee doubled back and checked the inside of the refrigerator. A half empty bottle of Chardonnay, a hunk of Brie, and a bowl of tossed salad were the only contents. So like Mick.

Smiling faintly, Dee made her way down the hall into the bedroom. At the doorway, she stopped cold. What the—?

Unlike the rest of the house, Mick's bedroom looked like a tornado had ripped through. Clothes were strewn all around: on the bed, the desk and the chair, the dresser—and worse; the floor. Mick's open closet revealed empty hangers and shirts hanging cockeyed. This was wrong. Very wrong.

Of all the things Mick was most careful with, his off-the-rack designer clothes ranked highest. The man's closet had always been a source of wonder to Dee. He organized the shirts by fabric and color and season. Though she loved shoes and her own collection was impressive, Mick's organizational skills had her beat. His shoes—Dee glanced at the closet bottom and barely suppressed a hiss—had always been arranged in boxes, by color and descending date of purchase. Not now. Now his shoes, like his clothes, were piled willy-nilly in an unorganized heap, out of their boxes.

The Mick she knew and loved would never have let brown leather be scuffed by black. And the suede . . . She shuddered.

All right, here was her first clue that something was out of the ordinary. But what did it mean?

And that smell . . . Sniffing, Dee followed her nose into the bathroom. The overpowering scent of Mick's many expensive colognes, all mixed together, made her cough and sneeze. What had happened in here?

Flipping on the light switch, she saw that Mick—or someone—had smashed every single bottle of cologne into his bathtub; shards of glass filled the white ceramic tub with deadly glitter. And as the jumble of scents would have hidden the stink of anything, including a decomposing body, the cop in her began looking for exactly that.

She checked the linen closet and the commode room, but found nothing. No body. A search of both the guest bedroom and Mick's exercise room yielded no cadavers, either. Dee breathed a bit easier, wondering at her paranoia. At least Mick wasn't dead. Still, something definitely was wrong. She just didn't know what. The Mick she'd known for over ten years would never have let his bedroom and bathroom remain in such awful disarray.

Back in the living room, she turned in a slow circle, looking for anything out of the ordinary. The dim lighting made sight difficult, and since the room faced the street, she didn't dare turn on a lamp. Every book, every framed photo, ever bit of bric-a-brac, seemed perfectly in place.

But, wait! She leaned closer. Was that . . . dust? When she ran her finger across the top of the coffee table, she left a trail. Dust. It was another thing over which Mick went ballistic. Around the station, the guys jokingly called him Mister Clean.

Everyone loved Mick, though. Despite his almost feminine beauty and unbelievable good luck, he was warm and caring, a cop who followed the rules yet somehow still managed to see the good in everyone. He had about him a sense of otherworldly courtliness, as though he'd been born in the wrong place and time. Dee had always envied this in her friend. Knowing she was ordinary, she secretly hoped some of his specialness would rub off on her.

She was making progress. So far her little foray had revealed three things—a dusty living room, a bedroom that looked like it belonged to a drunken fraternity student, and a bathtub full of cologne. But all of this meant . . . what?

Pressing the tiny button to light up her watch dial, she saw she'd been inside Mick's house a little over twenty minutes. She blew her breath out in frustration. All she'd learned so far confirmed only what she already knew: Something was badly wrong in Mick's life. After seeing his house, if she hadn't known better, she'd think he was the one whose life had gone down the toilet instead of hers.

About to leave, Dee paused. There was one other place to find clues, one other place. She'd nearly forgotten to search. The garage. It was a monument to organization. Mick had hired carpenters to build a workbench along the length of one wall, and tools he never used were hung on pegboard hooks there, arranged by color, size, and intent. A wall lined with metal shelves held an array of household cleansers, paints, and other assorted items, and in the left bay was Mick's prize possession, a fully restored 1967 Corvette Stingray. Mick only drove the car once a week, and annually in South Worth's Fourth of July parade. The rest of the time, the machine was kept highly polished and well covered. If the garage was out of order, she'd know Mick had gone off the deep end.

And then what?

Walking through Mick's small laundry room, she swallowed and opened the door to the garage. Squinting, she inhaled. Normal garage smell. That was good. Since there were no windows in the big, automatic door, she wondered if she dared flick on the light.

A scratching sound from the other side of Mick's car convinced her. If a rat had somehow gotten in here, the last thing she wanted to do was stumble over it. A brave cop she might be, but not when it came to rats. Rats ranked right up there with spiders and snakes. One, two . . . lights on.

Blinking in the sudden brightness, she saw the Corvette was parked in its normal spot, still covered with its custom-made blue cover. However, the work-bench, normally a pristine area more for show than actual work, was another story. Tools were scattered haphazardly, some of them covered with grease and dirt. The remains of a half-eaten sandwich that looked to be days, possibly weeks old, sat next to an empty bottle of . . . Budweiser?

Mick rarely drank beer. On the few occasions when he did, he preferred exotic dark beer from Germany. Jack, his significant other, had been known to indulge occasionally, but since he'd been ill Mick always went to his condo.

Dee moved around the bench, inspecting the mess, touching nothing, when another sound made her spin. *Rat?* She didn't want to find it, scare it, or kill it. All she wanted was to avoid the furry beast. As long as the rodent left her alone, she could safely promise she'd do the same.

Shuddering, she checked the floor. So far, so good. No sign of animal droppings. With a quick glance at the metal shelving, she determined nothing was out of place there, either. The only abnormality she noticed was the stacked cases of motor oil. Mick had always kept some on hand for the Vette, but he'd gone overboard. There had to be seven or eight cases! Way more than he'd usually buy.

What else? She needed to finish her inspection of the garage and get out.

The car. Mick's baby. She had to check the car.

At first glance, the Corvette looked tightly covered. A closer inspection revealed the tarp was askew, one corner of the front end folded up, revealing part of the shiny chrome bumper. Gingerly Dee lifted the cover the rest of the way.

Glossy paint, freshly waxed. The car, at least, remained exactly as it had been the last time she'd seen it. But was that good or bad? She still didn't know what to make of her discoveries.

Tucking the final edge into place, Dee bent low to tug the last part down—and met the gaze of the strangely dressed man crouched on the floor on the other side of the car.

CHAPTER TWO

Caught! Prince Cenrick of Rune froze, wondering if he should start talking or prepare to fight. But then, judging from the demeanor he'd observed as she'd stealthily searched Mick's garage, the slender auburn-haired woman had as little right to be there as he.

"Who are you and what are you doing here?" She gazed steadily at him, her voice cool and flat. Despite his size, she exhibited no fear. Rather, she rocked back on her heels and appeared ready to fight.

Impressed, Cenrick rose from his crouch and eyed the human woman. He made a rapid threat assessment. He saw no visible weapon, though metal shovels and tools hung on the wall easily within her reach. But if she was unaware he was Fae, she'd have no obvious reason to reach for those. And, in his experience, women rarely acted as warriors, despite their bluster. He judged her low risk.

Then why, when he was at least twice her weight, was she so bold?

18

"I might ask you the same question," he replied.

"You don't belong here. Breaking and entering is against the law."

He tilted his head, studying her. She was beautiful in the earthy way of human women. Even in this dim light, her hair gleamed with hints of fire and her eyes were the color of amber. He gave her a hint of a smile, extending the proverbial olive branch, and guessed: "Then you have broken the law as well."

Glaring, she acknowledged the truth of his comment with a dip of her chin. "So we're both trespassing. But Mick is my friend. I'm here because I'm worried about him. Your turn. Who are you and what are you doing here?"

Opening his mouth to speak, suddenly Cenrick found the room began to spin. Vertigo. Bracing his hand against a wooden workbench, he took a deep breath to steady himself. His legs felt weak, as though they could give out at any moment. "I . . ." Blinking, he struggled to focus on her question. "Mick's my distant cousin. We're worried about him too."

"Your cousin?" Her skeptical tone told him she didn't believe. "You look nothing like him. What kind of cousin sneaks around and hides in the garage?"

How to explain? He tried to keep his gaze on her face while the ground dipped underneath him. Clearing his suddenly dry throat, he tried to think, to dredge up a combination of words and string them together into a coherent sentence.

Since Fae couldn't lie, he countered her question with one of his own. "You claim to be his friend, yet

19

you're doing the same thing—skulking around without permission. How well do you actually know Mick?"

"Well enough to doubt that you're his family. I've known him a long time, and he's never mentioned you. Not once."

"We haven't seen each other in years."

"You're not his cousin." She crossed her arms. "I know all about Mick's lifestyle, so you don't have to pretend. Are you one of his . . . friends? You look like his type."

Flabbergasted, Cenrick started to shake his head. Never in his life had he been mistaken for gay. Despite Rune's relaxed views and easy sexuality, he'd never been attracted to men. Oblivious to his shock, the woman continued.

"Are you the guy Mick dumped when he hooked up with Jack? Are you the one who smashed his cologne bottles and messed up his clothes?"

Dumped? Hooked up with who? Since his legs still felt shaky, Cenrick kept his grip on the workbench and held up his other hand. "Hold on. The answer is no to both your questions. I prefer women, I'm not into men, and I don't know Jack. Furthermore, I just got here. I haven't even been in the house yet. I haven't smashed anything."

"You started with the garage?" She looked dubious.

"Yes." He swayed. Things were getting more and more blurry. He couldn't seem to focus.

She squinted at him. "Are you all right?"

Without thinking he nodded, but again the walls

seemed to dip and ripple. Grabbing onto the work-bench with both hands, he waited until everything steadied. "I'm not sure what's wrong. I . . ." He lost his train of thought.

She prompted him, "You were about to explain why, instead of calling Mick to let him know you're here, you entered unannounced and are snooping around his house."

"Was I?" He took a moment to collect himself. Finally he decided on the truth. "Something's going on with Mick, and I needed to make sure I had all the facts before I confronted him. I was asked to come here and check things out, without him knowing."

"Your family sent you to *spy* on him?"

"You could put it that way." Cenrick wanted to sit down before his legs collapsed, but unless he dropped to the floor, that wasn't a possibility. "Aren't you doing the same thing?"

Worrying her bottom lip, she gave a hesitant nod. "Yes, I'm on a fact-finding mission, same as you. Something *is* wrong with Mick," she agreed.

Cenrick's lightheadedness was growing worse. This was extremely odd as Fae were rarely sick and, when they were, healed rapidly. "Maybe we can work together on this. Help each other out. Share information."

"Work together?" She frowned. "I don't even know you."

His head felt like it was being pounded by a sledge-hammer. He shrugged. "I don't know you any better than you know me."

"Which proves my point." Her sigh seemed extraordinarily loud. "If you really were related to Mick, you'd know me. And you'd know Mick doesn't have any cousins."

Cenrick couldn't focus, couldn't concentrate, could barely breathe. His head felt like it was about to explode. "What do you mean, he doesn't have any cousins?"

Arms folded across her chest, the woman glared at him. "Because Mick is an orphan, just like me."

"An orphan? No, he's—"

They both froze as the automatic garage door made a sound. With a creak, the gears began to turn, chains clinked and the door slowly began to rise.

"Busted," the woman hissed, looking around frantically for a place to hide.

Cenrick cursed. With the way everything was spinning, he couldn't run. But he couldn't let Mick see him. Not yet.

"Come on!" Grabbing his arm, the woman yanked him down with her behind a bulky shape that Cenrick thought must be a covered car. Even though he'd worn his gloves as a precaution, he was careful to keep his distance from the metal.

The woman kept her hold on his arm. Oddly enough, down on the concrete floor, Cenrick found his equilibrium returned in a rush. This headache vanished as though it had never been. Headlights swept the garage as a large vehicle pulled into the driveway.

Beside him, hand still on his arm, the woman didn't move. Cenrick was glad. His heart was pounding so loudly he was afraid Mick would hear. He wished he had something to cover himself, aware that to his cousin he'd be easily visible. After all, Mick was Fae. Most Fae could spot another Fae's aura from fifty yards away. Cenrick could only hope the metal of the covered car would help obscure him.

Squatting, he pondered. An orphan? He shook his head. Since Fae couldn't lie, he wondered how Mick had managed such an outrageous story. And for what purpose?

The new vehicle parked outside the garage. Both its front doors and one back opened. Three people got out. Cenrick squinted and made out one Fae. Mick. But Mick's aura was surprisingly faint. The others were human, he decided.

"Get into the house." It was a female voice, new, pitched low, and it carried an unmistakable air of authority. "It's dangerous out here."

"Someone will have to help me." Mick's voice sounded weak and annoyed. Not like Mick at all.

"Something's wrong with him," came a whisper in Cenrick's ear. The woman he was hiding with. "And that's not his car."

"Shhh." Cenrick lifted a warning finger to his lips. Still crouched low, he continued to peer out.

"I don't see him," his companion persisted, her low voice worried.

"There." Cenrick touched her arm. "Look."

A blond woman and a muscular, dark-haired man came into view, both helping to support a taller and more slender man. Mick. Mick staggered slightly and looked paler than normal. Was he drunk, drugged, or merely ill? Or was this the result of whatever was stealing Fae souls?

"Look at him." Echoing his thoughts, Cenrick's companion sounded worried. "What's wrong with him?"

Cenrick shook his head in warning. Making a deliberate effort to soften the harsh sound of his breathing, he tried to make himself blend with the cement floor. Though Mick appeared to be the only Fae, and, thus, the only one capable of noticing his aura, he didn't want to take any chances. Best to err on the side of caution.

Evidently the woman beside him felt the same. Her hand still on his arm, she held herself motionless, watching the evolving tableau with narrowed eyes. The only sounds were the first man's footsteps, the shuffle of Mick's unsteady feet, and the staccato click of the blonde's high heels. Someone—Mick?—coughed.

The door into the house squeaked as it opened. The last person through, the blond woman punched a button and closed the garage.

Once the trio was gone, Cenrick's companion sat up, inhaling sharply. Cenrick saw a glint of silver. He realized with shock that she held a pistol. A revolver. A metal weapon. Which explained her earlier lack of fear. Despite himself, he recoiled.

"What?" Again, her amber eyes narrowed. "Don't tell me you're afraid of guns."

Already regretting his instinctive movement, he

24

jerked his head in a quick nod. "Not afraid. Wary. And with good reason. Where did you get that?"

"It's mine." The set of her chin was determined. "They took my service revolver, but this is my personal gun."

"Do you know how to use it?"

"Of course. I'm a cop, after all. Just like Mick." She got to her feet and, keeping a death grip on his sleeve, moved forward. "Come on."

"What are you doing?"

Without looking at him, she reached for the doorknob into the house. "I've had enough of this cloak-and-dagger stuff. If Mick's in some kind of trouble, I want to help him. I'm going in."

Despite the gun, despite the chill the sight of so much deadly metal brought him, Cenrick dug in his heels. "Wait. You need to calm down. Think for a minute. You might be a cop, but no crime has been committed." He knew this from his addiction to human television, especially the *Law & Order* shows— all of them.

To his relief, his companion hesitated. "You know, you're right. I can't go charging in there, weapon drawn." She reholstered her gun, and he breathed easier. "But damned if I'm letting them hurt Mick."

Letting him go, the woman marched over to the door at the back of the garage and opened it. Outside, the motion sensor activated. Dizziness rushed back, making Cenrick stagger as he tried to follow.

"Where . . . where are you going?"

"To the front door." Her cat eyes reflected the illumination. "I want to talk to Mick. I'm his friend. They can't turn me away." And she marched off, leaving Cenrick to chase after her.

Outside, he could breathe easier. The night air had grown slightly cooler, and the breeze carried the scent of flowers. His equilibrium partly returned. He looked up in time to see the woman vanish around the side of the house.

Because he had no choice, he went after her. He didn't even know this woman, but he might have to protect her. Such was his code. So he kept to the shadows where he had a clear view of the front door in case she needed him.

She pressed the doorbell. When the door opened, she stepped forward as though she meant to force her way in. A huge man blocked her, speaking in too low of a voice for Cenrick to hear what he said.

"I want to see Mick," she said. Her voice carried. "I'm not leaving until I talk to him."

The man stepped aside. She entered the house, the door closing behind her. Cenrick waited.

Though it seemed like an eternity, in reality less than five minutes passed before the door opened and she stepped back outside, her rigid shoulders and grim expression telling him of her anger. She hit the sidewalk at a fast walk, heading down the street and away from him. Cenrick jogged after her.

"What happened?" he asked.

She gave him a sharp glance. "She won't even let me talk to him."

"She?"

"The blond woman we saw. The one that's supposedly his girlfriend." Scorn curled her lip. "She said he was sick and couldn't come out of his room. When I tried to push past her, arguing that I should go see him, that goon blocked my way."

"Did he hurt you?"

"He didn't lay a hand on me." Her tone indicated she almost wished he had tried.

"Come on." Taking her arm, Cenrick steered her away from the house. Oddly enough, with each step he took he felt better. The dizzy feeling, the way his thoughts had felt disjointed, vanished. What was in that house?

A sound behind them made him turn. "Wait. What's that?" Cenrick said.

"Mick! He's calling my name." Pulling her arm free, the woman started back.

Cenrick ducked behind a massive pecan tree.

"Dee?" Mick appeared at the end of the driveway. Hands on his hips, he peered left, then right, finally catching sight of her hurrying toward him. "Stop right there."

She stopped, maybe twenty feet away. "Mick? Are you all right?"

"I'm fine." He glared at her. "I don't know what you're trying to pull, but I asked you to leave me alone. Go away!" he said.

"But—"

"No." He held up his hand. "Give me back my key."

Silently, she fumbled in her pocket and then tossed a key at him. He caught it neatly, closing his hand around the plastic part.

"Thank you. Now go away. Get out of here." He

turned and made his way slowly back up the driveway. A second later, the front door slammed.

The instant he was gone, the woman named Dee's shoulders slumped. She ran her fingers through her already disheveled hair, then turned and trudged back to where Cenrick waited.

"I can't believe the way he's acting," she grumbled, muttering to herself. "We grew up together, for Pete's sake. Not only that, we work with each other." She cast another look back at the house. "Or we did."

"What do you mean?" Cenrick asked. She looked at him like she'd forgotten he was there.

"It's a long story."

"I'd like to hear it."

She swallowed. "Yeah, well . . ." She sighed. "I've been put on leave as a precursor to being fired," she admitted. He could tell it cost her a lot to say the words.

"Being a cop is all I ever wanted. I was good, too." Her sharp look dared him to dispute her. "That's why I don't understand how anyone could believe the charges against me. They know me, respect me. Those charges are patently false. All the guys know I wouldn't do anything like that."

He studied her. "Is what they think important to you?"

"It's not only that." She bit her lip. "But, yes. Losing their high opinion hurts most of all."

"What were you accused of?"

As if he'd slapped her, she immediately withdrew. "I'd rather not go into that now. After all, I hardly even know you." Casting another look toward the house, she winced. "Those curtains just twitched. They're watching the front yard to make sure I don't come back." She turned and hit a button on her key ring, and a car parked several spots down made a noise. Its lights flashed.

"I'm out of here. Nice to meet you, and best of luck with your investigation or whatever it is." She walked off, heading for her car.

She was leaving?

"Wait."

Glancing at him over her shoulder, she hesitated. Barely. "Why?"

How could he explain to her that some gut instinct told him they could help each other? And that, being Fae, he always trusted his instincts.

"I need all the help I can get." He gave her a long look. "And you, I suspect, could use another friend."

She narrowed her eyes but didn't deny it. He admired her for that.

"Come on. Let's go someplace where we can talk."

"I don't even know your name."

"I'm Cenrick."

Her eyes narrowed. "That's an odd name."

With a shrug and a smile he acknowledged her words. "And you are . . . ?"

"Dee. Dee Bishop." Reluctance colored her voice.

"Pleased to meet you, Dee. Please hear me out before you make a decision."

Though she shot him a look laced with skepticism, she nodded. "Fine. If you can find some normal cloth-

29

ing you can follow me, and we'll go to that new coffee shop at the corner of Precinct Line and Main." Looking up and down the nearly deserted street, she cocked her head. "Where's your car?"

"I don't have a car, and these are all the clothes I have." He talked fast, hoping he could win her over before she decided he was a total crackpot. "We can take a walk. Talk. Decide if we want to work together."

Her frown deepened. Despite her displeasure, with her soft auburn hair and creamy skin, she was a very pretty woman. "I don't know . . ."

"For Mick," he added. "We both care about him, both want to find out what's going on. And"—he tacked on what he hoped would be the coup de grâce—"you have your revolver, after all. You're safe from me."

That convinced her. Relocking her car, she went with him.

He'd noticed a park a block over. Once they reached it, he took a seat on one of the stone benches. A nearby streetlight provided ample illumination.

Facing him, the woman crossed her arms. "All right, buddy. Talk. Your story has too many holes. Even if Mick *had* family, which he doesn't, no true relative would be skulking around in the garage. Explain yourself—and this better be good."

How much could he tell her? Though Fae could not lie, they could present partial truths, which sometimes worked just as well.

Her frown grew. "Damn it. Mick has been acting—"

Staring down into her suspicious face, he sighed. "My father thinks Mick might be involved in something . . . wrong."

"Wrong? Wrong how?"

He scratched his neck, aware he had to be careful. "There have been instances of people in our, er, family having something unspeakable done to them. Their brains have been . . . altered."

"That doesn't make sense. Explain."

He spread his arms. "I can't. We're not even sure how it's been done."

"And you seriously think Mick is behind this?"

"Not I. My father. And his advisor."

"Advisor? You talk like you're in the government or something."

"In a way I am. Which is another reason why I don't think Mick's involved. He knows better."

She started to comment, then shook her head, apparently having decided to let her questions on that topic go. For now.

"Mick wouldn't do anything without a reason." Her voice was instant, totally certain. "He's a cop."

"My father says everything points to him."

Chewing on her thumbnail, Dee Bishop considered his words. "But you don't believe it? Why are you here?"

"To find out the truth. There's even the possibility he's in danger. If he's involved, that is. I know my cousin." "Could he have been brainwashed?" Dee asked at last.

"Possibly."

She nodded. "He's not acting normal, certainly," she repeated. She stopped, swallowed, then lifted her chin and decided, "Something is definitely not right with him, and I want to learn why."

"Has anything changed in his life recently?" Cenrick asked.

"The major thing is that woman. You saw her."

"The tall blonde?"

"Yes. One of the other guys in the squad room said she and Mick were all over each other the other day. That would be different."

"Yeah, since Mick doesn't like women," Cenrick agreed.

"Right." Dee heaved a sigh.

Cenrick shook his head. "I knew Mick favors men, but I wasn't aware he'd gone public with it. I always assumed that with his job . . ."

Dee nodded. "He kept it quiet. A lot of the guys in the police department would be really surprised to know."

Cenrick regarded her thoughtfully. "Okay, then we need to check on the woman—where she came from, how he met her. Is she living with him?"

"I don't know." Dee cracked her knuckles, the sound loud enough to temporarily stop the crickets. Eyeing him, she cocked her head, as though considering some deep subject. He waited. After a moment she leaned toward him and his heartbeat stuttered.

"I normally work alone," she said. "Except for Mick. I don't do too well in teams. That's why I didn't go out for the Tactical Unit," she explained.

"I need your help," he replied.

"Are you still sticking with the 'Mick's cousin' story?"

He nodded. "I *am* his cousin. Honestly."

"What are your father's reasons for suspecting your cousin?"

Cenrick sighed. "Mick does have a rather . . . spotted reputation."

She waned that away. "I've heard. But that's in the past. Plus, it was all minor stuff."

"Car theft? Breaking and entering? You consider that minor?" He raised a brow.

Another step, and she was close enough that he could lift his hand and touch her if he wanted. Instead, he clenched his teeth and continued to wait, to see what she would do.

"Despite the fact that *juvenile records are sealed*, my gut instinct tells me you're okay," she said. He let his breath out. "But," she continued, "I'm also aware my gut isn't always right. You aren't telling me everything. I told you, I want the truth."

The truth? Warily, he considered. How much of the truth could he tell her without her believing him to be delusional?

"Look," she said, deciding for him. "If I'm going to trust you, I need to know. Tell me everything. All of it."

All of it? Okay, fine. What did he have to lose?

He began by explaining what he was. Fae. A magical being from another place that coexisted side by side with her world. He talked of Rune, his home, of his brother Alrick and his father the king. He talked of magic and of spells, and of how his people had been intermingling with hers for centuries. And when he finished his explanation, Dee Bishop looked blank, utterly at a loss for words.

He considered himself lucky. At least she hadn't immediately denounced him as crazy.

She was a trained law-enforcement officer. She dealt in realities. He'd known she would not find his words believable at first. But he hoped to convince her.

"You're saying you're from another dimension?" she asked. There was a certain carefulness in her tone. She spoke in the sort of voice one used on someone who wasn't quite right in the head. He didn't suppose he blamed her.

"In a way, yes. Why do you find it so strange? Over the course of history, your literature is full of mention of my people."

"Elves and dwarves? Faeries?"

"Yes."

"That's *fiction*," she exploded. "Come on. I can't believe I'm even standing here talking to you when you're clearly—"

"Delusional?" He lifted an eyebrow, daring her to refute his words.

"Possibly," she said. "Actually, definitely. Look, Cenrick. I've got enough of my own problems without adding your insanity to the list. I think it'd be best if we parted ways."

"I'm telling you the truth," he argued.

"It's ridiculous," she snapped. "And I've had enough. Just leave. Go."

He couldn't say he blamed her. Were their situations reversed, he'd probably think she was nuts. "All right, Dee. You leave me no choice—"

She stiffened, and one hand went for her weapon. "I'm warning you—"

He interrupted, "Hold on, I'm not threatening you!"

She didn't relax or take her gaze off him for a second. He admired that. Dee Bishop on alert was a sight to see. She struck him as supremely competent.

"Will you believe me if I show you?" he asked.

"No," she growled. "Now take your big self and your weird story out of here."

Cenrick sighed. Sometimes actions spoke much louder than words. Even though magic could cause strange things to happen in the earthly realm, he spoke the spell of crossing quickly, feeling that familiar tingling that told him the parting of the veil between worlds had begun. Then he grabbed her arm, knowing they must be touching in order to go together.

She tried to tug her arm away, but he held on fast. "What's happening?" she said. "Where are you taking me?" And in the last few seconds, while their surroundings wavered before finally blinking out of sight, she fought him. Her gun fell to the ground and was left behind.

Cenrick felt a sudden sense of rightness, though he knew his father and Mort would not be pleased. They wanted answers and wanted them quickly; taking the time to bring a human woman back with him wasn't in the plan. But if Mort sensed the same things in Dee that Cenrick had, he'd agree. She was unquestionably connected in all this, and he needed answers.

The more time he spent with this woman, the more Cenrick became certain he needed her help. Thus he had no choice but to show her Rune. He had to prove to her that the Fae existed. And he had the strangest urge to press his mouth to hers, to see if he could turn that scowl into a smile.

Instead, he tightened his grip on her wrist while her world vanished and his began to take shape. "I'm taking you home. I'm taking you to Rune."

CHAPTER THREE

As always, Rune was . . . more. More vibrant and colorful, the sky more sharply beautiful, the trees massive and leafy and proud. Even the scent of fresh-mown grass seemed larger than life. While they reformed, Cenrick inhaled, not bothering to hide his delight at the familiar aromas of home. Here he could feel the pulse of the earth, the energy that blazed through all living things felt vibrant and near.

He wondered how this human female would react, watched as she turned in a slow circle and took in her first glimpse of his home. He couldn't help but wonder what she'd remark on first. Would she exclaim over the glossy petals of the multicolored flowers, remarking that they stretched like neon velvet toward the sun's warmth? Or would she note the way each blade of grass grew separate, yet linked together in a thick carpet as green as scattered emeralds.

They'd arrived in the middle of the lush meadow of wildflowers that stretched from the massive oak forest to the castle that was his father's seat of power.

There were snapdragons and paintbrushes, daisies and carnations, and more—a floral smorgasbord of brilliant hues and intoxicating scents.

"What the . . . ?" Dee spluttered. She spun out of his grip, going into a crouch and instinctively reaching for a gun that was no longer there. "How did you do that? Where are we?"

Cenrick spread his arms. "My home. The home of the Fae."

"What?" She went still, though her frowning gaze continued to scan. "This is ridiculous. Am I hallucinating?"

"No." Watching her closely, he gestured to the meadow. "You are in Rune."

"How? How is this possible? What'd you do?"

Since the simplest answer was also the truth, he told her. "Magic. We've crossed the veil that separates our words."

Another glance around had her frown deepening. "Beam me up, Scotty? Just like that?" she asked. At his blank look, she made a rude sound. "*Star Trek.* Look, whatever you've done, stop it. I want things to be normal again. Real. Put me back where we were."

"In a moment." He touched her shoulder, making her jump. "Relax. Take a look around."

"I can't." And while they talked, her gaze scanned.

"Nervous?"

"Oh, please." She gave him a look full of scorn. But of course she was.

"Take a deep breath. Look around. Then tell me what you think of my home."

Glaring at him, she went still. Inhaled. Exhaled.

Loudly. The only other movement was the gentle breeze ruffling her hair.

"You want my opinion? Really?" she asked.

"Yes."

"Fine, then. It's so . . . silent," she said, the question in her voice unasked. "*Achingly* so."

Quiet? Startled, Cenrick considered. Then he remembered when he'd first visited the world of humans as a child, and how the noise there had overwhelmed me. It had not just been the obvious sounds, not just the traffic or the roar of the occasional jet flying overhead. Instead, he'd been bothered by the ever-present hum of the electricity always on, of the whirr and click and growl of the many machines constantly working. It had taken years for him to grow used to them.

He'd once asked Alrick if the noise bothered him. His brother had laughed and shaken his head no, telling Cenrick he needed to use his eyes before he used his ears.

Now, so many years later, this human woman saw with her ears first, as he'd once done. She'd noticed the silence before she even commented on the raw beauty of his home.

And she hadn't yet seen his people. "On earth, most Fae try to change their natural appearance."

"Why?"

He shrugged. "You'll see."

"So you understand what Mick is, as well as myself. I want your help. I need it. If seeing Rune gains your trust, both Mick and I—as well as my people—benefit."

She did a double take. "Mick? Are you saying he's . . ."

"Fae. Yes. We're related, remember? I was telling you the truth when I told you we're cousins."

"How is that possible? We grew up together in Trixon's Children's Home. Mick's an orphan just like me."

Cenrick sighed. "He's Fae. He was left in the human world by his irresponsible mother. By the time she decided to go back for him, he was nearly grown."

"Then he *knew?* All this time, he knew he was a . . . Fae? And he didn't tell me?"

"He couldn't. Not if he wished to remain in your world. We are forbidden to reveal such a thing without good reason. Not only would humans believe us insane, but if the Mage of Rune learned of it we would be yanked back across the veil and punished."

She opened her mouth to speak, then closed it. Cenrick couldn't help but smile. Then, because she still looked dazed, he touched her shoulder.

"Please, take a look around Rune. I promise you we won't stay long."

"I—"

"Please."

With a sigh, she did as he requested. With the shadows of the ancient forest behind them, and the palette of color stretched as far as the eye could see, it might be easy to overlook the gold-cobbled path that ended up the hill to the glittering fortress that Cenrick called home. At first, her mobile features showed no visible reaction, but he kept watching and saw the change come over her as she gradually began to absorb the amazing natural beauty surrounding her. Her lovely eyes softened with curiosity rather than hostility or fear, and her lips curved into the beginnings of a smile.

Finally. After all, Rune was a wondrous place.

She did as he asked, but as she did she tugged at one ear with nervous fingers. She turned, her amber gaze darting here and there, taking in everything. Now she saw the scarlet butterfly, the sapphire dragonfly warring with another the color of turquoise. Now she took in the massive oak forest, the carpet of grass, the splash of the flowers. The castle.

Watching her, he knew what she'd say next. The heady perfume of this fragrant meadow had caused many a female, human and Fae, to exclaim in delight. To lie down and—

She sneezed. Once, twice, then again, with explosive force. Then she cursed. "Damn allergies."

For a startled moment, he simply stared. Then, dragons help him, he laughed.

She was sniffling and wiping at her nose, and her smile had completely vanished. "Amused, are you?" she asked.

"Yes." He grinned at her.

She sneezed again. "I don't know why. Allergies aren't any fun." Her eyes were red. She wiped at them. "My eyes are running. Can we get out of here, away from all these flowers? Otherwise I'm going to be really miserable."

A woman who didn't like flowers? Dee Bishop was different, that was for sure.

"As you wish." Indicating the path, he motioned for her to walk before him. "After you."

The woman glanced at her watch, narrowing her watery gaze and squinting at the dial. "The damn thing's stopped working," she realized. "I just replaced the battery too. It must have been defective."

Peering at her wrist, Cenrick shrugged. "I'm surprised it even crossed the veil with you. That's unusual. Mechanical things seldom cross to Rune, and when they do, they don't work. Your watch will probably be just fine once we get back to your world."

"Okay." She sighed. "I've seen Rune. You've accomplished your purpose—I now believe you're a Faerie. I'm still not sure about Mick, but I believe you."

He stared at her. "Why aren't you sure about Mick?"

"I've known him all my life. We're both orphans. If he had family somewhere, anywhere, I can't believe he wouldn't have told me." She shook her head.

All her frowning had made a tiny line appear on her brow. Cenrick caught himself about to smooth it with his finger.

"Also, I can't believe Mick's a . . . that Mick's . . ."

"Fae?"

"Right." She spread her hands, but each time she looked at him, her gaze skittered away. "Mick's . . . Mick. He's a cop. He's my friend. He's . . . human."

He simply arched a brow.

"What the difference anyway?" she finally asked. "This place looks like Oregon, sort of. And you—and Mick—both seem normal. Other than his good-luck, that is."

"We are beings of magic." Struggling to find the right explanation, Cenrick watched her for signs of disbelief. "Our people live at the grace of yours."

"Explain."

"As long as someone somewhere believes in magic, we can exist. Man, woman, child, it matters not."

"So you're saying you have . . . powers."

He put his answer as simply as he could: "*Yes. We do. Would that upset you?*"

"No." Her direct gaze told him she spoke truth. "I'm only angry because Mick and I told each other everything."

"He didn't tell you this."

"No." Sadness mingled with her fury. "I'll never understand why not."

"We're forbidden to do so, unless we have good reason."

"Like now?" she asked.

"Yes. Like now."

She seemed to digest this with a nod, then continued to scan the world around her, her face impassive. She jiggled her leg, tapping her toe, shifting her weight from one foot to the other.

"What's wrong with you?" Cenrick asked.

Her brows rose. "What?"

"You're"—he waved his hand—"fidgeting."

"Oh, that. I always do that when I'm feeling impatient—jiggle my leg, tap my foot, drum my fingers on the nearest available hard surface. The guys back at the station always teased me about it. 'Dee's ready to go,' they'd say." Her sheepish smile faded. "Sometimes, I really miss my job."

He didn't understand. In Rune, work was work, play was play. "Why?"

"Because we were like family." She blinked rapidly. "Some of those guys still call me, but I won't take their calls. I'm too embarrassed."

"Over what? You said you'd done nothing wrong."

"True." She looked miserable. "But someone thinks I did, or they wouldn't have suspended me. I couldn't bear to see doubt and disgust on those guys' faces."

"Come on." He held out his hand. "There isn't anything you can do about it now. Let me show you Rune.

She shook her head. Her frown returned, along with the tiny line in her forehead. "This is absolutely lovely, but I really don't have time," she said. "Seriously. I need to go back."

Blinking, he wasn't sure he'd heard correctly. "What?"

"All this." She waved one hand dismissively at the lush surrounding landscape. "I'd love to explore this place if I was on vacation, but I'm not and there's no time. So, take me back. Now."

He blinked. This had to be the first human he'd ever met who, once seeing Rune, wasn't overcome. "I told you, time passes differently here for humans. Though we might spend hours in Rune, when we go back to your world, it will be like a matter of minutes. You have all the time you want."

One arched brow told him she didn't believe him. "Only for humans?"

"Yes. Fae exist in the here and now."

"That makes no sense. This *feels* wrong, no matter

44

what you say. We're wasting too much time here. Let's go."

"In a moment. There's one more thing we've got to do before we can leave. I want to look at the ones who've been harmed. You may know some of them, as they were Mick's friends. My father didn't give me time to do so before I traveled to your world and—"

"I don't know . . ."

He tried a different tack. "I would think that, as an officer of the law, you'd want to see the people you're going to help. And though you don't want to think of Mick as a bad guy, there is some evidence that points to that."

The woman sighed, rubbed the back of her neck with her free hand. "I live," she said stiffly, "to protect others." Again she checked her watch, shaking her head when she realized what she'd done. "Sorry, checking the time is a habit of mine. Will this take long? And don't say time is relative."

"No. This shouldn't take long," he replied.

She nodded then asked, "You honestly believe Mick is behind all this?"

"I don't see why he would do these sorts of things, but my father and his most trusted advisor seem to think so. If he would just let my father question him . . ."

Considering Cenrick, Dee cocked her head. She seemed to come to a decision. "Mick took an oath to protect and serve, just like I did. What I've seen means Mick's been lying to me about nearly everything. I want to see the victims. Maybe I can get a better understanding of all this."

"Good," Cenrick said. "Take my hand. The afflicted ones are with the Oracle, a great sorceress who resides across the Plains of Lothar. Getting there will require another spell."

Chin up, Dee held out her hand. And as Cenrick gripped her fingers with his own, again he felt that click of connection, of rightness.

Three words, repeated twice. They were ancient words, the meaning of which were no longer known. But they were powerful. An instant later, the lush meadow of his home faded, and another breath, another heartbeat later, they reformed in an alpine meadow. The sparse grass and delicate flora thrived in the thin air. Here, the breeze carried a chill, the likes of which reminded Cenrick of Rune's winter.

"Ah." Dee sighed, pleasure obvious in her face. "This reminds me of Colorado."

This time, at the close of their journey she didn't immediately yank her hand free of his. Oddly, Cenrick found he liked that.

"This way." He pointed to a narrow path winding up the side of the mountain.

"Don't we need an appointment or something? Surely we can't just barge in on this person if she's important, especially if she's caring for sick people."

He had to laugh. "She's the Oracle. She foretells the future. She'll know we're coming."

Dee fell silent as they headed toward the path. Once there, Cenrick released her hand and indicated she should precede him. They began to climb. Cenrick couldn't help but admire her shape as she continued on ahead.

When they reached the top, Dee turned to face him, her chest heaving with exertion. Again, he found himself enjoying the view.

"Are you all right?" he asked.

"I'm good. A bit out of breath, but fine. You, you're not even winded." She pointed her finger accusingly. "But then"—her gaze traveled over him—"you work out a lot, don't you?"

If by "working out" she meant exercise, he supposed he did.

"Yes," he managed to answer, surprised that a simple look from her caused heat to crawl over his skin. "Plus, we Fae are a very fit race."

The cool breeze ruffled her short hair. Cenrick turned away, staring blindly at the sand-colored cliff walls.

"The Oracle lives there." He pointed up sheer rock. "See those steps?"

"In a cave?" Dee sounded shocked. He glanced at her, nodding.

Above them, a hawk screeched. Dee jumped.

"That is Tinth." Cenrick smiled, feeling slightly relieved. "The Mage of Rune's pet hawk."

Hearing her name, the huge bird landed on a boulder before them. Tinth's bright eyes looked curious as she cocked her head and watched them approach.

When they were within five paces of the hawk, Tinth spread her massive wings and took off, screeching as she flew ahead, spiraling up and finally disappearing inside the cave.

"She leads the way," Cenrick said. "Come on."

Silently, they climbed the steps. Once they reached

the third plateau and could go no higher, they began a descent into the largest of the caves. The air was cold, and the scent of heavy incense drifted up the passages. Torches flickered, placed at strategic intervals along the rock walls.

Below, the tinkling of bells sounded, a magical breeze swirling through the caverns and stirring the hundreds of crystal wind chimes and shell ornaments hanging from rock ceilings and walls. For centuries the Oracle had used them for decoration, as had those Oracles who preceded her.

Little had changed in this place since Cenrick's last visit, even though twenty human years had gone by, and finally he and Dee came to the great central cavern deep within the mountain. They stepped through the cool darkness and into a soft shimmer of light that proclaimed the Oracle's presence.

"Welcome." Clothed in her customary white robe, made of a material so rich the touch of it would feel sinful, the great seer kept her hood raised, her face in shadow. Even Cenrick, Crown Prince of the Fae, had never seen her features. It was said the sight of the Oracles beauty drove even the most learned Fae mad. Her eyes glowed scarlet with impossible power.

"Greetings, Oracle," Cenrick said. "I have brought Dee Bishop with me, from the human world."

"You have come to see the soulless ones," the Oracle replied.

"Yes."

"It is fitting." The brilliant red of her glowing gaze found and lingered on Dee. "You found her," she said cryptically. "One who . . . lives to protect others.' "

Dee seemed surprised. "Yes, that's true. How did you know?"

"I have seen you." The Oracle glanced at Cenrick. "And you. Good. Only the two of you working as one can halt this great evil."

A prophecy. Cenrick looked at the small human woman and was pleased he had acted on instinct. The Oracle was never wrong.

Dee crossed her arms, considering. "Working together, huh? Haven't you seen that I work better alone?"

"Not this time." The Oracle's gossamer robes shifted in an insubstantial breeze. "Alone, one would surely die."

"A vision?" Dee seemed skeptical.

The red of the Oracle's eyes flared brighter, changing from cherry to plum. "I speak truth," she said finally, turning away, "but I cannot speak prophecy—not with humans. Their machines make seeing within their world difficult." The seer seemed to grow, to loom over them, but then Cenrick blinked and she seemed normal-sized again. Perhaps the vision was a trick, the result of the shadows cast by the flickering torches.

The Oracle seemed to float ahead of them into another passageway, calling over her shoulder, "Come with me."

"Where?" Dee asked, looking at Cenrick.

The Oracle answered. "We go deep into the bowels of the earth. There I keep the soulless ones. Come, both of you, and see what has been done to our people."

Silent, they followed as she led them farther and farther down. Around each jagged corner, torches flickered on the walls and lit the way. The air became thinner and cooler the deeper they descended.

Finally, the Oracle stopped. "They are here," she said. She waved her arm, the white fabric glistening as much as her ruby eyes glowed. "Here, where magic once coalesced, they gather around the Pool of Dreamers hoping the power of the waters will restore them."

Her words gave Cenrick hope. "Have they begun to heal?"

"No." Though her voice rang with authority, sorrow threaded needle-sharp through the Oracle's tone. "Look for yourself." And she stepped aside, her brilliance fading as she appeared to blend into the stone walls.

Even though Mort had warned him, Cenrick was shocked when he saw his people. *The soulless ones*, they had been called, and now he saw exactly why. They milled aimlessly, like beautiful cattle. Nothing of their spirit remained behind their dull eyes. Even the murky water of the underground pool sparkled far more brightly.

Worse, their inner malaise had rotted more than their bodies. With horror Cenrick saw that their auras, which should have been shining with the brilliance of copper and gold, were black, ruined, horribly, awfully damaged.

His people. Though he didn't know all of them intimately, in Rune all were connected. They were like family, like friends. His people.

"How many are there?" he asked.

"Forty or fifty," the Oracle replied. "Though their number grows daily."

"How many *friends* does Mick have?" Dee sounded shocked.

It took Cenrick a moment to understand her meaning. "Not that kind of friend."

"Still, Mick knew all these . . ." She waved her hand in front of her.

"Nay," the Oracle's repeated Cenrick's assertion. "This sickness began with those closest to Talmick, yes. Since then, the disease has spread. And there are men and women here, both those that prefer their own sex and those who desire the opposite. The only similarity is that they are all Fae."

Dee persisted. "Have they all lived in my world? Or did some of them become infected here in Rune?"

The Oracle's eyes glowed softly, telling Cenrick she understood why Dee questioned. It was Dee's nature as a police officer to get all the facts.

"They were all in your realm."

Again Dee glanced around the room. "Really? Then how many Fae would you estimate live undetected among humans?"

"The number is unknown."

"Can you guess?"

Cenrick stepped in. "I would say thousands."

Dee nodded, though she was clearly surprised. "How many Fae live here in Rune?"

"No one knows."

"You don't count? Take any sort of census?"

"No."

When Dee opened her mouth for another question, the Oracle lifted her hand. "Enough. Prince Cenrick, look at your people."

"Prince?" Dee stared. "Did you forget to tell me something?"

He gave a half shrug. "Does my social standing matter?"

The puzzled look she gave him answered for her. "You're the strangest man—er, Fae—I've ever met. You'd better go, *Prince Cenrick*, and see your people."

Throat tight, Cenrick moved among them, touching one man's shoulder and realizing with shock that this hollow shell was all that remained of a man named Galyeon, whom Cenrick remembered from his youth. He had been a cheerful sort, always ready with a joke or a laugh. Now, empty eyes peered out from a gaunt face.

A great sorrow filled him. "Do they ever speak?"

"Not at all." He heard echoes of his own emotion in the Oracle's rich voice. "I do not believe they can. If they could, I would ask them who has done this to them, and how."

Dee watched, her expression puzzled. "I thought Fae healed fast."

"Not from this," the Oracle said, "This is not normal."

Galyeon shuffled away, and rage pushed back Cenrick's sorrow. "I will stop this," he vowed. "No matter what it takes to do so."

"What of you?" Eyes glowing from within the shadows of her hood, the Oracle stared at Dee.

Dee's inner struggle showed on her face. On the

one hand, she'd sworn to protect and serve. On the other, this was Mick. They might have to go up against her best friend and childhood companion.

"You say this is some sort of illness?" she asked. "Something that could be transmitted unknowingly?"

"That is one possibility. But only one scenario."

Dee's expression went blank. Cenrick guessed she was puzzling out some of the others explanations.

Finally, she lifted her chin.

Moving to stand beside him, she looked from him to the poor, empty Fae, her expression resolute. "We will stop this. I can promise you that."

"How?"

By that one word, the Oracle seemed to be throwing down a gauntlet. Dee stepped forward and accepted it.

"I'm a cop, she said. "To protect and serve. That's my vow."

Cenrick didn't bother pointing out Mick was also a policeman, and that, if he truly was behind this, he'd not only broken his vow, but condemned his soul to a thousand hells.

Suddenly Dee let out an awful gasp. "Look! That looks like Peter. No way—it can't be him!" She hurried across the room.

Cenrick followed, close on her heels.

Skirting the murky pool of water, Dee threaded her way through unseeing, motionless Fae. When she reached a tall, blond-haired man who stared like the others unseeingly into the distance, she staggered and gave a low cry. "Peter." She grabbed his arm. "Peter, what's happened to you?"

The one called Peter gave no response.

"How do you know him?" Cenrick asked. He studied the man, not recognizing him.

Dee looked up, meeting his gaze. Cenrick saw her lovely eyes glisten with tears. "He is the man I was to marry until he broke off our engagement. This means he's Fae also, doesn't it? Which means everyone I know has been lying. And now this." Her voice shook. "If Mick did this to him, I'll . . ."

Peter shuffled off, mindless.

"I can't believe this." Dee looked tortured. "Why am I suddenly learning that I've been surrounded by Fae?"

Good question. Cenrick watched the Oracle, waiting to see if she would answer. Instead the sorceress walked off, lost in her own thoughts. Cenrick waited while she composed herself.

After a moment Dee turned, looking for Peter, finding him standing on the other side of the cave facing the stone wall. "Poor, poor Peter," she said.

Cenrick took her arm. "I'm sorry."

"Yeah." She bit her lip. "Me too."

"Do you still love him?"

"Not in that way." She sighed. "But I still care."

"You didn't know the man you planned to marry was Fae?" Cenrick asked after a moment.

"I didn't even know there *was* such a thing until you came along."

Which was another question for Mick: Why had he found it necessary to hide things from her? Why had Peter? Many Fae had relationships with humans, always with full disclosure. Cenrick didn't understand why it should be any different with Dee.

"We will stop whoever or whatever is doing this." She sounded fierce.

"Yes, we will," he agreed. "And once we have, maybe Peter will become himself once more."

She nodded, no doubt hearing the words he didn't speak, the words reassuring her that once Peter had been restored to his former self, he'd want her once more. Cenrick wondered why the thought made his chest feel so tight.

"Can we go?" Staring up at him, Dee resembled a slender warrior ready to do battle.

"We can go." He took her hand. When she leaned into his touch, even if ever so slightly, he knew she too felt need of comfort. He couldn't blame her. What had been done to these people was the stuff of nightmares.

"Are you ready?" he asked.

"Yes," she said, gripping his fingers hard. "But I want my gun back. It'd better be where we left from."

They rejoined the Oracle, who'd remained on the other side of the pool. Without a word, the seer clapped her hands. "Go," she ordered.

And just like that, they went.

This time, millions of stars rushed past, and the wind roared before their feet touched solid ground. But then, back in the cricket-filled field, the night seemed much the same.

Dee glanced first at the sky, then at her watch. "You were right. It's working again. Though I'll have to reset it once I find out the correct time."

"Don't worry. All the time we spent in Rune was less than a heartbeat here."

She looked doubtful but didn't argue. Rubbing her hands together, she took note of the position of the moon. "Maybe you're right. That's pretty cool."

He smiled. "I know."

She turned in a slow circle. "Now to find my pistol."

Though he couldn't touch the metal, he helped her look.

They located the weapon in the tall grass near where they'd been standing earlier. With a sound of satisfaction, Dee scooped up the black revolver and inspected it before slipping it back into her holster. Then she rubbed her hands together.

"All right. Well, it was nice meeting you." And she began to walk away.

Stunned, Cenrick stared.

"Wait!"

She glanced at him, but continued walking.

"Didn't you hear the Oracle? We've got to work together. I told you the truth, as you requested. You agreed to help me."

"So I did," she tossed over her shoulder. "Guess you'd better hurry if you want to catch up."

He jogged to her side, his usual good humor reasserting itself. Until he had a better plan, he'd go with whatever she suggested. "Where are we going?"

"We're heading to visit Jack."

"Jack?"

"Yes, Mick's significant other. Though they don't live together, he and Mick are very close. If anyone can tell us what's going on with Mick, he can."

Cenrick fell into step beside her. "Will he talk to you?"

"Of course he'll talk to me." Her fierce voice seemed at odds with the vulnerability in her eyes. "Jack likes me. I'm Mick's best friend."

"*Were.* You *were* Mick's best friend," he warned.

"No, that's where you're wrong. I don't toss away my friendships that easily. He's in some kind of trouble and, though he won't admit it, he needs me."

He had to admire her loyalty. They'd reached her car and she unlocked the doors, motioning for him to get in. Slipping on his gloves, Cenrick did. Dee waited until he'd fastened his seat belt before turning the key.

"Jack lives near downtown, in those new condos they built off the river. Twenty minutes max by car."

Cenrick settled back to enjoy the ride. "Maybe he'll have something new to tell us."

"True." She shot him a glance. "But first we need to stop by my place so you can change clothes. I can't take you anywhere dressed like that. Peter left some of his things there. I'm thinking they'll fit you."

CHAPTER FOUR

Watching the way Cenrick prepared to get into her car made Dee curious. First he pulled on long, black gloves. Then he adjusted his sleeves, making sure every inch of exposed skin was covered. He checked his trousers—or leggings, or whatever they were—tugging them and tucking them into the tops of his boots. She couldn't help but notice everything was made of cloth; he wore no leather. Maybe he was allergic.

Finally he settled in his seat and fastened the seat belt.

She turned the key, still watching him. "What was all that? The gloves, the adjusting of your clothes, everything?"

He looked a bit sheepish. "I can't touch steel, so I have to make sure I'm well-covered."

"Oh. That makes sense." She thought of Mick. He'd had similar elaborate rituals, making him the subject of a lot of good-natured teasing over the years. "Mick used to do the same, though I never knew the reason why."

"One of the down sides to being Fae." He glanced at her, his dark eyes bright. "I've been working for years trying to find a solution, some sort of antidote, but without any luck. Fae and steel are incompatible."

"You know, I seem to remember reading something about that once, somewhere. Must have been in some fairy tale."

He grimaced. "Very funny."

"Sorry." But she wasn't. Wisecracks were a good way of dealing with stressful situations. Finding out that her best friend had been lying to her all these years had simply added to her frustration. Not that she'd let this Cenrick know. The less he knew about her, the better.

Biting her lip, she began backing out of her parking spot. If she focused on Cenrick, she wouldn't have to think too much about her own situation. "What about leather?" she asked.

He gave her a blank look. "What?"

"Leather. I noticed everything you wear is woven. Even your shoes are cloth. Do you have something against leather?"

"That's made from cattle, and we don't wear animal skin," he said. As if that explained everything.

She thought about Mick, remembering his extensive wardrobe. "I could swear Mick wore leather shoes."

Cenrick shrugged. "Maybe they were imitation."

Forcing herself to relax, Dee concentrated on the road. Driving felt good. Doing something, taking action. She felt empowered being on the move again.

They stopped at her place. Pocketing the keys, Dee

left Cenrick in the car while she ran in and grabbed a pair of Peter's khakis and a t-shirt. She handed them to him through the car window and turned her back to give him privacy while he changed.

Try as she might, she couldn't keep from imagining him naked. All corded muscles and tanned skin, with his long dark hair and bedroom eyes he'd tempt a saint into hell.

Whatever else she was, when it came to sex, she wasn't a saint.

"All right," he said. "I'm ready."

She sucked in her breath when she saw him. The t-shirt clung to his broad chest, accenting his narrow waist. With regular clothes on, his masculine beauty seemed otherworldly, more . . . Fae.

Damn.

How would Jack react to her showing up unannounced and uninvited? She hadn't seen him in a while, but they'd always gotten along. Though, that had been before Mick gave her the brush-off. Normally she'd call first, sound him out, but this time she needed the element of surprise. She wanted answers, especially since she'd seen what had happened to those poor Fae who were Mick's other friends.

Was Mick involved in what had been done to them? No. Mick was too kind, too good-hearted to do anything so ruthless, so evil. Wasn't he?

But then, Mick was also apparently an accomplished liar. She'd thought she knew him, believed they were best friends. But not only had he pretended to be an orphan like her, he'd also pretended to be human when he wasn't. And when she'd needed him the most, he'd bailed.

She had to wonder.

Cenrick fell silent while she drove, staring out the window. After ten minutes, she realized it was a comfortable silence, similar to the ones she'd enjoyed in the past riding around with Mick. *As though she and Cenrick too were old friends.* Odd.

She sighed. Her connection to Cenrick was most likely transference, her putting all her feelings for Mick onto this stranger.

Even close to midnight, downtown bustled. Even in the summer, the trees were awash with twinkling lights. No matter the season, Sundance Square always looked festive. Throngs of people crowded the sidewalk, visiting the various bars and restaurants and movie theaters.

Jack's condominium was part of the new, upscale downtown development along the river, a trendy place for the upwardly mobile. Dee pulled into the covered parking garage, took a ticket, and located a spot between a Mercedes and a BMW.

"Come on." She waited for Cenrick, tapping her foot impatiently. When he reached her side, she locked the car and took off, adopting her normally brisk stride. Beside her he walked silently, as though his feet didn't touch the ground. She wished she could master that trick, walking without making any sound.

The double glass doors ahead sparkled. They pushed them open and stepped onto luxurious carpet. Once inside the building, they rode the elevator to the thirtieth floor, Cenrick still silent. He'd pulled off his gloves and untucked his pants from his boots. He looked relatively normal—except for his size and unusual way of moving.

Dee pondered for a moment. He moved like a large predatory animal, even though he was a big man. With him at her side, she felt protected—like she had a bodyguard. She wasn't sure she liked feeling that way. It was an unsettling feeling for a cop. Of course, it was strangely reassuring as a woman.

Once they reached Jack's floor and walked quietly down the patterned, carpeted hall, she pointed to number 3331. Even the doors in the building were elegant, with gleaming brass fixtures and ornate, scrolled numbers. "There's Jack's place. I'm going to ring the buzzer alone. I want you stay out of sight of the peephole."

"Why?"

"He doesn't know you." She shrugged. "And in case you're right about Mick and Jack knows something, I don't want to alarm him. Let me handle this."

Cenrick nodded. For the first time she noticed his pallor. Actually, his skin appeared slightly green, as though he were on the verge of puking.

"Cenrick? Are you all right? What's wrong?"

"Sorry." He took a shuddering breath. "Now *I* am the fish out of water." Dragging a hand across his mouth, he narrowed his eyes. Perspiration beaded on his forehead. "I don't like this place."

She glanced around their elegant surroundings.

"Why not? This is the best place to live in town. What's not to like?"

He shrugged, giving her a sheepish half-smile. "The space—it feels confining in here. Like being in a giant beehive. Not natural. I'm Fae. I need space."

The big guy was claustrophobic? Interesting. Dee filed that information away. "I'm sorry. This shouldn't take too long. Maybe you'll feel better once we're inside Jack's place. It's very spacious."

Keeping an eye on Cenrick, she rang the doorbell—once, twice, listening for a response. She waited, tapping her toe on the carpet. "Hmmm."

Cenrick leaned against the wall, his eyes closed. Even from ten feet away, she could see he was perspiring profusely.

She rang once more, keeping her finger on the buzzer. Finally, she admitted defeat. "Still no answer. Just our luck. Jack's not home.

"Maybe he's over at Mick's." Cenrick straightened, frowning. "I know we just came from there, but . . . And I wonder if he's Fae."

"I doubt it." Still, despite Dee's denial, her stomach burned. What was up here?

"He could be," Cenrick argued. "Mick seemed to befriend others like himself."

"He hung out with me. Not everyone is Fae," she snapped. "Some of us are just plain human." She turned her attention back to the buzzer, trying one final time. Nada, zip, zilch.

A door opened two doors down. A tall, elegantly dressed man emerged, glancing at them. "Looking for Jack?" he asked.

"Yes." Dee smiled, recognizing him from one of Jack's numerous parties. "He doesn't seem to be home."

"He never is." The man shrugged. "I haven't seen him for a couple of weeks." Wearing expensive slacks and a well-cut jacket, he walked toward them. "I guess he's just busy, busy, busy. Like we all are." Smiling, he eyed Cenrick appreciatively.

"You don't have any idea where he might be?" Dee asked.

The man shook his head, his gaze touching on her with disinterest before rocketing back to Cenrick. "None whatsoever. Maybe he decided to do some traveling. He always wanted to see the Caribbean."

She sighed. "Thanks."

Too busy fighting claustrophobia to notice the other man's blatant appraisal, Cenrick leaned against the wall, his eyes closed. The man walked past. He lifted his hand in a casual wave, giving Cenrick one last lingering look before he turned the corner. A moment later, Dee heard the ding of the elevator opening.

"Are you okay?" she asked.

"Yes." Cenrick exhaled. "Though I'll be better once we're back outside."

"Come on, then." She started off down the hall, keeping an eye on him. "That guy thinks Jack's on vacation. It's possible, though I doubt it, since he and Mick usually go together."

"When was the last time you saw him?" Though he kept pace, Cenrick still looked nauseated. He untied his shirt, exposing more of his gleaming, muscular chest. Catching her looking, he gestured. "It's hot in here."

She felt her face heat, trying to remember what they'd been discussing. Jack. Focus on the topic at hand. "I haven't seen Jack in awhile, which makes no sense. Unless . . ." A thought occurred to her. "They broke up? Maybe that's why Mick's been acting so weird. Losing Jack might be enough to send Mick off the deep end."

"Wouldn't you know?"

Surprised at the question, Dee gave Cenrick a rueful smile. "Once, I would have. Until a couple weeks ago, Mick told me everything." Catching herself, she amended her statement: "Or very nearly everything."

Hearing herself speak the words, Dee was struck by a sense of loss so strong she nearly staggered. How could Mick have hidden so much of himself from her? How much of what else she knew about him was false?

And Jack . . . Was Jack Fae too? Had he succumbed to the same mysterious illness as Peter and the others, becoming the ones the Oracle called soulless? Cenrick had said the damaged Fae were all Mick's friends. But how could she tell which were Fae and which weren't? Looking at Cenrick, she saw an extremely handsome man, but not a magical being. Not someone unmistakably magical like one of the elves from *Lord of the Rings*.

And Mick? He looked like any other cop she'd ever worked with. A regular guy. Hell, most people didn't even know he was gay, never mind a Faerie.

They reached the elevator. Cenrick hit the button. "Let's go. I need some fresh air."

Once they stepped inside, Dee studied Cenrick, looking for obvious hints she might have missed. She saw nothing. "How come you don't have wings?" she asked.

That got his attention. He stared at her. "What?"

"Wings. I thought faeries had wings."

He snorted. "Not in real life. Some human invented that. What brought this up?"

"I can't believe Mick is Fae. I couldn't tell and he never told me."

"Why would he? Most Fae come to the human world to live a normal—at least by your standards—life. Mick was left there by accident, and by the time he found out he was Fae, human seemed more normal. He wouldn't have wanted to risk it."

The elevator stopped at the fifth floor. No one got on. Again, Dee punched the L button for the lobby.

Cenrick sighed, drawing her attention. Studying him, with his amazingly broad shoulders and rugged, sexy features, she grimaced. "You know, I can't see any family resemblance between you and Mick."

Mick was ordinary looking. Average height, average build, sandy-brown hair, regular face. Cenrick, on the other hand . . . He brought Conan the Barbarian to mind, even dressed in his wrinkle-free khakis and tight-fitting t-shirt. Talk about the "it" factor. This guy had it in spades.

"Different sides of the family." He shrugged, his face carefully blank.

She studied him again, trying for her usual detachment, but the feminine side of her couldn't help but appreciate him again. He could have been a movie star or romance novel cover model, with that thick hair—hair so dark it was almost black, tumbling all the way to his shoulders. On some men, this might signal trouble, but on him it looked just right.

The rest of him was just right, too. His physique was amazing. At the gym she'd seen men work for years trying to obtain such a build. He had broad, muscular shoulders, and a narrow waist with—she was willing to bet—a set of pecs and abs that would make any champion bodybuilder jealous.

Not to discount his face. Good Lord, no. His gorgeous high cheekbones, ruggedly chiseled features, and amazing eyes the color of molten chocolate made him so beautiful that looking at him almost hurt.

Almost.

She sighed as the elevator doors slowly opened. Yep, Cenrick of Rune was absolutely mouthwatering. *If,* she amended hastily to herself, one was in the market for a man. Which she wasn't. Hastily she averted her eyes. Good thing she hadn't seen him naked.

"Something wrong?" he asked, stepping aside to let her exit first.

"Nope." Pushing past, Dee cleared her throat, slightly embarrassed to be caught looking, and gave him her best detached look: the frozen, don't-mess-with-me stare she'd spent years perfecting in foster home after foster home. Girls that looked like her, even when she'd still been a child, learned quickly how awful men could be. Only around Mick was she able to relax. And later around Peter, who'd teased and joked his way past her defenses.

The Ice Princess, they still called her around the precinct. To be honest, Dee had always been proud of that moniker. Hell, being aloof was the only way an attractive woman could make it in law enforcement, or in any male-dominated career for that matter.

All her life she'd had to play down her looks. She'd taken care to ensure that words like "Barbie doll" and "advancement-by-couch" were never applied to her. Though her auburn hair was thick and healthy, she kept it cut short, wearing it tucked neatly behind her ears. She chose loose, nondescript clothing to hide her admittedly curvy figure, and saved the dangly ear-rings and heels for out-of-town weekends with Peter, the man she'd thought loved her.

Obviously, she'd been fooling herself. Both about Peter and her job. And about Mick, her pretend-brother.

She forced her thoughts back on track. Mick and her job were two monumental problems somehow in-tertwined. Though she'd become a cop mostly be-cause of Mick, she'd always given her job one hundred and ten percent. She was a good, no . . . an excellent cop, and all the guys respected her.

Or, they *had* respected her. Now the taint of false accusations would flush her career right down the toilet unless she could clear her name. Odd, how the word of one known prostitute was enough to make the department open an investigation. The hooker had accused Dee of roughing her up and demanding a cut of her income. Dee barely even remembered the last time she'd arrested the woman. The lies were no doubt part of some elaborate scheme to get even.

When the first complaint was filed, Dee's direct supervisor, Lieutenant Cowell, had told her the suspension was only a formality: "Of course we have to open an investigation. You know the drill. Take a few days off, let Internal Affairs look into it, and this will all be over before you know it."

She'd believed him. After all, Dee was an honest cop. She'd never in her life done anything even skirting the borders of unethical.

Taking her boss's advice, Dee had simply gone shopping that first day of her paid suspension. She'd imagined she'd be back at work by the end of the week.

Then a second civilian had come forward. This time, his accusations were harder to dismiss. A respected business owner, his coffee shop was near her patrol area. His accusations of Dee demanding protection money were so ludicrous, she couldn't believe anyone would take them seriously. Unfortunately, the police department had no choice.

That time, Lieutenant Cowell had referred Dee's questions to Internal Affairs. Police Chief Ferguson had left a message on her machine, asking her to avoid the press until the situation was resolved. And then he'd finally called her into his office.

She supposed she should count herself lucky they hadn't made her turn in her badge yet. Everyone knew that once that happened, your career was over. Still, it wasn't as if she could ever regain her old standing in the department. These types of accusations, even once disproved, could hang over a cop's head forever.

Yes, Dee's neatly ordered world had been turned

upside down. None of this made any sense. Sometimes she'd found herself wondering if she'd inadvertently stepped into an old episode of *The Twilight Zone.* She'd even caught herself looking around corners, half expecting Ashton Kutcher to jump out and yell "Punk'd!" In short, she wanted to wake up from this bad dream.

She glanced over at Cenrick, who appeared lost in his thoughts. Things had gotten even more surreal recently. Now she had to deal with alternate realities, a Fae prince, and the knowledge that a horrible, atrocious act had been committed against this man's people. Possibly by Mick.

Keeping ahead of Cenrick, Dee pushed through the double glass doors and felt like a one-woman cyclone. She hated this unfocused feeling; as a cop, she was used to taking action.

"One dead end." Cenrick's slightly accented statement made her start.

"True." She wiped her suddenly damp palms on her jeans. They reached her car and she pressed her key fob, unlocking the doors. "So, we've got to think of something else."

Sliding in the car beside her, Cenrick nodded. "Any thoughts?"

"Not yet." She forced a smile, turning the key in the ignition. The engine roared to life and they pulled out. "I'm thinking we should circle back and check out the house. Maybe do a stakeout."

"A stakeout?"

"Watch the place without Mick and his new friends

knowing. Maybe they'll leave him alone long enough for one of us to get in and talk to him."

"Sounds good." He rewarded her with another one of his breathtaking smiles. "Let's go."

She drove the speed limit, using care not to break any laws. The last thing they needed was for one of her former coworkers to pull her over.

"Look." Cenrick pointed at the horizon in the general direction of Mick's place. "What's that?"

A soft glow lit the sky. God knew what it was. Light like that usually meant spotlights and crowds. If there'd been smoke, she'd have suspected a fire.

She pushed the accelerator harder, gradually picking up speed. When they reached the end of the Mick's block, Dee pulled over to the curb. Though they were still four houses down, Mick's place appeared lit from within, lit up so brightly it positively glowed. A quick check assured her there were no spotlights or exterior lighting of any kind.

"What the—?" She eased down the accelerator, moving forward, one hand on the butt of her gun. But the weapon felt wrong, the size and weight different than she was used to. It was because she was carrying her personal gun rather than her service revolver.

"Hey, what are you doing? We don't want to attract their attention."

Cenrick's husky voice brought her back to reality. Even though her adrenaline was high and her heart was pumping, she wasn't a cop; not right now. She couldn't just pull up in front with a squeal of tires and barge in with her weapon drawn. No crime had been committed. No one had called for help. Even if they had, some other uniform would have to answer. Dee was suspended. She had no right. She eased off the gas pedal.

"Sorry. Habit." She flashed Cenrick a quick, sheepish smile, deliberately unclenching her fingers from the steering wheel. "You're right. We'll drive by slowly and then circle the block."

As they passed in front of Mick's, the brightness was almost blinding.

"Don't you think the neighbors would notice?" Dee asked. Even after she'd turned the corner, Dee could still see the light in her rearview mirror.

"Perhaps it's only visible to those attuned to magic."

Dee felt obliged to point out that she could see it. "And I'm quite possibly the least whimsical person you'll ever meet."

"You've been to Rune, using magic to travel across the veil. That alone may have made you attuned to such vibrations."

Dee shrugged. "Whatever."

As they turned back onto Mick's street again, she pulled over to the curb and parked, killing the ignition.

"What are you doing?" Leaning forward, Cenrick squinted through the window at the glow. "We're too far away to see anything in detail."

"This is as close as we can get. That's the point of a stakeout—to observe without being noticed. If I park across the street, they're bound to notice two people sitting in this car. Either they'll investigate, or call the cops."

"They wouldn't call the cops." Cenrick sounded positive.

She supposed he was right. Criminals never wanted the law around. "Either way, anything that attracts attention to us will ruin this. I don't see any other option." And with a sigh, she settled back in her seat, trying to make herself comfortable. Unlike television, real-life stakeouts were frequently long and boring.

"I think we should leave the car here," Cenrick decided. "We'll go on foot and just stroll by the place, as though we're neighbors taking a nighttime walk."

"Won't work." She shook her head. "If Mick sees me—he knows damn well I don't live in this area."

"You can always be trying to visit him again. You would visit if things were normal." He gave her a grim smile.

"He told me to stay away."

"Normally would that stop you? More importantly, do you have a better idea?"

She supposed he had a point.

"All right. We can try it," she agreed grudgingly, one hand on the door handle. "If blondie is watching, there won't be a problem. I don't know her. I've never met the other man either."

Outside, Cenrick took her arm, making her jump. He explained: "Part of the camouflage. We need to look like a married couple." She didn't bother to point out that most married couples she knew rarely touched.

The first pass was unremarkable, other than the way the house appeared. If she'd had a whimsical bone in her body, Dee would have said it looked otherwordly, like an intergalactic UFO about to blast off.

They managed a nonchalant saunter to the STOP sign, crossed the street and continued down the other side. From there, they had an unobstructed view of Mick's house. But other than the neon yellow glow, the house looked unremarkable. Nothing stirred, no breeze blew through the curtains, not even a bird sang or a single squirrel scampered up one of the oaks that ringed the lawn. The same vehicle, that combination SUV and truck, was parked in front of the garage. Dee saw no sign of Mick's Ford Explorer. She dug in her pocket, located a scrap of paper,

"Even the insects avoid the place." Cenrick pointed at the house next door. It had the front porch light on, drawing a small cloud of moths and assorted other flying insects. Mick's house, illuminated a hundred times brighter, was completely bug-free.

"Strange," he murmured, as though speaking to himself. "What kind of magic could do this?"

"Or machine." Dee felt obliged to point out that magic wasn't behind everything in the universe. "I think that glow comes from some sort of machine."

"Machines and magic don't mix, Dee. Whoever is harming Fae is stealing their magic. I doubt any manmade machine could do that."

She didn't see why, but also saw no reason to argue. Not without proof. If machines such as CT scanners and MRIs could exist, who could say someone hadn't invented a magic-stealing machine? Someone evil.

"One more pass."

As they turned to head back, another car pulled up in front of the house. Two men got out.

"Not men," Cenrick corrected, as though he'd read her mind. "Fae. I can see their auras, though they're weak."

Not wanting to be noticed, Cenrick and Dee slowed their pace to a virtual crawl, though they had to keep moving. The two newcomers didn't even glance over. Instead, they walked up the flower-trimmed sidewalk toward Mick's house. No, *walked* didn't even begin to describe the way they moved. They *marched,* moving stiffly like robots.

At the last moment, something, some sound or intuition, drew their attention. They froze, swiveling their heads to look at Dee and Cenrick. Now Dee got a good look at them. Her skin crawled as she realized what had happened to them. Oh, they were Fae all right. They were still beautiful, to be sure. Much more up Mick's alley than the blond, sharp-faced woman. But they looked drained of spark, empty of life. They were well on their way to becoming soulless.

Dee made a strangled sound. Cenrick growled low in his throat.

After one disinterested look, the men continued forward. Mick's front door opened. Even brighter light spilled out, illuminating the sidewalk like some giant, malevolent spot. Looking neither left nor right, the two Fae stepped inside.

When the door closed behind them, Cenrick cursed. "Did you see that? They're becoming soulless."

"I know," Dee answered truthfully. "However and whatever, the process has already begun."

"Lothar's plains!" Cenrick's arm tensed under her hand and a muscle worked in his jaw. "But how? How is this being done?"

"And why? Why in Mick's house?" Though she hated to admit it, she'd never been one to lie to herself. "Mick has to be involved somehow. But I don't understand. After growing up longing for a family of his own, I can't believe he'd intentionally harm his own people."

"After all you've seen, you still doubt?"

"I don't doubt that he's involved. But . . . it's entirely possible that Mick's under their spell, you know. He might be in trouble too."

Cenrick opened his mouth to say something, but just then, the glow vanished. Mick's house had gone dark.

CHAPTER FIVE

Cenrick looked at Dee. She stared back. Then they both turned to Mick's house, which sat silent and dark as if a giant switch had been flicked to cut off the glow.

It was black, but not empty. Cenrick would swear the blackness pulsed. He shuddered. Though he didn't like to remember, he'd seen this utter and absolute darkness once before, while helping Alrick fight the warlord from the future. The shadows around Mick's house danced and swirled and . . . *breathed*. Evil was at work here. This darkness signified more than a mere absence of light. Cenrick sensed the absence of magic as well. And while his heart screamed impossible, his scholarly mind couldn't help but wonder how.

Everything that lived had some small concentration of magic. Even in the human world, traces of magic remained in every living thing, from the smallest blade of grass to the tallest, towering oak. But now, in this swirling black air around Mick's house, there was none. No magic. Nothing. Only a complete and utter void, as though someone or something had sucked all magic from the immediate vicinity.

If such were true, Mick must be dead. Or worse, one of the soulless.

Intrigued and puzzled, Cenrick moved away from Dee toward the house. Immediately he fell to his knees, and wave after wave of negative energy swamped him, sapping his strength.

"Cenrick?" she called.

He could only point toward the house, praying she'd understand.

She crossed to his side. "Take my hand." Reaching out, she threaded her fingers through his. Right away, he felt better. Protected. Her touch restored his strength, allowed him to climb to his feet.

Her touch? How was this possible?

Experimentally, he pulled free. Instantly everything went blurry as before. The thing—whatever it was—again hammered at him.

He grabbed her hand, once more holding on as though she was his lifeline. In a way, she was.

"Your touch . . ." He lifted his head. "Helps me."

"Let's get out of here." Dee moved quickly. One arm under his, supporting him, she helped him get back to her car. With fumbling urgency, they got the passenger door open and, without him touching any metal, he dropped himself into the seat. Without another word, she cranked the engine, slammed the car into drive and took off.

He felt better as soon as they turned the corner. Better still by the time they reached the main road.

One stark truth now stood out—going anywhere near Mick's house was extremely dangerous for him.

Except—he shot her a glance—when Dee touched him. Somehow, she blunted the effects of the magic-stealer. He didn't understand how such a thing was possible.

"Are you going to live?" she asked. Something, some catch in her voice, made him turn to face her. The streetlights illuminated her delicate features and lush figure, and suddenly he wanted her.

What the hell? This was wrong. More than wrong, it was completely bad timing. They were partners, coworkers in a way. She'd be afraid if she saw his desire.

No. He could control this, *would* control it. He'd just survived a magic-stealing attack. He'd channeled the rush of adrenaline into desire. That was very natural and normal, and now that he understood, easy to control.

He hoped.

But analyzing the why and how didn't change his desire for her.

"Yeah," he managed to say. "I'm okay." His swollen body pulsed, despite his attempts to think non-sexual thoughts.

"I'm not," she replied, her voice shaky. She pulled into a deserted parking lot, drove around to the back and parked. Cenrick tried to concentrate on the fact that she'd left the engine running, but all he could think about was how badly he wanted to touch her. The seat creaked as she swiveled to face him.

"What *is* this?" Her eyes widened, pupils dark, and

he suddenly knew she felt the same overpowering need. "What's happening to me?"

He swallowed. "I don't know. Maybe you'd better just drive."

"Drive? I can't. I can't concentrate on the road. All of a sudden, all I can think about is how large you are." She took a deep, shuddering breath. "How tightly corded your muscles. You're . . . you're *beautiful,* Cenrick of Rune. And I want you."

Each husky murmur was like oil poured on a fire. Staring back at her, he clenched his gloved hands to keep from giving in to his desire. He could feel his blood pulse, heavy and urgent, in his body, which was thick and ready.

"I—" He tried to articulate a warning, but couldn't.

"Damned if I'm not"—she licked her lips, the sensual sight sending his heart into overdrive—"aroused as hell. As aroused as I've ever been."

Unable to help himself, he moved closer. "Touch me," he growled, his face inches from hers.

She shook her head, then reached out her hand to do as he asked.

He had to warn her, to tell her this wasn't real. This was an after effect. Now, with his magic channeled into his libido, the overflow was surely radiating out from him, affecting her. This wasn't real. She didn't want him, not really.

But dragon's lair, how he wanted her.

He opened his mouth to tell her the truth. She kissed him. And as her lips moved over his, he felt himself sinking into need. He wanted to refuse her, to help her resist, but he couldn't make himself push her away. Merely being kissed by her made him more aroused than he'd even been.

Somehow, he broke free. "Dee—"

"I want to climb on top of you, take you inside me, swallow you whole." She sounded stunned, amazed, and excited all at once.

He tried again. "Dee . . ."

But she climbed atop him, settling herself on his swollen arousal. Even through his braes, he could feel her warmth.

Damnation.

He shuddered, pushing himself against her before he managed to get himself under control.

"Stop," he begged, his voice ragged.

"I can't." And again she moved her body, nearly shredding the last tattered remnants of his self-control.

"Dragon's blood!" Cursing, he lifted her off and pushed her away. "Stay there," he bit out. "This is not you or me. It's magic."

"Magic. Hmmm. Okay." She kissed his hand, her tongue doing things with his fingers that had him longing to rip off his gloves. "I'll show you magic. If you won't help, I'll do what has to be done."

"No—look away from me, open your window and breathe. Please!"

When he forced her hand away, she did as he requested. He punched the button to lower his own window, and followed his own advice.

The moon seemed brighter than normal. He could even make out the shape of the craters on its surface.

That was odd. And the stars twinkled brightly like cut diamonds on black velvet.

"Are we done?" Dee asked. She sounded more like Dee, again, less like the seductive siren.

"No. Not yet. Keep breathing. Concentrate on the moon," he said. And following his own advice, he thought they had a prayer.

Gradually the urgent desire that had overwhelmed him vanished.

"Cenrick?" Dee said. She sounded confused. "What just happened? We . . . I . . . why did we . . . ?" Her voice faltered. She looked away, her color high. "I am *so* sorry."

"Don't be. It's not your fault." He gave her as succinct an explanation of his theory as possible, how they were reacting against the magic-stealer, and ended with his own apology.

"That's great." She made a sound, something between a snort and a sigh. "And now I'm afraid to look at you or touch you. That was intense. What if that need comes slamming back?"

"It won't," he promised, hoping he wasn't wrong.

Exhaling, she massaged the back of her neck. "Okay, that's over. Now what?"

Now? Now he felt an overwhelming exhaustion. A need to sleep so strong he could barely keep his eyes open. "I don't know about you, but I could use some rest."

"Yeah." She put the car into drive and pulled slowly around the parking lot and back out onto the street. "Do you have a place to stay?" Before he could respond, she shook her head. "Of course you don't. Looks like you're sleeping at my place."

She sounded apprehensive, and he couldn't help but smile. Thank god they'd bested this before they'd gotten there. "Thanks. And maybe in the morning we can come up with a better plan."

"Yeah." Her sideways look was laced with speculation. "But first, we need to figure out what happened to you at Mick's. Did that soul-stealer thing's influence extend to you even outside the house?"

"Yes." He made the admission grimly. "Whatever it was, it reached right inside of me and attempted to rip out my core. Pretty powerful stuff. I couldn't move, couldn't think."

"If it's a machine, they must have turned it all the way up. And those other two Fae were able to walk, so whoever was doing it must have waited until they were inside."

Those two were now soulless. Neither could say the words.

Still not entirely convinced of Dee's machine theory, Cenrick frowned. Magic and machines didn't mix well. "Since it's obvious Mick's involved up to his neck, I have to talk to him. My father will want him back in Rune, too, to stand trial."

"But how can you even think about approaching him when you get zapped like that?"

A muscle worked in his jaw. "That's why I need a better plan."

Dee sighed. "One thing is for sure, whatever the power is in Mick's house, it's dangerous to you."

"Yes." But Cenrick had a brief thought. "Except, your touch seemed to somehow block the effects. I'd like to investigate that as well."

Dee shook her head. "How is that possible? I don't have magic."

"I don't know. Regardless, I've got to stop that thing, and quickly."

"*We*," she corrected. "*We*'ve got to stop it. And I think I know how." Fishing in her pocket, she pulled out her cell phone and punched in a speed dial code.

"What are you doing?" Cenrick asked.

"Calling Mick. Even though all the evidence seems to point to him, there's one small problem. He's Fae too, and he's in there. If that thing affected you outside, how can he shield himself from it inside? I want to talk to him, to see if I can get him to meet with us off premises. And I want to make sure he's . . . healthy."

He watched silently, knowing that if Mick was behind this atrocity, he'd have figured out a way to protect himself. If not, it was probably already too late. Unless his cousin had developed some sort of shield, no Fae could withstand a direct hit against magic like that and remain the same.

"No answer," Dee said finally, clicking the cell phone closed. "But at least that woman didn't answer. I still think she's behind all this."

"An accomplice? She is human, not Fae. We will need to find out who she is."

Dee grinned. "Oh, I've already started." She pulled a small notepad from her console. "I wrote down the license plate number of the truck. It's all we have to go on for now, but maybe if I run a trace, I can figure out who she is."

"How will you do that, since you don't currently have access to the police computer network?" Cenrick wondered.

Her amusement was a thing of beauty, and that hit him like a fist in the gut. "There's always the Internet. The amount of information you can learn on the Web is amazing. Most times, we cops curse it because people can be so vulnerable and not even know. But now?" She shrugged. "After I catch some sleep, I think I'm going to put my home computer to good use."

She turned her car into a parking lot. "Here we are," she said. "Home."

The place where she lived was not at all what he'd expected. The three-story beige apartment building had been designed in a Southwestern style and was obviously an upscale community. Despite that, he couldn't get over how each building looked exactly like the others in the huge complex. Made of wood, brick, and stone, they clustered together in a valley with several hundred other buildings. A sea of red tile roofs stretched as far as the eye could see.

She must have caught a glimpse of his expression. "What? You don't like it?"

"It's better than Jack's place," he admitted. "But still, pretty confining."

With a shrug, she unlocked her front door, stepping aside to let him go past. Fighting exhaustion, he stumbled inside.

He stopped short in amazement. Entering her living room was like entering another world. Was this the real Dee, hidden behind her professional and competent facade? If so, he suspected he might be in trouble. She already attracted him physically. The woman who'd decorated this room would be fascinating mentally as well.

The scent hit him first. Heady and sensual, it made his head spin. Sandalwood? Vanilla? He wasn't sure.

His second impression was visual, of vibrancy and comfort. Her huge, overstuffed golden sofa was covered in plush, jewel-toned pillows. Interesting little knickknacks scattered around the room evoked other countries—from his travels in her world he recognized India and Saudi Arabia, as well as Spain, Morocco, and Puerto Rico. This room welcomed him. This room felt like home. He turned to stare at her, not bothering to hide his shock.

"Do you like it?" Flicking on the light, she closed the door, grinning.

"Yes. I do." Giving in to his fatigue, he crossed the room and tested the feel of the couch. He immediately sank down. "Nice."

"Glad to hear it, since that's going to be your bed." She flicked on a few more lights, and he saw her dining area was decorated similarly.

He eyed the sofa, doubting he'd fit. Maybe if he removed all the pillows. She caught him looking and gave another faint smile.

"Come on, the kitchen is through here." Touching one more switch, she led the way.

Curious, he followed. Ah, here was an area that

seemed more suited to the woman she presented to the world: a spartan, utilitarian room that contained no personality and appeared to be seldom used. The countertops were pristine and uncluttered. The sparkling white appliances looked brand-new, and reminded him of the decorating magazines he'd seen his brother's wife read. The room looked as though she rarely set foot in it—which made no sense. She had to eat, didn't she?

Opening the fridge, she peered inside. "You hungry? I've got enough for a couple sandwiches."

Suddenly, he realized he was starving. "Sure," he said, watching as she reached into the refrigerator and withdrew lunch meat, cheese, and bread. Placing all the sandwich fixings on the counter, she went back for two cans of cola.

"Do you want ham?"

"No meat. Just cheese."

"No meat? Why? Are you a vegetarian?"

"Yes. Most of my kind are."

"Jack ate meat." With that, she carried the food to the table, slapped together a couple sandwiches and dumped a bag of potato chips on a paper plate. Then, handing him one can of cola, she popped the top on the other and took a long swallow. "Dig in."

Seeing him eye her, she laughed. "Your expression reminds me of how I used to feel in a new foster home when they served something weird for dinner. I'm guessing you don't eat a lot of sandwiches, right?"

"True." But it wasn't that. He couldn't tell her he'd been pondering her rather than the meal. Her words had made him imagine a younger, more vulnerable Dee. All her contradictions fascinated him.

He grabbed his dinner and took a bite. Chewing slowly, he watched her inhale her sandwich, several handfuls of chips, and her entire can of cola. Meanwhile, he could barely keep his eyes open he was so tired.

"Great. Now I'm going to sleep." She yawned, pushing herself out of her chair. "But first . . ." Crossing to the wall, Dee picked up the phone and dialed. "Trying Mick again," she mouthed. A moment later, she shook her head. "Still no answer. I'll toss some blankets on the couch for you, then I'm going to bed."

With a wave, she left him alone to the remains of his sandwich, lights still on. He heard the sound of her bedroom door close, wondering how he felt her absence so sharply.

Who knew? Scratching his head, he finished off his meal and then set about stripping the couch of pillows and arranging his blankets. Luckily it was extra long and wide, and it would accommodate him. When he removed his clothing, he relished the feel of the cotton sheets against his bare skin. Lastly, he turned off the lights.

As he lay there in the spice-scented darkness, again he pondered Dee. He'd never met anyone like her, human or Fae. The face Dee presented to the world was no-nonsense and efficient. But her apartment felt sensual and exotic.

He fell asleep dreaming of her veiled and dancing for him, the sheer fabric of her costume giving him tantalizing glimpse of creamy skin and toned legs.

* * *

Dee woke with a start, blinking at the bright light. She glanced at her alarm clock and groaned, shoving back the sheet and swinging her legs over the side of the bed out of reflex. If she didn't hurry, she'd be late again.

Abruptly she froze, as the reality of her life came crashing back. She wasn't going to be late. She didn't even have a job to rush off to. Even worse, she had a full-grown Faerie sleeping on her couch.

Ouch. She needed coffee. She wondered if the Fae drank coffee. One thing was for sure, she wasn't worth anything without her daily shot of caffeine.

Stepping into a pair of jean shorts and a tank top, she brushed her teeth, applied deodorant and used a damp comb to tame her unruly hair. Finally feeling ready enough to face Cenrick, she opened her bedroom door. The damn thing creaked. She'd never noticed that before.

Stepping quietly, she moved into the living room. Cenrick was up, sitting on her striped-down couch wearing—she averted her eyes hastily—absolutely nothing.

Oh. My. God.

"Er, excuse me." Averting her eyes, she kept her back to him, aiming for the kitchen and the coffeemaker. Coffee. She needed coffee.

"Good morning," Cenrick said. He sounded normal, completely unabashed.

Fumbling with the coffee filters, she nodded. "I, um, didn't realize you weren't dressed."

"That's all right." He didn't sound concerned. "I always sleep in the nude."

Measuring out grounds, she hoped the sounds she heard meant he was getting dressed.

"Hurry up, coffee," she muttered.

"What?" Cenrick asked.

Unable to resist a quick look over her shoulder, she saw he'd replaced all the pillows back on the couch. But—she goggled at him in disbelief—he was still buck naked. And sexy as hell.

He met her eye and grinned. Then, to her shocked consternation, he began heading toward her.

Crap!

"No!" she yelped. "Hold on. Aren't you forgetting something? Like your clothes?"

"Oh, that." He dismissed her concern with a shrug, leaning on the counter that separated her kitchen from the other room. "It's warm this morning. No hurry. I'll put them on later."

"No, put them on now. Please." She forced herself to meet his eyes, sternly ordering her gaze to sink no lower.

He looked at her as if she'd lost her mind. "Why?"

The question floored her. "Because . . . because . . ." She sputtered. "I don't like you walking around like that."

He seemed equally surprised. "You don't?"

"No." The more she talked, the more flustered she grew. "Please. Get dressed."

Shaking his head and muttering about the oddities of humans, he turned to do as she'd requested. Dee caught a quick glimpse of a perfect male behind as he headed back toward the sofa, where he must have left his clothes. She sagged against the sink.

Luckily, her coffeemaker beeped, informing her the brew was ready. Hastily she poured herself a full mug. Two heaping spoonfuls of creamer and two packets of artificial sweetener later; she was good to go. Closing her eyes, she inhaled the rich aroma before she took the first sip, prepared to savor the taste as she always did.

"I've never tried coffee."

She jumped, splashing and scalding her hand. Cenrick. He'd practically sneaked up on her while she was distracted, and had spoken from maybe three inches away. He was so close, his breath actually tickled her ear. Hastily she set her mug down and moved to the sink, ran cold water on her poor hand.

"Don't do that," she snapped. Drying her hand on a dish towel, she snagged her cup and took another gulp. "You want coffee? You can have coffee." And without waiting for him to answer, she plucked a second mug from the cabinet and filled it.

"Cream? Sugar? Artificial sweetener?" she asked. Taking a deep breath, she faced him.

"I don't know." He grinned at her, looking entirely too good with that lock of black hair falling over his forehead. "I'll take it the same way you do, I suppose."

She nodded, inwardly wincing. He was still half-naked, though he'd complied with the spirit of her request to dress by putting on Peter's trousers. Seeing him bare-chested and barefoot, looking completely at home in her kitchen, provided more of a wake-up jolt than ten cups of caffeine.

She took another chug of coffee and grimaced when she realized she'd inadvertently drunk from his. "Here." Handing it to him, she added, "Most men take it black."

Gaze locked on hers, he nodded. Raising the mug to his mouth, he drank, his throat working as he swallowed. Dee's mouth went dry. Damn.

Carefully she moved past him, refilling her cup and heading for the kitchen table. "Let's talk," she said. She pulled out a seat. He did the same, taking the chair across from her.

Cradling her mug in two hands, she sipped. The niggling bit of desire she felt each time she looked at him made her decide to cut to the chase. "About Mick—I think I've come up with a workable plan."

He raised a brow, then motioned for her to continue.

"I'll go undercover. Maybe If I pretend to be Fae I can get into that house, but I won't be hurt by whatever is going on there like you would. I've got wigs and colored contacts from my days working undercover in Vice. Once I'm in, I can find out what Mick's up to, whether he's a willing participant in this or—"

"Not possible." Cenrick cut her off, his voice certain.

"Why not?"

"Because no matter what you do, any Fae will instantly know you're human."

"How?" She rubbed her eyes. "What am I missing? Don't tell me you guys have some special scent or something."

"Not a scent. An aura. Remember I told you I can see other Faes' auras and they can see mine? Human auras are completely different."

"Auras. Of course." She sipped coffee and tried to regroup. So much for her plan. Life kept getting stranger and stranger. "Shifting veils" separating her world from his; an alternate reality, one in which elves and faeries existed; magic spells, soul-stealing machines—if she didn't know better, she'd suspect she was under the influence of some mind-altering drug or in the throes of a really bizarre dream.

A dream. Wouldn't that be nice? Maybe she would wake up and find out she hadn't been accused of being a crooked cop. She'd still have job and her best friend Mick, and a normal life.

"Stop," she muttered.

"Stop what?"

"Nothing." She drained her mug. Pushing to her feet for one last refill, she checked his. He'd barely drunk any. Fine. More for her.

Once she'd finished doctoring her refill, she carried it back to the table and sat down. "Okay, you've nixed my plan. But I still want to go back to Mick's. For one thing, I want to know why that glow went out."

"I think that glow only occurs while souls are being taken," Cenrick said. Expression serious, he studied her. "What about the license plate number you wrote down? Shouldn't we check on that?"

"Great idea," she said. "I forgot." She jumped up and crossed to the corner of the dining room where she kept her computer on a small desk. "Give this thing a minute to boot up, and then we'll see."

She got on the Internet—thank goodness for DSL—and went to the Web site of the data service she used and logged in. Then she did a search by license number, and less than ten seconds later a name appeared on the screen. "Natasha Klein." Now she brought up a powerful search engine. She got dozens of results. "It seems Mick's new friend is a top-level scientist with NASA."

"NASA?"

"Our space agency. It's in Houston. She's apparently also done some work for Lockheed. Now, let me make sure this is the same person." Clicking on link after link, she located a picture of the esteemed scientist. "Bingo. That's her."

"Well done." Cenrick's eyes were full of admiration. "Human technology is almost as good as having an Oracle and a Mage."

"Almost as good?" Dee laughed. "It's *better*. After all"—she clicked the PRINT button, labeling a manila folder—"your people weren't able to learn any of this. At least now when we head over to Mick's we know exactly what we're dealing with."

CHAPTER SIX

As they had the last time, when they reached Mick's they drove on the opposite side of the street. But this time they parked much closer, only two houses away. A sickly yellow glare again emanated from the house and lit up the cloudy afternoon sky.

"The glow is back," Cenrick said.

"Yeah, and something's happening. I wonder what."

Tonight the place was a hive of activity. A large, white, windowless van was parked in the driveway. Two goons, with Blondie supervising, were unloading several people.

"Can we drive closer?" Cenrick asked.

Dee glanced at him curiously. "I can, and I'd like to write down the van's license number, but I'm not sure it'd be a good idea for you to go. Remember what happened to you last time. I don't want whatever it is that's sucking magic out of Fae to affect you."

His expression set in grim lines, he drummed his

fingers on the dashboard. "Go. If I start having problems, I'll let you know."

"Fine." She pulled closer, stopping directly across from Mick's. "You'd better hope they don't notice us." She kept a notebook in the glove box, and while she jotted down the license number, he watched the goons.

"By the Plains of Lothar!" Cenrick cursed. The narrow-eyed glare he shot Dee was full of fury. "Look at them! Just look!"

The soul-stealing was again in progress. Like zombies from some grade-B horror flick, a small cluster of Fae shuffled forward, vacant-eyed and slack-jawed, and the goons were herding them toward Mick's front door.

"Are they under a spell, or have their souls already been stripped?" He shook his head. "Even here I can feel that thing—whatever it is—attempting to pull the magic from my body."

She shot him a look. "Magic, or your soul? Which is it?"

He shrugged. "They're one and the same. All the magic we Fae have resides in our souls. It's our core, our very essence."

A thought occurred to Dee. "Without it, how do the soulless manage to live?"

"I don't know," he replied.

They both fell silent as the blond woman appeared, motioning for her hired muscle to hurry. "Natasha Klein," Cenrick repeated slowly. "It's good to put a name to the enemy."

Dee nodded. "Knowing she works for NASA and

with Lockheed—she *has* to be the one who developed the machine."

Cenrick didn't argue. He must finally be coming around to her machine theory.

Once the last stragglers had been herded away, Natasha motioned to the van. Immediately it drove off. While Dee was trying to see the driver, Natasha and the others disappeared inside the house. The garage door closed behind them.

Dee looked at Cenrick. Then they both turned and stared at the house. Except for its still pulsing glow, the place might have been an ordinary suburban home.

Cenrick looked frustrated. "We've got to get in there."

"I know. But since you shot down my plan . . . Cenrick, look!"

Natasha had come outside. Alone. They watched as she strolled down the driveway toward the mailbox. Dee tensed, poised for action. Beside her, she sensed Cenrick doing the same.

"Let's jump her now. She's alone and far enough from the house." He fumbled with his door handle.

"No!" Dee grabbed his arm. "I'm sure her muscle is watching. Those guys have got to be her bodyguards."

Just then, proving her words, one of the big guys strolled out the front door and stopped by Natasha's SUV. Arms crossed, he waited while she retrieved the mail. Even from this distance, Dee could see he was armed.

Natasha walked over to him, and the two conferred for a moment. Then, to Dee's disbelief, the bodyguard opened the SUV passenger door. Natasha climbed in. Once he'd closed the door behind her, he walked around to the driver side and got in.

"They're leaving." Dee couldn't believe it. "Talk about lucky breaks."

Cenrick nodded. "Which means only one guard is left. And all those messed-up Fae."

"And Mick." Dee couldn't keep the hope out of her voice.

She and Cenrick exchanged a glance. She understood exactly what he was thinking, and said it for both of them. "Excellent odds."

In the dim illumination of the streetlight, his aristocratic features looked even more handsome. He smiled as the SUV backed out and drove off. "It's time."

"Yep." Dee opened her door. "I'm going in. You wait here."

The look he gave her told her that would be a cold day in Hell. "No. I'm going with you."

"What?" Door halfway open, she turned to look at him. "You can't. The house is still glowing. That means it will affect you."

"Maybe, but . . ." He pushed himself up out of the car, leaving her to hurry after him. "It's a good time to test my theory."

"What theory?"

Giving her a mysterious smile, he shook his head. "Wait and see."

"Cenrick—"

"Shhh. Are you ready?"

Glaring at him, she grabbed his arm. "What if you get in there and it zaps you so badly you can't leave?"

His gaze was dark as he looked down at her. Smiling grimly, he said, "Then I guess you'll just have to rescue me, won't you?"

"Was he joking?" She glanced up at him, unable to tell.

His expression was impassive; he didn't blink. "Come on, Dee. Time's running out. We're going to have to do like my brother Alrick usually does—act without a completely thought out plan."

"That doesn't sound good." Dee watched him closely. While he seemed to truly love his twin, every time he spoke of Alrick, she sensed discord.

Cenrick shrugged as though he didn't care, but the look in his eyes told her different. "All his life, Alrick has made a habit of acting first and thinking later. Though we're twins, I'm the opposite."

"And that works for him?"

"He's known around Rune as a great warrior."

Gaze still locked on his, she softly touched Cenrick's arm. "And you? What are you known for?"

Once corner of his mouth curled in a bitter attempt at a smile. "Me? I'm known for being a scholar, Dee. And since I have no better idea, I'm resorting to my brother's way of doing things. I don't know what else to do. Some scholar, huh?"

"You still think we should try?"

"We don't have a choice."

"But we do," Dee grumbled.

"Look what happened to you last time. You almost

passed out when you even got close to the place," she reminded him.

"I'll be fine. Nothing hurt me the time before that, when we ran into each other in the garage."

"The house wasn't glowing then." She looked around. "And . . . what's that awful smell?" It was an overwhelming odor, sickeningly sweet and full of decay. And God help her, she knew what the smell meant.

Something had died here.

Cenrick sniffed. "Pretty powerful smell. Do you think it's coming from his garden?" he asked.

"No." She took a look around. "It's too awful to be plants."

"All of the shrubs are dead and shriveled," Cenrick pointed out.

She took another look. More than merely dead, Mick's beloved plants looked scorched, as if a nuclear explosion had ripped through the yard. The grass too had gone brown and lifeless.

"Mick's gardens." She felt stunned. "Those were his pride and joy. There's not a single bloom left living."

"Maybe it has something to do with that awful smell," Cenrick suggested. But he didn't sound convinced that was the only thing. He must know, as she did, that such an odor could only come from a decaying body. She could only hope it wasn't Mick, and from the set line of his mouth, she guessed Cenrick hoped the same.

Carefully they skirted the side of the house. The motion sensing light in the front of the garage clicked on, but no one came out to investigate. The ground felt damp and spongy underfoot, despite the dead grass, or maybe because of it. It was like some horrible chemical had seeped into the soil, polluting everything within reach.

The smell grew stronger. Waves of nausea and dizziness made Dee's head spin. She hoped Cenrick was all right.

Taking a deep breath and fighting not to gag, she leaned on the brick for a moment. Every instinct screamed at her to leave. As a cop, she'd learned to trust such instincts. "I don't like this," she said.

Cenrick made a sound of frustration and reached for the back door. "Look, quit worrying. Last time, that thing—whatever it is—took me by surprise. Now, I'm better prepared." He tried the knob with his gloved hand. To her surprise, it turned.

"They left it unlocked?" Shaking her head, she swallowed her trepidation and followed him inside. "This is beginning to feel like a trap."

She'd barely spoken when the glow flared brighter, pulsed. Sickly yellow-green light flooded the kitchen, bathing Cenrick's face. He staggered.

"Everything's spinning," he said through clenched teeth, sounding in pain. He inhaled deeply, once, twice—a loud rasping in the quiet.

"This is what I was afraid of," Dee cried. She grabbed him. "You'd better hope your theory works."

As soon as Dee touched him, the cloudiness vanished from his eyes. He grinned. "I think it does."

Keeping her hand on his arm, he was able to stand. A moment later he slid his fingers through hers. "Don't let go," he told her.

"You seem better." She squinted up at him. "Just because I touched you? What's up with that?"

He flexed his other hand. "I don't know. I don't understand why, but you protect me."

She scoffed. "Either that, or they've turned off the machine."

But the evil, pulsing glow still filled the room.

She sighed. "If you're okay, let's see what we can do to get to Mick. I'll make sure not to let go of you," she promised. And side by side, they moved forward.

Despite the glow, the house appeared deserted. In fact, the house was so silent they could hear the ticking of the kitchen wall clock.

"Mick's bedroom is this way," Dee whispered. "This still feels—off. Wrong."

"—Bad," he said at the same time. "I agree. But we have no choice."

Hand in hand, down the eerily lit hall they went, peering into the rooms they passed. They saw no sign of the bodyguard who'd been left behind, nor of the Fae they'd seen shuffled inside. Worse, when they reached Mick's room, the unmade bed was empty.

Cenrick cursed. "He's not here."

"No, but I am." It was a stranger's voice, one from the hall behind them. "She said you'd come."

Dee spun, pulling out her gun. In her haste to draw the weapon, she yanked her hand free of Cenrick's. Immediately he fell to the floor, gasping.

The newcomer rushed her. Pivoting, Dee danced away, bringing her revolver to bear on him. "Freeze," she ordered.

The man laughed. "Point that gun all you want,

lady. I'm not sure how a Fae like you can hold metal, but I've got the machine amped up to full power. She wanted him, and you'll be an added bonus."

Dee had been right—this was a trap. That explained why neither Natasha nor her helper had even so much as glanced at Dee's parked car. And *they wanted Cenrick*. She glanced at him, thrashing weakly on the floor near the doorway. No way could she get to him, not yet.

Seeing the direction of her gaze, the guard laughed and pointed. "In a second you'll be just as helpless as he."

He thought her Fae. That meant he was human, though she supposed it didn't matter. He wasn't too bright, and one shot would take care of him either way.

"Put your hands over your head," she yelled.

The guy didn't move.

"Do it. Now!"

Instead, he took a step toward her. "Any moment," he repeated, his expectant gaze fixed on her face. He didn't seem to know or care that she had a .357 Magnum pointed at him.

Dee's hands tightened on the gun. "I said *freeze.*"

He kept coming.

No choice left, she squeezed the trigger, but the guy dropped and rolled a half-second before. Her bullet went wild. The man crashed into her legs. She went down; her gun flew across the carpet.

The man grabbed her. She elbowed him in the stomach and, with a cry of pain, he released her.

On her hands and knees she went for her gun, but he got there first and snatched it.

Damn.

The guard's laugh was full of triumph. Her gun in his hand, he pointed it at her. "Now *you* freeze," he snarled.

Dee froze. She had to get to Cenrick and touch him, but first she had to disable Natasha's guard.

A quick glance at Cenrick showed he lay face down, unmoving. Thinking quickly, she dropped to her knees and began to moan as though she finally felt the effects of the machine.

"See?" the man taunted. "Now you're mine." And as he came closer to gloat, she knew she had him.

"Oh, yeah? Guess again." Using her shoulder, Dee pushed herself to her feet and rammed him. Surprised, her enemy fell backward, dropping her pistol and hitting his head on the wall. He crashed to the floor and lay there, unmoving.

First, she grabbed her gun. Then she went for Cenrick. Grabbing him by both arms, she pressed against him. "Come on Cenrick, come back to me," she said.

He didn't move, and she began to feel a teeny bit worried.

"Cenrick? Are you there?

No answer. Crap.

Checking her watch, she saw they'd been inside the house nearly half an hour. No telling how long before Natasha and reinforcements returned.

The unconscious guard stirred. *Great.* Now what should she do?

She heard the answer as though someone whispered it. *Touch Cenrick again. More.* Right now her only contact with him was through her hands. She supposed it couldn't hurt to try.

Another quick glance at the guard assured her he was still out. Good. She climbed on top of Cenrick, stretching herself until her entire body touched him.

Body to body. Soul to soul. Again, she could have sworn she heard a whispering voice.

Beneath her, Cenrick moved. "Dee?" he rasped, his voice weak.

"Right here."

"By the Plains of Lothar," he groaned.

She rolled off him, keeping one eye on the guard as she stretched out by Cenrick's side. "Are you all right?"

"Now I am." He flexed one hand. "My strength is returning."

The guard made a snuffling sound.

"Cenrick?" Dee sat up, keeping her hands on his arms. "We've got to go."

He rolled over. "No." He closed his eyes. "Not until we find this machine."

"And Mick," she reminded him. "We have to find Mick."

His eyes opened and he agreed, "And Mick." He brought his hand up to cover hers. "Keep touching me." To her relief, his voice almost sounded normal again. "Can you help me up?"

"Sure." Doing as she asked, she pointed to the unconscious guard. "He's out, but I don't know for how long."

Cenrick nodded. "Okay. Come on, let's find and destroy the blasted thing." And still gripping her hand, he led the way down the hall.

"I feel . . . something," Dee whispered.

"Like what?"

"I don't know, but it raises the hair on my arms."

"Maybe the machine's properties are affecting you," he worried.

Though they searched the house, they found no sign of any mechanical device, nor of Mick or the other hapless Fae who'd arrived earlier.

"That machine has got to be here," Cenrick said.

"The guard mentioned he'd turned it up, so it's got to be nearby," she agreed. "No one else but us was here."

Except that voice she'd heard. Should she mention that?

"Magic." Cenrick made the word sound like a curse. "They used magic to move those Fae, the machine, everything."

"But the house is still glowing."

"It's fading."

She squinted. "You're right. Since the machine is gone . . ."

"The glow has gone with it." He motioned toward the back door. "Come on, let's get out of here."

They fled to her car and drove off without incident.

"I don't believe this." Dee wanted to hit the steering wheel. "Where could they all have gone?" she asked.

"I don't know," Cenrick replied, sounding as unhappy as she. "But that's the thing about magic. They could be anywhere in your world."

"But not Rune?"

"No." He sounded confident, though he'd thought for a moment. "A machine like that would never make it across the veil."

She breathed a sigh. "One less place to search. Any idea how we can find them?"

"I'll need to contact the Mage. Tracking them down will benefit from magical help."

She nodded, turning onto the street that led to her apartment complex. "You know," she said, "up until now, I really believed that Mick wasn't involved."

"After today, there's no doubt."

"It's *possible* he's being coerced," she said.

"But you don't really believe that, do you?"

She didn't answer. What could she say? The man she'd grown up with, who'd been the closest thing to a brother she'd ever known, was now a criminal.

"When we find him—" A cold fury made the certainty in Cedrick's voice chilling.

"*If* we do."

"Oh, we will. Not only will we find Mick, we'll find that machine of his and destroy it."

Dee barely glanced over. "Do you think so?"

"We have no choice."

"But how?"

"All magic leaves a trace. Mort or the Oracle will be able to find it."

Dee glanced at him. He gave no signs of the desire that suddenly hammered her, the same urgent, insistent lust as the last time they'd faced the soul-stealing machine. It had taken every bit of willpower to keep from attempting to seduce him then. Now, only the embarrassing thought of what she'd done last time—and how he'd pushed her away—kept her from climbing atop him right there in her car. Again.

She studied him, but she saw no obvious signs of need. He regarded her the way one would a working partner, with no swollen body part or eyes dark with passion.

She shouldn't be so disappointed, so hurt. But she was. Her breasts felt heavy, her body sensitive and restless. She found it difficult to concentrate on the subject at hand. Magic. They'd been discussing magic, and getting the Mage or the Oracle to help them.

"Are you saying we'll have to go back to Rune?" she asked. She pulled into a parking lot outside her apartment and parked, pocketing her key and avoiding touching him.

"I don't think we have a choice."

"But not tonight, right?"

He smiled, a flash of white in the darkness. "No, not tonight."

Dee shivered. Even the husky timbre of his voice strengthened her need. And here he was, obviously too weary to think about it.

Climbing out of the car, she hurried up the sidewalk to her apartment ahead of him. The last thing she wanted was to make a fool of herself again. Within thirty minutes of unlocking her front door, she planned to be in her room getting ready for bed. Alone. Cenrick followed her into the apartment, apparently too exhausted to even speak.

After a quick stop in the kitchen to grab a glass of

water, Dee hurried down the hallway, tossed a good night over her shoulder, and headed for her bedroom. Any other night, she might have closed the door to keep him out.

This night, she left it open.

CHAPTER SEVEN

Keeping himself from making love to Dee was the most difficult thing he'd ever done, bar none. The instant she touched him, desire slammed into him the same as before, a direct result of having his magic drained from him and then returned in a rush. But this time, feeling the first twinge of lust stir his body, he prepared himself to fight it. For her. Dee. He'd humiliated them both once. He would not so dishonor her again. Old-fashioned, true, but there it was.

One look from her and his body burned, one accidental whiff of her light floral perfume and he was hard. Yet, though his heart pounded and his blood ran like fire through his veins, he gave no outward sign of his inner battle. He was able to maintain his iron control until they got home and she went to bed.

But then she'd left her bedroom door open when she usually closed it. Was it an invitation? The mere thought started sensual images playing in his mind.

Dee, Dee, Dee.

Would his desire be so strong for another woman? He couldn't help but wonder.

No.

Somehow, he was certain of the answer. While these magical repercussions might send his libido into overdrive, the strength of this need was based solely on the woman. Dee Bishop.

Knowing this, he got no sleep. For hours he paced the confines of the small apartment, wondering how such a thing could be possible. Finally, hours after she'd turned out her light, he made the couch ready and attempted to sleep. At last he succeeded.

In the morning he awoke from a dream of holding her in his arms to find his arms empty. Dee's sharp scream, quickly cut off, brought him to his feet. He yanked on his trousers, grabbed his dagger and ran.

Bursting into the kitchen, his blade drawn, he prepared to do battle. Both Dee and the silver-haired man talking to her looked up in surprise.

"Cenrick?" Dee crossed her arms. "What's wrong?"

"I heard you scream."

"Oh, that?" She gave a self-conscious laugh. "This man scared the hell out of me. He appeared just as I was measuring out the coffee."

"It's Mort," Cenrick told her. "The Mage of Rune." Mort spread his hands and looked rueful. "Sorry."

Cenrick sheathed his dagger, shaking his head. "Looks like I won't be needing this. Greetings, Mort. Your arrival is timely as always."

"I wonder how he knew we needed to talk to him." Dee's question made both men smile.

"He knew because that is his job as the Mage of Rune." Clapping the older man on the back, Cenrick saw Dee had poured Mort a cup of coffee, too.

"Have you tasted that?" he asked.

Mort shook his head.

"Vile stuff." Cenrick indicated the mug. "I tried it once. That was enough."

Mort took a small sip, then nodded. His grimace made Dee laugh. "You're right. This is bad."

"It's an acquired taste," she said. And as if to prove it, she took a deep drink. She told Mort what happened at Mick's the day before."

Mort nodded again, eyeing his coffee before taking another wary sip. "You say you found nothing when you entered Mick's house?"

"Yes. Nothing. Though we watched several Fae arrive, they were not in the house when we searched."

"We took out the one guard," Cenrick continued, his tone terse, "yet we couldn't locate Mick or the machine."

"Machine?" Mort went still.

"So we believe. The guard we incapacitated alluded to a machine."

"I see. But you could not find this machine anywhere?"

"No." Cenrick shook his head. "Despite the way the house glowed, that thing was gone."

"Then, they moved it."

"Yes. Magically, I think. Though I don't know who cast the spell, or when."

"Spell?" Dee turned troubled eyes on Cenrick. "So that's what I felt. I figured it was the machine. Power crackled across my skin. Like the willies. Whoever cast it had to be really powerful."

"You speak as though you felt the magic," Mort said. He watched her closely, his expression giving away nothing.

"I did," Dee said. "Though I didn't know what it was at the time. But I sensed the power."

"Magical residue," Cenrick spoke up, wondering how such a thing as she said could be. Humans *never* felt magic.

"What about you?" the Mage asked, looking at Cenrick. "Did you feel this too?"

"No," Cenrick admitted. "Whatever the machine does affected me too greatly. I was weak and incoherent. If not for Dee . . ."

"A human female." Mort sounded puzzled. "Describe what you felt." Though his voice was deceptively casual, the mage didn't fool Cenrick. And he watched Dee with an intensity that would have frightened a lesser woman.

But not Dee. She lifted her chin and considered. *His Dee.*

His Dee? Still reeling from the thought, Cenrick nearly missed her reply.

"I felt . . . a black hole," she said slowly. "I've read about them, even watched a film about them somewhere. That's what this felt like: a powerful eraser. All matter that comes into contact is absorbed into . . ."

"Itself." Mort completed her sentence, deep lines appearing in his forehead. "And this affected the prince but not you?"

113

"Yes. Of course. He is Fae and I'm not. That's the entire reason, plain and simple. I'm just an ordinary human."

Mort shook his head. "Not ordinary. Not if you can feel power."

Dee shrugged.

"Then there's the way her touch can heal me," Cenrick put in. "And, when she's touching me, I'm shielded from that machine."

"What?" Eyes full of excitement, Mort peered from Dee to Cenrick. "What do you mean?"

In a few short sentences, Cenrick explained.

"This is not possible," the mage breathed, his gaze focused inward. "The legend—" He drew himself up abruptly, cutting off his own words.

"What legend?"

But Mort only shook his head. "I will have to consult with the Oracle. If I'm correct, then we have a chance of winning. If I'm not . . ." He didn't finish the words, but they all knew what he meant to say.

All would be lost.

"What about the machine?" Cenrick asked. "Can you find it?"

"I will try. Again, as the Oracle told you, we have limited success seeing into the human world. And, if this is a machine, magic will not locate it."

With that, he snapped his fingers and vanished.

Dee looked at Cenrick, brows raised. "Now what? What do you think we should do while he 'tries'?"

"Gather more data." He drummed his fingers on the tabletop, apparently having decided to ignore the coffee she'd poured him. "We can't diagnose the problem without knowing all the factors."

She made a sound of frustration. "Again with the math crap. You sound like a scientist—like that Natasha chick probably would." Her eyes widened. "You know, I've never asked. Besides being prince, what exactly do you do in Rune?"

"Do?"

"You know, what kind of work? What's your occupation?"

"I'm a scholar," Cenrick said.

"That's all?" She sounded disappointed. "You're one of those eternal students?"

He frowned. "What do you mean?"

"I thought maybe you'd be a professor, or work in a lab. Or maybe act as a doctor."

"We don't have any call for that sort of thing in Rune," he replied. "There are mages and scholars and warriors."

"Warriors." She chuckled. "Like Conan the Barbarian?" "You resemble him, you know."

Since he had no idea who this Conan was, Cenrick couldn't comment.

She cocked her head. "Do you have a sword?"

"I have an excellent blade, one forged for me in the mines of Gristo."

"I thought you Fae couldn't touch metal."

"My sword is not metal. She is made of crystal." He crossed his arms, wondering if she would understand. "Though I am an accomplished warrior, I am a man of peace. If there is a way to deal with problems without bloodshed, I seek to find it."

"And if there is not?"

"Then blood shall flow like a river."

At his words, she looked away. "I've taken an oath to uphold the law," she said.

"What law? Are you speaking of this situation? Human laws do not apply."

"Yes, they do." She lifted her chin. "Natasha is human."

"Not any longer. If she's stealing souls . . . It's possible she's using magic."

"How?"

"I'm not entirely sure," he admitted. "If I go back to the library at Rune, I can research all this. I can—"

"That would take too long," she guessed. "We don't have a lot of time, do we? We're going to have to do the best we can without a bunch of research. I don't want Mick to end up like those other people, those soulless ones." She shuddered. "If he hasn't already."

"And Peter?" The words were out before Cenrick had time to think them through. "You must want to help him, too."

The look she gave him was steady and without guile. "Of course. I want to help each and every one of those people. But Mick is closest to my heart. He's the nearest thing to family I've ever had."

He himself had always been surrounded by family. Cenrick couldn't imagine how lonely a life like hers must have been. And Mick—what must that have been like, finally learning he wasn't alone after years spent believing the opposite? Was that the reason Mick had for hurting the ones who cared about him— revenge, for leaving him by himself so long? Or was there another, deeper motivation? Until he could get Mick alone to explain, he'd have to wonder.

Dee drained her cup and spent a moment staring into its depths, then echoed his thoughts. "There's got to be a way to find Mick. We just have to think of the right plan."

Pushing his chair back and getting to his feet, Cenrick nodded. "There *is* one option."

"Let's hear it."

"They want Fae to drain. We can flush them out if we use me as bait."

Before he'd even finished, Dee was shaking her head. "Of all the bad ideas I heard in my six years on the police force, a civilian attempting to use himself to attract criminals is the worst. Not only that, but you've seen how that machine affects you."

"I wouldn't go alone. We're partners, a team. I'm safe as long as we're touching," he reminded her. She stared at him, clearly considering, so he pressed his advantage. "Dee, I don't have much choice. I'm a Prince of Rune. My people are being hurt. I have to take a risk, especially if by so doing, I can save them."

"True, and it's a good start," she agreed. "But say you really do flush them out. Then what? Where do we go from there? You're a planner, I know. What's the whole plan?"

A frown creased his forehead as he worried.

"You heard the Oracle," he said. " '*Only the two of you, working as one, can halt this great evil.*' We have to get moving, and this way we'd be working together."

"That could mean anything. And I don't think she would want you to risk yourself stupidly, especially if you're the only one who can stop this. You can't take a chance on being captured and having your soul stolen!"

"I can and I will, unless you can come up with a better plan."

"I don't have one. Not yet," she admitted. "But give me time."

Her doorbell chimed as Cenrick was about to speak.

"What now?" she groaned, going to the door and peering through the peephole. "Damn. Two men in dark suits and sunglasses. They're either Men in Black and I'm misinformed and they're tracking down fairies instead of aliens, or they work for Internal Affairs. What the hell do they want with me?"

"You are being investigated, aren't you?"

She nodded. "But I've already answered all their questions at the station. Internal Affairs doesn't make house calls. Something is wrong here."

"You can always pretend not to be home."

She hissed him to silence. "I'm not hiding like I'm in the wrong. I haven't done anything."

"Then open the door and get it over with," he replied. He crossed his arms.

Dee sighed. "You're right."

Cenrick moved back, preferring to stay out of sight. As he disappeared down the hallway, Dee opened the door.

"Ms. Bishop?" The taller of the two men stepped

118

forward, holding out a laminated ID card. "Chad Riddick, Internal Affairs."

After making a big show of examining his card—it looked legit—she finally handed it back to him. She said, "I've already talked to your department, last week. *At the station*," she emphasized.

Riddick cleared his throat. "We understand coming here is highly unorthodox, but we're acting on a tip."

She nearly groaned out loud. IA working the field? Now she'd heard everything. She kept her face expressionless. "What can I do for you?"

"We'd like to ask you a few questions. May we come inside?"

"Sure." She stepped to the left, letting them past her.

Closing the door, she took a deep breath. Though Cenrick was nowhere in sight, it was reassuring to know he was there in case she needed him. But even thinking that stunned her. She'd always worked better alone. Since when had she needed someone to watch her back?

The two men regarded her expectantly.

"Please, sit," she said. Indicating the sofa with a wave of her hand, she dipped her head. "I'll be more than happy to answer any questions I can."

Prowling around her living room, Riddick examined each knickknack, lifted some to study more closely before setting them back down. His partner sat, leaning forward and staring.

"I'm Jones," he said, when she stared back at him.

Riddick finally joined Jones on the couch. Then, and only then, did he pull a notebook from his pocket and flip it open. "Now, Ms. Bishop," he began, stopping when she held up her hand.

"Just a moment. Before we start, I have to tell you up front—as I did the other IA guys last week—these charges against me are completely bogus." Taking a deep breath, she plunged on. "I don't know how or why I'm being targeted, but I'm an honest cop. A good cop. I did nothing wrong."

They nodded politely. No doubt they'd heard all this before from others, likely many times.

Clearing his throat, Riddick started again. "The investigation against you is ongoing. But we're not here to discuss those allegations."

"What?" This made no sense. Puzzled, she eyed them. "What do you mean you're not here to discuss my case? How do you expect me to clear my name if you guys won't investigate?"

Jones lifted his hand. "I can assure you, we are investigating."

"Then what—?"

"There is the distinct possibility that more charges are being added to the list." For the first time Officer Riddick appeared uncomfortable, tugging at the collar of his uniform. "Though, obviously, that depends on what kind of evidence we unearth."

Now he'd totally confused her. "Other charges? Evidence? What are you talking about?"

"We're here about another officer. Mick Morsi."

Her stomach somersaulted. "What about him?"

"You were close?"

Were? "We're best friends."

"Then you should know Mr. Morsi didn't show up

for work today or yesterday. Nor did he call in sick. His supervisor says that's not like him at all."

"That's unlike him," she agreed. "But what does that have to do with me? Maybe he's really ill. Unable to phone. I wouldn't know. I don't understand how Mick's problems warrant a visit to my home from Internal Affairs."

Riddick's smile was a mixture of smugness and malice. "Well, that's the thing." He leaned back on the couch, his hawklike gaze never leaving hers. "Morsi's live-in girlfriend, one Natasha Klein, filed a missing persons report yesterday. She claims she doesn't know where he is either. But she says she saw you and some other man lurking around the house. She thinks you might have had something to do with Mick's disappearance."

It took half a second for his words to sink in. When they registered, Dee exploded. "You're crazy! There's no evidence. Mick doesn't have a live-in girlfriend. Did you bother to search his house? Have you even looked for him?"

Riddick ignored her outburst. "We have corroboration of Ms. Klein's claims."

Dee went very, very still. "Show me," she said.

The younger officer handed up a manila envelope. Opening it slowly, Riddick withdrew a stack of photographs and passed them to her.

Looking at them, Dee couldn't believe it. All of them were of her and Cenrick skulking around the sidewalk in front of Mick's house. In the photo, the house didn't glow at all. But Natasha had been watching. Taking pictures.

"Is that you?" Riddick asked, relentless.

What could she say? Throat tight, Dee handed back the pictures and nodded. "Yes. But the mere fact we were at his house doesn't mean we had anything to do with Mick being gone."

"Really? You don't find this odd?" Riddick commented. "Mick Morsi, an important witness regarding the corruption charges against you, disappears a few days before he's scheduled to testify. And even after he asked you to stay away, you're seen around his house?"

Crap. Talk about a set-up. She could feel the noose tightening around her neck. "Those photos prove nothing. I can't believe you think I had something to do with hurting him."

The two men exchanged glances. Finally Riddick spoke up. "Let's just say you're a top suspect. You're the only one we know of who has probable cause."

"But you have no evidence." Yet. Doggedly, she continued to defend herself. They had no evidence yet. Though she could safely bet that soon some compelling evidence would come along courtesy of Natasha.

And Mick?

She concentrated on breathing slowly, evenly. Damn, if she hadn't severely underestimated the blonde and her cohorts.

The Internal Affairs officers stared her down, no doubt hoping she'd spontaneously confess. Shaking her head, Dee stalked to the door, yanking it open as she stepped to one side.

"I'm going to have to ask you to leave," she said.

Riddick didn't move. "Being uncooperative won't help your case any," he warned.

She pointed outside. "I'm telling you to go. Don't bother to come back unless you have a warrant."

They left without another word. The look Riddick shot her as he walked past was one Dee was familiar with. She'd given it to numerous perps over the course of her career.

And though it gave minimal satisfaction, she slammed the door behind them.

"Dee?" Cenrick appeared. "Are you all right?"

"I'm fine." Wrapping her arms around herself, she told him what had transpired.

"Mick was reported missing?" He ran his fingers through his hair. "Well, he's more likely not 'missing.' They've used their machine on him."

"Why is he involved in this?" Dee asked. Her voice shook. "He must have a reason, something we don't know."

"Mick was likely involved from the beginning, when it was safer. I think the balance of power has shifted. It's all Natasha now. Mick's become a pawn. I think she used him to get things set up. Once he delivered the Fae and she knew she could get more, she didn't need Mick anymore."

"It's possible Mick didn't know what she was planning," Dee said, obstinately loyal but not caring. "And once he found out, maybe he tried to stop her."

Cenrick gave a slow nod. "I'll let you have that small hope, though I don't have the same faith that you do."

She studied him. "Explain. I thought you and he were close."

He swallowed. "We were—once. But Mick harbored a lot of bitterness against the Fae. He was furious when he learned his mother had left him on earth without a second thought. His anger grew as he came to know his family and realized no one had ever even looked for him. In time, he came to believe the Fae held him in contempt. This was why he ultimately chose to live in your world permanently."

Expression stunned, Dee lifted her chin. "Despite that, I know Mick.

He just . . . wouldn't do something like this."

"Why not?" Cenrick watched her closely. "The Mick I know was in one kind of trouble after another."

"That was before he became a cop, right?"

"Years before."

"That's what I thought. All *my* Mick ever wanted to do was stop injustice. If he could have become a superhero, he would have. Growing up in the orphanage and in foster homes, he saw what kind of people prey on kids. Mick wanted to fight them. He was passionate about the subject. I joined the police department because of him."

She took a deep breath, then continued. "That's why the idea of him preying on other Fae makes no sense. *She's* behind all this, this Natasha Klein. We've got to find out what she's done to him. 'Missing,'" she fumed. "She better not have made him soulless."

Cenrick nodded. "Then we'll go with my plan I'll flush them out."

"I don't know—"

"Do you have a better idea?"

"No," she admitted. "But what's going to make this

more difficult is that we're probably under police surveillance now. They'll be watching this house and following me around."

He seemed surprised. "Why?"

She laughed, a sound utterly without humor. "If they really think I've killed off another cop, if I make one false move, I'm dead. There won't be a cop out there who isn't itching to get his hands around my throat."

"Surely they won't judge you without a trial."

"Oh, they will. It's human nature. All this started with corruption charges. Natasha's taken quick steps to ensure I have no credibility and no friends. I just haven't figured out why."

"That's simple," he said. "Obviously she's worried about you foiling her plan. Now if we can just find out how, we'll be better equipped to succeed."

Dee sighed. "Let's make another run by Mick's house. Perhaps Natasha and her machine have returned."

Cenrick looked nervous. "What about the police? If they're watching . . ."

"I'm a good driver. If they try to tail us, I'm sure I can shake them."

Dee saw no tail. Either she'd been wrong about the surveillance or Internal Affairs hadn't had time to set anything up yet. No one followed, and she drove quickly and unerringly to Mick's house. When his street materialized in front of them, in the late afternoon light she saw his house once again softly glowed.

"Look at that. They *must* be back."

Cenrick sat up straight. "This time, we've got to get inside without them knowing."

Dee parked the car in a different spot, one around the block. Together they got out. Cenrick held out his hand. She took it.

As they approached the front sidewalk, a police car screeched up, lights flashing, siren wailing.

"Freeze!" a voice yelled.

Dee groaned. "What now?" she muttered.

"We're bringing you in for questioning," the uniformed officer said, hustling her and Cenrick to his car. "Come with me, please."

Dee dug in her heels. "I need to know why."

His eyes met hers over the top of his sunglasses. Flat and cold, they were furious eyes, those of a cop holding in his anger. "Mick Morsi's Explorer was found, blood all over the front seat, Dee. He left a note in the glove box that said if anything happened to him, to look at you."

CHAPTER EIGHT

Eight hours later, they were finally released. Wear 'em down interrogations. Dee was intimately familiar with it now from the perp's perspective as well as the cops'.

"They can talk to me all they want," she explained to Cenrick while driving away from the police station. She kept her shoulders back and her chin up, as was her way, but he could see exhaustion radiating from every pore. "I'm only a suspect. Without hard evidence, they have nothing."

"They can't arrest you?"

"Not yet." She didn't sound optimistic. "I swear, if I can find Mick, I'm dragging him down to the police station myself."

"Not if he's soulless."

"We need to go back to his house," she decided. "Though, we've picked up a tail."

Cenrick stared at her. "You need to get some sleep. It's one o'clock in the morning, and you're spent."

Because he was right, instead of arguing she swore

long and low under her breath, using curses he'd only heard uttered by drunken soldiers in the raunchiest human bars.

She noticed his surprise. "Cops. I learned those words from other cops. Sorry." She looked embarrassed.

When they arrived at her apartment, the Sunday paper had already been delivered. She scooped it up off the doorstep on her way in, then tossed it on the floor near the couch. While she went to her bedroom to change, Cenrick dropped onto the sofa. The headline on the front page caught his attention:

LOCAL POLICE OFFICER SUSPECT IN PARTNER'S DISAPPEARANCE.

He grabbed it and unrolled the paper. At least they weren't calling it murder.

"Dee, come here," he said after reading a bit.

"What?" She hurried back into the living room.

"Take a look at this." He showed her the article. "They found Mick's Explorer, just like your police department said."

"But . . . this doesn't make sense. How'd a reporter get tipped off so quickly? We only just left the police station. The printer needs several hours' lead time, which means this was fed to someone long before I ever talked to the police."

Snatching the paper out of Cenrick's hands, Dee began reading. She was horrified. "Oh my God. The informant, whoever that may be, must have thought I'd confess. It's a damn shame when a supposedly unbiased newspaper practically accuses me of Mick's murder." She slammed the paper down on the kitchen counter. "I wonder if other media have picked this up and are running with it? I can't believe this."

"They aren't accusing you. They just mentioned you were a suspect. And nobody used the word murder."

She laughed bitterly. "They can't—they don't have a body."

Scanning the story again, he whistled. "I wonder what's with the blood all over the front seat. None of the soulless were hurt—at least, not their bodies. Maybe Mick staged this."

"He wouldn't," she replied. "Mick hates pain. He's incapable of cutting himself voluntarily, even to stage his own death."

"Are you certain of that?"

She thought of Mick and his squeamishness at the sight of blood, any blood. "Positive. If that blood matches his type, someone hurt him."

Cenrick sighed. "Well, that's entirely possible, the way things are going. And I suppose we don't even know what is involved with turning my people into husks. Maybe taking blood *is* involved."

She stared. "What have I gotten into here? Are we talking about vampirism? Some kind of ritualistic sacrifice?"

He shrugged. "I suppose there's a possibility either one might be involved. I just don't know."

"Great." She rubbed her temples. "What now?"

Cenrick leaned back where he was sitting. "I wish we knew why getting you out of the picture is so important to them. There's got to be something we're missing." He gave her a long look, considering. "I suppose we've got to get back into that house."

"Yeah. But with the police watching my every move, that's pretty damn impossible."

He glanced at her. "Go to bed, get some rest. Things will look better in the morning. They always do."

"Better in the morning, huh? You know, once that cliché used to be true, but not anymore. These days, every time I wake up things have gotten worse."

He held out his hand. She hesitated for the space of a heartbeat, then meshed her fingers with his. Holding on to him felt good. It felt right. She wished she had enough nerve to ask him to come to bed with her. But that wasn't fair to either of them. Using sex merely for distraction was never a good idea, at least for her.

Hand in hand, they walked down the hall to her room. At her door he pulled free, staring down at her with an inscrutable expression. Was he about to kiss her? Heart pounding, she waited. But he only murmured a quiet good night, and turned away, leaving her feeling like a fool.

She went into her room, alone again. Like she'd been all her life.

Though she thought she'd toss and turn all night, once she crawled between the sheets, she drifted off into that shadowy realm between sleep and wakefulness. Images haunted her, misty forms too indistinct to identify, and others, starkly sensual, of she and Cenrick.

She must have slept, because the next thing she knew, an earsplitting buzz startled her awake. The phone on the nightstand was ringing loud enough to wake the dead.

She bolted upright, confused and disoriented, squinting at the clock. It was still the middle of the night. A phone call at this hour couldn't be good.

Heart pounding, she grabbed the receiver. "Hello?"

"Dee. listen to me." It was a man, whispering urgently. She'd know that voice anywhere.

"Mick?"

He didn't respond. "You're in danger. They're going to come for you. You've got to get out."

"Who are *they*, Mick? Where are you and who is this Natasha? What's she doing to you?"

He coughed, sounding as though he were gasping for air. "No time to explain. Please, Dee, get out while you can."

"Are you in danger?"

Silence.

"Mick, are you in danger?"

"I don't think so." Still whispering, he sounded . . . confused. Then, more firmly: "No. I'm not."

"Are you helping those people harm the Fae?"

He made a sound, a harsh intake of breath. "You know? How?"

Her heart sank. He hadn't denied it. "Never mind how I know. I want to know *why*. How could you do something so horrible? What's going on with you?"

"I can't talk now. And you've got to go, Dee. Quickly."

"Run away? I can't. They're setting me up."

"I know." He sighed. "I wish I could help you more, but—"

"You're involved! You can. Talk to me. Let me meet with you somewhere, anywhere. Your choice."

Silence was the only response.

"Mick, please. Talk to me," she begged. But instead of an answer, she heard a click as he hung up the phone. She checked the number. The caller ID read UNAVAILABLE. Of course. Mick knew better than to call from a traceable number. She wanted to throw the phone against the wall.

"Who was that?"

Bleary-eyed, Cenrick stood framed in her doorway. Wearing only a pair of silky red boxers she remembered Peter hating, he looked sleepy and gorgeous and sexy as hell. His long, dark hair was tousled, standing up every which way in unruly tufts. With her adrenaline already pumping, Dee pushed away a sharp stab of desire and inhaled sharply, telling herself not to lose focus.

When she didn't immediately answer, he moved closer. "Dee? The phone. Who called?"

"Mick," she said firmly, suddenly conscious of her aching breasts and the way her nipples poked at her cotton pajama top. Cenrick took the last couple of steps, stopping at the side of her bed. Peering down at her, he ran a hand through his hair.

"Mick? Where is he?"

"I don't know. Caller ID wasn't helpful. But he said he was calling to warn me."

As she repeated Mick's words, again Cenrick dragged his hand through his hair, making an even worse mess of it. She was tempted to help him out, but she knew running her own fingers through his looks would be a terrible mistake. At this moment, merely touching him would destroy what was left of her tattered self-control. She couldn't give in to temptation.

But, so what if she did? She was tired of fighting this attraction. Right now, Cenrick's masculine beauty was the only good thing left in her life. And if there was anything she'd learned growing up the way she had, if something good came along, she'd better enjoy it. Happiness was fleeting.

He shifted, looking down at her. She knew the exact moment when his focus changed from discussing the phone call to registering the fact that she was nearly naked, with hunger burning in her eyes.

"Dee?" He touched her arm, making her jump. "Are you all right?"

The huskiness in his voice had her peering up at him through her lashes. What she saw in his face made her heart skip and her breath catch in her throat. *Desire*. As raw and hot and urgent as her own.

Her heart turned over in her chest. She concentrated on keeping her breathing steady and regular. Did she really want to do this? The answer was a resounding *yes*.

Cenrick sat down on the edge of the bed, causing the mattress to dip and her mouth to go dry. How simple it would be to roll toward him until she could wrap herself around his muscular body. Once they touched, they'd combust, she knew, and they'd make wild, passionate love. Even thinking about it had her biting back a groan.

Yet she held back, unwilling to make the first

move. Even though she knew it wouldn't absolve her of guilt if anything happened between them, she wanted him to initiate it.

"I wonder why he called now, in the middle of the night," Cenrick mused.

"He had to be calling me on the sly," she said, rehashing their conversation, feeling rather desperate. "You should have heard him, whispering. If he wasn't in danger, why whisper?"

"True. So, he didn't want his cohort, Natasha, to hear him?"

"Exactly."

Cenrick stared off into the distance, thinking. He looked a thousand miles away. He wasn't going to touch her.

Dee's heart sank, and her throat ached. Either his self-restraint was greater than hers or he just flat out didn't want her. She again remembered the feelings from her childhood spent waiting to be adopted.

Fine. She could deal with this. But if she didn't move, and move quickly, she'd make a complete and utter fool of herself. Edging out of her bed, careful not to touch him, she headed for her closet. She could swear she felt his gaze burning her.

Doing her best to pretend he wasn't there, she pulled a pair of jeans up over her short pajama bottoms and grabbed a T-shirt with a built-in bra. Keeping her back to him, she got dressed, finally stepping into flip-flops. Thus armored, she turned and faced him, hoping her expression looked as remote as she desired.

He stared at her, his expression perplexed. "What are you doing?"

"Getting dressed so I can go," she said in a lofty voice.

"Go where?"

Crossing to the dresser, she stared into the mirror and dragged a brush through her hair. "Mick's house." On her way to the bathroom to brush her teeth, she glanced at him over her shoulder, eyeing his boxers with a disdainful raised brow and said, "And if you want to go, you'd better get dressed quickly." She closed the bathroom door behind her.

As exit lines went, not half bad. He'd never know the way emotion and need tumbled inside her.

Leaning on the counter over the bathroom sink, she let her rigid posture sag. She craved this man with a strength and urgency she'd never before felt, not even with Peter. Worse, she knew their combination was impossible. Cenrick was a Fae prince, while she was . . . nothing. She had no family, no friends— not even a job. Even Mick, the man she'd called brother, had deserted her.

"No pity parties," she told herself firmly, rolling her shoulders.

Brushing her teeth, washing her face, and rolling on deodorant: all the motions of an ordinary morning should have helped her regain her equilibrium. But it was still so early in the morning, and her body knew she ought to be in bed.

With Cenrick.

She sagged against the counter. Back to that again?

What on earth was wrong with her? She covered her face with her hands. She was an emotional wreck.

Reaching for a towel, she blotted her face dry and sighed. Sometimes she couldn't win for losing. Cenrick was dressed and waiting when she emerged.

"Let's go."

She strode past him, proud of herself for appearing so aloof, and scooped up her car keys. He followed her, waiting silently while she locked the door behind them. If she hadn't known better, she would have thought he was brooding.

Outside, the pre-dawn air was cool. The stars sparkled brightly in the cloudless sky.

Dee drove fast, with a precision she'd learned in the police academy. Beside her on the front seat, Cenrick stared out the window at the night landscape that flashed past, and didn't speak. Which suited her fine. She wasn't in the mood for talking either.

As they got off the freeway, she heard the sound of sirens in the distance. As she neared Mick's subdivision, the sirens grew louder. A fire truck roared up behind them, lights flashing. As Dee pulled over to let it pass, several more followed.

"Two or three alarms," she mused. "That's not good."

"What?" Cenrick looked confused.

"That means they're calling more than one city for assistance. Look. Smoke, that way." She pointed, an awful certainty making her chest tight. "That's right where we're going. Mick's house."

"I've got a bad feeling about this," Cenrick said.

"That makes two of us."

"You don't think . . . ?"

She smiled grimly. "Unfortunately, I do."

Numerous fire engines, an ambulance, and two police cruisers, all with lights and sirens blaring, passed them. Dee checked her mirrors and pulled back onto the street

The scent of smoke grew worse as they pulled into the gates marking the beginning of Mick's subdivision. Ahead, a glow lit the sky, similar to the one caused by Natasha's machine. Dee wondered who could see it.

As they attempted to turn onto Mick's street, they found it crammed with fire trucks, emergency vehicles, and police cars, making it impassable. A roadblock had been set up, and worried neighbors clustered at each end of the street.

Four houses down, an enormous blaze raged. The flames engulfed not only Mick's house, but the houses on either side.

"Damn it." Dee opened her car door. "I don't believe this." She started to get out, but Cenrick grabbed her arm.

"Wait," he said. "Going out there might not be safe for you."

"Why, because Mick just called and said as much?" She shook her head. "It was probably a trick. That phone call was probably a last ditch effort to get me to stay away."

Cenrick stared at her. "You don't find this odd? Mick calls you, and less than an hour later his house catches fire?"

She stared back at him. "You know I've got to go. I

can't sit here and do nothing while his house burns to the ground."

She got out of the car. Cenrick did the same, a look of resignation on his face.

Though she knew the firefighters would disapprove of her getting too close, she approached anyway, Cenrick at her side. Fire trucks were everywhere; completely blocking the street, a cacophony of engines and sirens, hoses spraying and blaze roaring. Blue, red, and white lights flashed from the trucks, a startling contrast to the leaping orange flames. Black smoke billowed everywhere, turning to gray as the hoses blasted the fire with water.

Despite that onslaught, the inferno blazed on, flames arching high and wide, unstoppable. Showers of sparks threatened to ignite more trees, other roofs, additional houses, if the steady flow of water wasn't able to curb the conflagration. The closer Dee got, the more intense the heat.

"Get back," someone shouted. A group of firefighters moved back in a wave. There was a shower of sparks as the roof collapsed.

"Was anyone in there?" Dee asked, grabbing the first person she could. "Did everyone get out safely?"

"We don't know." Grim-faced and soot-stained, the firefighter shook off her hand. "By the time someone sounded the alarm and we got here, the structure was already too unstable, the fire too intense. We tried to send someone in, but he couldn't make it."

One of the cops caught sight of her and hurried over, looking harried. "Dee, what the hell are you doing here?"

It was Chad Warwick, one of her former pals.

"I wanted to check on Mick," she replied.

He shook his head. "Sometimes I wonder about you. Did you ever stop to think how this would look?"

Confused, she stared at him. "How what will look?"

"You're under investigation. Mick goes missing, an incriminating note is found, and then you show up at his house to watch it burn to the ground. Don't you think they're going to wonder if you torched the place?"

"You know me better than that," she snapped. But her heart was pounding. "And I didn't know his house was on fire until I got here. Mick called me."

Now it was his turn to stare. "No way."

"Yes. He's not missing. He called me tonight, just a half hour ago."

"From here? Not possible."

"I don't know where he was. Caller ID didn't say. He blocked the call."

Chad crossed his arms, regarding her steadily. She could tell he didn't believe her.

"Start another hose," someone yelled. Another truck moved into place, more firefighters jumping off. While they worked feverishly to unravel the hose, another man pushed through and headed toward Dee. Even at this distance, she recognized him. Ted Harstan, the Fire Chief.

As he approached, she could tell he wasn't happy to see her. "Chief Harstan." Dee dipped her head, smiling pleasantly. "How are you?"

"Dee Bishop." No answering smile softened the craggy planes of his face. "You need to move along. You don't belong here. But then, it's a known fact arsonists can't resist returning to the scene of their crimes."

"Arsonists?" Reeling from his words, Dee was glad of Cenrick's steadying arm. "What are you saying?"

He ignored her question, continuing in a hard voice, "I'm warning you right now. We will have investigators looking into the cause of this fire. If arson is determined, and I think it will be, you'd better hope you have an alibi."

An alibi? "He's my alibi." She jerked a thumb toward Cenrick. "Are you formally accusing me of setting this fire?" She couldn't believe this. Yet the Chief's rigid posture and scowling face told her he meant exactly what she thought.

"Not formally," he replied. His accusatory glare cut to the bone. "But you're my main suspect." And with that, he stalked back to his men.

With a sad shake of his head, Chad Warwick watched him go. "I told you. You shouldn't be here."

"What the hell?" Dee exploded. "Why does everyone in this town find it so easy to believe I'm a criminal?"

Chad looked over his shoulder. "Motive, Dee," he said. "Motive." He walked away, leaving her standing staring after him, her stomach tied in knots and burning.

"Maybe we should go." Cenrick tried to turn her away, back toward her car. As he did, flashbulbs exploded. Reporters! Three cameramen, each from a different network, came at her, shouting questions while filming her with the raging inferno as a backdrop.

"What do you have to say to the allegations about your connection to Mick Morsi's disappearance?" a stocky woman from Channel Four News called out.

Stunned, Dee could only shake her head. Not waiting for an answer, the other reporters yelled out their questions, each vying loudly to be the one she answered.

"Did you set this fire?"

"What do you know about the blood in Mr. Morsi's Explorer?"

Meanwhile, the cameras continued to roll.

Dee tried to push her way past, but they blocked her.

"Come on." Cenrick turned her into his chest, shielding her, using his big body like a linebacker to push through.

They made it to her car. Hands shaking, Dee managed to get the key in the ignition and start the engine. She drove without seeing where she was going. Drove until the smoke and the sirens and the commotion was several blocks behind.

Then, pulling over, she turned to face Cenrick.

"You realize what this means, don't you?"

He nodded. "With the house gone, they won't be back. Wherever they've moved their machine, it's permanently gone. We'll have hell finding it."

"And Mick." She ran her fingers through her hair, wishing she could stop trembling. "And they're trying to pin one more thing on me. My credibility is shot to hell. They've won."

"Not yet. We'll figure something out." He leaned

close. She was pretty sure he meant to kiss her cheek, but she turned her head at the last moment, and his mouth slanted across hers.

Shuddering, she put all of her frustration into the kiss, all the feeling in her soul. It might be a mistake, but she needed this more than she'd ever needed anything. She needed him to make love to her.

CHAPTER NINE

The instant their lips touched, heat flared. Desperation driving Dee, she put everything into the kiss, hoping, praying that he wouldn't turn her away. After a second of stunned shock, he took control, deepening the kiss, his tongue mating with hers.

Desperation fled, desire, urgent and hot, taking its place. She wanted him—right here, right now. Had she really thought she could control this? When they'd been dancing around their attraction for days?

Luckily, she still had the capacity to reason. After all, they were back in her car, parked on the side of a very public street.

"Cenrick." She broke away. "We can't. Not here."

He nodded, gazing down at her. The heat blazing in his eyes was almost enough to change her mind.

"My apartment. We're five minutes away."

"Get there quickly." The raw desire in his voice made her shiver.

"Oh, I will," she promised.

They made it in four minutes. Exiting the car, they

hit the sidewalk running, taking the front steps two at a time. As they reached the landing, she dug her key out of her purse and headed for the door.

Cenrick grabbed her arm. "Wait."

Impatient, she danced from one foot to the other, anticipation making her edgy. "Why? What's up?"

"Look." He pointed.

Her front door was slightly ajar. When they'd left, she'd been careful to lock it.

"Someone's been in my apartment!" She pulled her gun from its holster and flicked off the safety. "Let's go."

"No." He touched her arm, forestalling her. "I'm going first."

"But I'm armed. You're not."

"You can cover my back." And without waiting for an answer, he pushed the door open with his shoulder.

Taking a deep breath, Dee plunged in right behind him. Inside, chaos reigned.

"Look at this." He shook his head. "What the—?"

With a touch on his arm, she got his attention. "We check the place out first, see if anyone's still here. Then we can take stock of the destruction."

Prowling from room to room, they searched everywhere. As she'd suspected, the intruder was long gone.

"Now," she said, holstering her gun. "Let's see what they've done." Vicious, random destruction. Her apartment had been completely trashed.

They started with her living room, her favorite area. The multihued pillows had been slit, their stuffing flung all over. The plush sofa had been slashed.

All that remained of the cushions were ribbons of foam and cloth. The intruder had even taken care to destroy the prints on the walls, smashing the glass and using the shards to shred the art.

In the kitchen she saw that the contents of her refrigerator had been flung all over the countertops and walls, running in great globs of goo to the tile.

"If I didn't know better, I'd think this looks like the work of teenagers. It's random destruction for no reason."

He gave her a thoughtful look. "There's a reason. They're trying to intimidate you."

"Who? Natasha and her pals?" She grabbed paper towels, handed some to him, and got busy cleaning the kitchen. After a moment, he joined her.

"After what happened to Mick's, I'm actually surprised they didn't set fire to the place," he said, scrubbing.

"Ah, but then I wouldn't have been able to see their handiwork." She couldn't keep the bitterness from her tone. "What I want to know is, why? Why are they targeting me? What have I done to hack them off?"

"Your association with Mick."

At her snort of disbelief, Cenrick smiled. "Somehow, some way, you're a threat to their plans. We have to take heart in that."

"You know," she mused. "When I was a police officer and I investigated robberies and break-ins, the victims always said they felt violated. While I sympathized, I didn't really get it. Now, I know exactly what they meant." She picked up the phone, started to dial;

then, shaking her head, she punched the OFF button. "I can't believe how this is affecting me." Looking down at her hands, she saw they were trembling.

Cenrick put his arm around her shoulders and drew her close. "Hey, at least you haven't been hurt. Count your blessings."

"I know, I know." She made a face. "You're right. And nothing's missing, at least that I can tell. But this was my home. My first real home. Growing up the way I did, when I finally got my own place, I took pains to make each room exactly the way I wanted. And now someone's gone and taken that away."

He hugged her, offering a silent comfort.

Though she told herself she wouldn't cry, the hot ache at the back of her throat and the stinging in her eyes proved her wrong. For a moment, for just a tiny slice of time, she allowed herself to hold on to Cenrick, taking comfort in his solidness and breathing in his masculine scent. Then she pushed herself out of his arms and lifted her chin.

"You know, if I'm looking on the bright side, at least they didn't touch my shoes." She laughed.

He stared. "Your what?"

"Shoes." With a small shrug, she gave him a sheepish smile. "I'm fond of designer shoes. Expensive ones. I save for months to buy one pair. I have a bit of a collection." She led the way to her bedroom closet, opening the door to show him the rows and rows of boxes. "They left these alone, thank goodness."

"They probably didn't know they mattered to you."

"True. I'm sure if they had, they would have destroyed them." She trooped back into her living room, eyeing the mess. She sighed and held up the phone she'd carried with her.

"I keep putting off the inevitable. I need to call this in." At his blank expression, she elaborated: "I need to make a police report, so this is documented."

She dialed the number she knew by heart. Susan Best, the dispatcher on graveyard duty, took the report and promised to send out an officer. Her unemotional voice and the way she didn't even ask if Dee was okay, told Dee the poisonous lies about her had spread throughout the entire department.

Again, as if he could sense her despair, Cenrick came to her. This time he took her hand. They sat side by side on her ruined couch and waited for the police.

In twenty minutes, the doorbell chimed. The responding officers were Ben Lieber and Linda Lacey, two officers Dee knew well. She and Linda had even gone out for drinks once or twice. They'd both lamented how hard it was to be a woman in a man's world, though both were determined to make it.

At least Linda was still in the game.

Lieber, an older man with a bald spot, was decidedly unhappy to be there.

"Point of entry?" he asked, his tone suggesting that perhaps she'd trashed the place herself.

"Over here." Cenrick showed him the broken door frame.

"I can't believe you of all people don't have a better dead bolt," Officer Lieber commented, shooting Dee a harsh look.

"I know." Dee felt a bit sheepish. "I'm getting a new one now, believe me."

"Get two," Linda said. And as the other woman smiled sympathetically, Dee felt some relief. At least not everyone in the police department believed the false stories.

Officer Lieber, however, clearly did. Clearing his throat, he planted himself in front of her, his aggressive stance and hostility evident. "Do you have a list of what's missing?" His pen poised over paper and his narrow-eyed glare told Dee exactly how much he disliked even talking to her.

The sad part was, she couldn't blame him. Once she'd have felt the same, were their situations reversed.

"Whatever happened to innocent until proven guilty?" At Lieber's shocked expression, Dee realized she'd spoken her thoughts aloud. Good. She was tired of being tarred and feathered without a trial.

"Do you have a list?" Linda stepped up to fill the silence. Through most of this, her gaze had been going to Cenrick.

Again, Dee could relate. Before all this had happened, she herself had been ready to jump his bones.

"No list. As far as I can tell, nothing is missing. I don't think this was a robbery."

"Really?" Lieber drawled. "Then, pray tell, why the break-in? Just to inconvenience you?"

Dee ignored him, focusing on her friend Linda. "Intimidation."

Lieber laughed, a mean sound. "Don't you mean payback? Payback for dishonoring your badge and our department?"

"Ben, that's enough." Linda snapped. "If you can't be professional, why don't you wait outside."

"Sounds good to me. It stinks in here." Stalking to the door, Officer Lieber left.

"Thank you," Dee said softly. "You don't know how hard this has been for me."

"Look." Officer Lacey waved away her thanks. "At the department, a lot of people don't believe the charges. Gossip has dozens of witnesses saying you took bribes, that you were running a racket, selling drugs, you name it."

"One hooker, and some guy I've never even met." Dee shook her head. "I swear to you, I wasn't."

"Tell it to Internal Affairs."

"I have." Swallowing, Dee looked the other woman square in the face. "I'm going to find out who set me up and I'm going to clear my name."

Linda looked hopeful. "Yeah? You'd better do it fast. They're talking about calling a grand jury and setting up a hearing next week. If they indict you . . ." She didn't have to finish. Dee knew her career was over if she was indicted.

"They don't have enough evidence to go to a grand jury." Not unless something more had turned up, something Dee hadn't been told about. "I'd better call Lieutenant Cowell."

"You do that. In the meantime, we'll make our report." Linda opened the door, turning one last time to check out Cenrick before looking at Dee. "And Dee? A word of advice. Look into Mick's so-called girlfriend. If she's for real . . . Well, I heard she used to be a scientist at some hush-hush government lab."

And with that, Officer Lacey let herself out.

Once she was gone, Dee stared at Cenrick. "Do you believe that? They know about Natasha."

"They know what we do, that she used to be a scientist." He shrugged. "They don't know about the Fae or the machine that's stealing Fae souls."

"And they think Mick is dead. And that I'm evil incarnate." She laughed, a sound without humor. "Come on. Let's head over to the hardware store and pick up a couple dead bolts."

When they returned, new door assembly and dead bolts in tow, Dee sighed again as she surveyed her wrecked living room. "I'll make us a pot of coffee, even though it's kind of early yet. I need my caffeine fix." Standing on tiptoe, she placed a casual kiss on his cheek, wondering if he'd totally forgotten what they'd started in the car. Now that the initial shock of the break-in was over, making love with him was all she could think about again.

As she moved away, he grabbed her, claiming her mouth in a savage kiss. *Thank goodness.* Letting the package fall to the floor, she wrapped her arms around his neck.

"Cenrick," she gasped against his lips.

"Now is not the time for reason," he told her, his breathing harsh. "I need to feel you, your sleek softness and rounded curves. I want to make love to you, to bury myself deep inside you."

She started to speak, and he shushed her.

"Nothing else matters for this instant. Just you and me."

Her moan was one of acquiescence. He was right:

YES!

Sign me up for the **Historical Romance Book Club** and send my TWO FREE BOOKS! If I choose to stay in the club, I will pay only $8.50* each month, a savings of $5.48!

YES!

Sign me up for the **Love Spell Book Club** and send my TWO FREE BOOKS! If I choose to stay in the club, I will pay only $8.50* each month, a savings of $5.48!

NAME: _____

ADDRESS: _____

_____

TELEPHONE: _____

E-MAIL: _____

☐ **I WANT TO PAY BY CREDIT CARD.**

☐ VISA   ☐ MasterCard   ☐ DISCOVER

ACCOUNT #: _____

EXPIRATION DATE: _____

SIGNATURE: _____

Send this card along with $2.00 shipping & handling for each club you wish to join, to:

**Romance Book Clubs
20 Academy Street
Norwalk, CT 06850-4032**

Or fax (must include credit card information!) to: 610.995.9274.
You can also sign up online at www.dorchesterpub.com.

*Plus $2.00 for shipping. Offer open to residents of the U.S. and Canada only.
Canadian residents please call 1.800.481.9191 for pricing information.

If under 18, a parent or guardian must sign. Terms, prices and conditions subject to change. Subscription subject
to acceptance. Dorchester Publishing reserves the right to reject any order or cancel any subscription.

JOIN NOW!

Desire, wild and fierce and urgent, swept everything else away.

"Touch me," he growled against her mouth.

Her breath caught. Her heartbeat stuttered. Hesitantly, tentatively, she trailed her fingers over his chest, down to his flat belly and the band of cloth at his waist. Finally, skimming over fabric, she touched him *there,* gasping as she felt the fullness of his arousal through his trousers. He moaned as she cupped him.

He tugged at her shirt. Still stroking him, she lifted it, pulling it over her head and tossing it away. She loved being half naked and pressed close to him.

"You next," she gasped against his mouth. She tugged at the collar of his shirt, tearing it.

Eyes burning with desire, he shrugged it off.

She gave him a slow smile. "The pants have to go too," she added.

He stood still as she tugged his trousers off him. Unable to resist stroking him, she bit her lip as he pushed his rigid flesh against her hand. About to lower her mouth to taste him, she made a sound of disappointment when he stopped her.

"It's your turn," he growled, motioning to her pants.

Keeping her gaze locked with his, she shimmied out of her jeans. One simple flick of her wrist, and she sent her panties sailing across the room.

"Come here." He tugged her to him and they tumbled onto the shredded couch.

She gasped as he settled her over him, her body heat combining with his. She'd only made love half a dozen times in her life, most of those with her fiancé Peter. Never had it felt like this.

Placing his hands at her waist, he slid her up the length of his sex, to the top of its swollen head. Then, while her damp folds enveloped him, he took her nipple into his mouth and lightly bit. She moaned. He suckled. She lifted herself up and with one swift motion, took him deep inside her.

He clenched his teeth. "By the Goddess . . ."

When she began to move, she forgot all her past. She gave herself over to the sensation, helplessly tightening herself around him with each upward stroke.

"Ah, Cenrick." Increasing her pace, she made love to him with wild abandon. Her shuddering release came an instant before his. She was still clenching in the throes of ecstasy as he groaned and poured his seed into her. Her last thought before she collapsed on top of him was that she'd finally found the magic that had been missing from her life.

While the sun rose, Cenrick held Dee and savored the scent and feel of her while she slumbered. He tried to understand his emotions. Confusion and elation battled equally inside him. How had this happened? Completely unexpectedly and at the worst possible time, he'd found the one woman whose spirit resonated with his. In Rune, they called these soul mates.

How Alrick would laugh. Especially since Cenrick had teased him without mercy when Alrick had said the same about his own human soul mate, Carly.

Finally Dee snuggled close, a tight fit on the large couch, and Cenrick slept.

Feeling strangely happy to be so domesticated, he woke and moved from the couch without waking her. Stepping over the shredded pillow, he went out to get a breath of fresh air. Judging from the position of the sun, it was late afternoon. As he turned to go back inside, he came face-to-face with a large manila envelope taped to the front door. Dee's name was written on the front in black ink. After thoroughly inspecting the thing, he carried it inside. If magic had been used around the paper, he couldn't detect any.

Still dozing, Dee had snuggled into the ruined sofa. She groaned when he turned the blinds and flooded the room with bright sunlight.

"Wake up," he said. He waved the envelope at her. "Someone left you a present."

Blinking, she pushed herself up. "What the—?"

"It was on your front door." He dropped it in her lap.

She ripped into it carefully, peering inside before gently shaking the contents into her lap. A square of lined notebook paper fell out. When she unfolded it, she found a key taped inside.

"Something's written on the paper. 'Mailboxes and All,'" she read. "That's up on Hemphill Street." Rubbing her eyes, she climbed off the couch, wincing when she surveyed the remaining mess from the day before. "Give me a minute to wash my face and brush my teeth and we'll go. We can grab some coffee on the way out. Five minutes," she promised, and dashed into the bathroom, closing the door.

True to her word, she appeared a few minutes later wearing jean shorts and a tank top. "Ready?" she asked.

All he could do was stare. "You look . . . beautiful," he managed. Though he would have thought their lovemaking the night before would have satisfied him for a bit, he felt his body stir.

She laughed, swatting at his arm. "Right. Come on, let's go."

He followed his usual precautions when getting into her car and she waited patiently. Once he had buckled up, she drove slowly from her parking spot, waving to the unmarked police car across the street.

"Watch. He'll follow us."

The white car pulled out behind them.

Dee drove slowly, signaling each turn. "I'm giving him time to get complacent before I lose him," she confided.

Once they left her neighborhood, she began to pick up speed. While she drove, she was focused, watching both the road and her rearview mirror.

They entered the freeway at a sedate forty-five miles per hour, according to the speedometer. Once on, she moved into the middle lane, gradually increasing her speed. The unmarked police car stayed with them.

Admiring her competence, Cenrick studied her. She seemed calm, cool, and in control. Then he noticed her hands gripped the steering wheel so tightly that her knuckles showed white.

"Hold on," she said. Immediately, she yanked the wheel. From the middle lane, she cut left, roaring past four cars, then swung across two lanes and passed several more. "Now we'll lose him."

He turned to look. He saw white cars, black cars, and various other vehicles, all moving the same direction. He couldn't see their tail. "Where is he?"

"Three cars back, right behind us." She gunned the accelerator, slipping into a slot between a tractor trailer and a minivan. "Hang on." They shot forward.

"There's my exit." She pointed to a sign ahead. "Downtown, half a mile."

Glancing back, he saw their tail was trapped behind a delivery truck in the middle lane, boxed in on both sides yet still in view.

"He can still see us. How are you going to lose him?"

With a fierce grin, she stomped the accelerator. "He's about to get out of his box. Once he does, he'll pull in behind us. Which is good, because I'm going to make it impossible for him to follow me off the exit. You'd better hang on."

True to her prediction, their tail finally passed the delivery truck and shot into their lane, two cars back.

"Here we go."

Horns blared as she shot across two lanes, narrowly missing a station wagon. Tires screeched, then they were clear, barreling down the exit. Trapped, the police car continued on.

"That took care of him." Sounding satisfied, she slowed and made a right turn. "Here we are. Hemphill Street."

The four-lane street was lined with shops. People crowded the sidewalks, and traffic moved slowly between stoplights.

"There it is." She pointed. "Mailboxes and All. In that two-story mini-mall right next to the Sonic." They pulled into a lot and parked.

He couldn't resist glancing the way they'd come. "No police car."

"Good." Unbuckling, she grinned. "That means we lost them."

He smiled back, resisting the urge to kiss her. "Where'd you learn to drive like that?"

"Special training. I thought I wanted to be on our SWAT team once." With a shrug, she pocketed her car keys. "Since I don't work well in groups, I opted out. Come on."

The inside of the mini-mall was packed with men in Hawaiian print shirts, women in halter tops and shorts. Kids wheeled all around, laughing and running.

"Summer in South Worth," she said. "Lots of tourists. I think the Mailbox place is this way."

When they reached the storefront, Dee nodded at the clerk, refusing his offer of help. Eyeing the wall of mailboxes, Dee pulled out the key. "Let's see. We need 2467. Ah, here we are."

The box was on the bottom, nearly at the end of the row.

The key fit. The lock turned and Dee pulled open the metal door. Inside was a narrow manila envelope. She looked left and right as she withdrew it, relocked the box and pocketed the key.

"Got it. Let's go." And grabbing Cenrick's arm, she leaned into him as though cuddling.

Though he knew she was putting on an act, his

heartbeat sped up. "Aren't you going to see what's inside?" he asked.

"Not here." She whispered into his ear. "Pretend like we're a couple, will you?"

Puzzled, he put his arm around her shoulder and drew her close. "Why?"

"If anyone's watching for us, I'd like to be less conspicuous, though your size makes that difficult. If they're looking for you, they won't expect you with a woman. And vice versa."

"I see." Moving through the mall, he kept an eye out for any suspicious characters. No one appeared to be paying them the slightest bit of attention.

Outside, the humid air felt like a slap in the face. The parking lot was full, with two more cars waiting in line to take each empty slot. A huge bus rumbled past, the diesel fumes making Dee sneeze.

"Damn allergies." She shook her head. Cenrick hid his smile, thinking of Rune and the flowers.

As they crossed the pavement, making their way toward her car, he heard a muffled sound and the window of the pickup next to him exploded.

"What the—?"

"Get down!" Throwing herself on top of him, Dee knocked him to the ground. "That was a gunshot. And they've got a silencer."

Their attacker squeezed off another shot, this time striking the side of a candy-apple red BMW parked on their other side.

"I can't see where he is," she muttered. "I don't know what direction we should run."

They were trapped. Unable to flee. Their only option was to fight back. But how? Cenrick tried to think. He couldn't use magic here, surrounded by so much metal machinery. And, against bullets, his crystal dagger would be all but useless.

"Stay down," Dee grunted. "Damn, I wish I had my gun. I left it in the glove box."

"If we stay low, maybe we can make it to your car."

"Maybe. But first I've got to figure out where the shooter is hiding. And pray no one else wanders into his line of fire. There are a ton of tourists with kids out here today. I don't want any of them hurt."

He hadn't thought of that. Shifting his weight, he muttered an ancient curse. "Haven't enough innocents been harmed? These people keep destroying Fae lives. Why harm humans, too?"

"Most likely this is a hired gun. Natasha probably paid someone to come after us. Either that or"—her voice was grim—"somebody in the police department decided they hate me enough to kill me."

Startled, he looked at her crouching next to him, so beautiful, so tiny, so fierce. He couldn't let them harm her. "Let's make a run for it. I'll shield you with my body."

She made a strangled noise low in her throat. "If anything, *I* should shield *you*. Metal bullets will hurt me, but they're poison to you."

"They can kill us both just as easily." He pushed himself up to see if he could spot any sign of the shooter.

Again he wished, as he'd wished a hundred times in his life, that he was more of a warrior like his brother. Alrick had been the golden boy, Rune's equivalent of a superstar athlete, while Cenrick had been more of a quiet scholar—a nerd.

But with no time to dwell on this, Cenrick ducked behind a car before cautiously peering around the back bumper.

Immediately, their assailant fired again. This time, the bullet ricocheted off a concrete pillar behind them.

"Oh!" Dee jerked and grabbed her side, staring down at her abdomen in surprise. Blood spread over her shirt and hand. "I've been hit. In the stomach." She gasped again. "Gut shots are never good."

Cenrick looked desperately around for something, anything, some kind of weapon he could use. He found nothing.

Dee moaned with pain. He grabbed her, trying to staunch the flow of blood. As she slipped into unconsciousness, going limp in his arms, he heard footsteps moving closer. The shooter, coming to finish them off.

He did the only thing he could. Despite the metal all around him, he grabbed Dee's shoulder. Quickly, urgently, he spoke the words of the spell to take them to Rune, and prayed it would somehow work.

CHAPTER TEN

Materializing in Rune, Cenrick let out the breath he'd been holding. "Thank the Goddess!" he said.

He stepped onto the path that led to the palace, and he saw that Mort waited as though expecting him.

"She is hurt," he said.

Mort gasped at all the blood.

Carrying Dee in his arms, Cenrick strode past the mage, hurrying toward the castle. Above, Tinth screeched and circled. Mort hurried to keep up.

Once they'd gained the steps to the castle, Cenrick turned to look at the older man. "Can you save her?" he asked.

The mage looked from Dee's unconscious form to the hallway that led to his quarters. "Bring her to my room, and let me try."

Try? "Trying is not enough, old man. You must save her." Cenrick was already moving forward, making the seemingly endless journey down twisted deserted hallways until he reached the mage's double-paneled door.

Mort threw the doors open. Inside the room, a hearth fire burned merrily to banish the chill. "Place her on that pallet," he ordered.

Cenrick complied, gently arranging a still-unconscious Dee on the surface, and squinting at the older man suspiciously. "One might almost assume you were expecting us."

Mort's expression was grave. "As when your brother brought Carly here after that explosion which nearly took her life, Tinth came before you, warning me to make ready. My hawk told me of the metal bullet that pierced Dee's side."

Moving the bloodstained material away from the wound, Cenrick nodded absently. All his life, most of Rune had wondered at the mage's communication with his hawk. Now, Cenrick had to worry about Dee.

She moaned and he froze.

"Moving the cloth pains her, but it must be done," Mort said, placing a basin of warm water near the pallet and handing Cenrick a cloth. "We must clean the wound so I can remove the bullet."

Gently Cenrick washed away the blood, turning the water red as he wrung out the cloth. "The wound still bleeds, but it's as clean as I can make it."

"Then leave us," Mort commanded. Slipping on his gloves, he waved a hand.

"No." Dropping the cloth into the basin, Cenrick stayed put.

The mage sighed. "Then hold her hands, in case she wakes. I can't have her moving when I'm working."

Heart in his throat, Cenrick did as Mort requested. Her small hands were cold and lifeless, which terrified him. He kept his gaze on her face while the mage searched for the bullet.

"I found it!" Triumphant, Mort held up a bloody piece of metal in his gloved fingers. "Now that the metal has been removed, my magic can heal her. She should be good as new."

Good as new. While the mage worked, Cenrick thought of the shooter. He wanted to go back, right now, and find the man who had done this to her. And when he did . . .

Suddenly, he remembered the envelope. Did she still have it? He remembered she'd slipped it into her back pocket. He glanced at Dee, who was still unconscious. Perhaps whatever was inside would reveal clues to their enemy's whereabouts.

"Finished." Satisfaction rang in Mort's voice. "You can let her go now."

Cenrick placed her hands at her sides. Then, gently, he slid his hand under her backside, locating the brown envelope and pulling it from her pocket.

"What is that?" Mort regarded him curiously.

"This is what we were retrieving when someone shot at us." Peeling back the flap, he opened the envelope.

Inside, he found several photographs. The first was of some kind of machine, the second showed the blond woman Natasha standing next to it, her expression coldly triumphant. In the third Mick had joined her, looking solemn. And the fourth—oh, the fourth—showed the Fae known as Galyeon strapped into the machine and screaming. Galyeon was now one of the soulless.

"How long before Dee wakes?" he asked.

Mort shrugged. "I don't know. But I promise to make certain she feels no pain." He indicated his stock of herbs and potions. When something he saw in Cenrick's face must have alarmed him, he added, "You cannot wake her now. She will suffer."

Looking at her, so pale, so still, Cenrick believed the mage was right. "I know." He took a deep breath. "But as soon as she is able, I must show her these."

"May I?" Mort held out his hand.

"They show the machine that steals Fae souls." Cenrick handed him the envelope.

Poring over them, Mort grunted. When he'd finished, he looked at Cenrick, eyes glowing with determination. "It is this machine that you must find and destroy," he agreed.

"We," Cenrick corrected. "Dee and I."

"Time is of the essence." Mort glanced at Dee, still unconscious. "She will not be capable of movement for many days, and I have new information which . . ." He swallowed hard.

"Information?" Cenrick said. "What kind? How did you get it?"

"I sent Tinth to watch."

Cenrick rubbed his jaw. "Your hawk? What did she see?"

"They have your father. They mean to destroy the King of Rune."

The entire world seemed to freeze. Cenrick felt himself go very, very still. "The hell they do. How was this allowed to happen?"

"Tricks and lies." Tears shown in Mort's tired eyes, reminding Cenrick of the great friendship the mage shared with the king. "I do not know for certain if this Natasha knows who she has captured. Your father was trying to act as a spy and got caught up in her web."

"Explain."

"Simply put, he dressed in human clothing and began visiting some of the bars Natasha and her cronies frequent. He met her and didn't know who she was. She, it seems, recognized him as Fae."

"How?"

"There are several Fae who are always with her. No doubt they saw his aura."

"His aura is so bright," Cenrick agreed. He felt his chest constrict at the thought of that brilliant aura snuffed our forever. "I'll have to go without Dee."

Mort nodded, though his expression remained worried. "Yet . . . the Oracle said it would take two to vanquish this thing."

Both men gazed at Dee, who was still unconscious. Cenrick said, "Aye, and without her, I will have no protection against Natasha. Yet each moment I delay, more Fae souls are lost. Time can only be manipulated so much." Cenrick shifted restlessly. "I must try soon. My father's life is at stake. I see no other alternative."

"Your highness—Rune cannot lose you also."

"Someone must take this risk, and I believe it must be me." Cenrick set his jaw.

"Wait!" It was Dee, her voice weak. She raised her head. "I'm part of this too. No way are you leaving me here."

Cenrick crossed to her side, placed a gentle kiss on

her forehead. "You must heal. That will take more than mere hours."

She gazed up at him, eyes bleary from pain. "Time," she croaked. "Change time." Then she lapsed once more into unconsciousness.

Cenrick looked to the Mage. "Can we? One more time?"

"We can try." Mort nodded. "If she awakens again, we must give her this draught to ease the pain."

Cenrick dragged his hand across his face. "She has a point. When you send me across the veil, you can control the time of our arrival—without too serious consequences, right?"

"Hopefully. I can try to arrange your arrival so no time is lost." The mage swallowed. "But remember, magic involving time is unreliable and cannot be exactly controlled. Plus, the consequences could be . . ." He shuddered.

Nodding, Cenrick pulled a chair up to Dee's side, taking her hand. "It is worth the risk. I'll wait here while she heals. Then you can try to send us back to the same time, the same place, and hopefully only minutes will have elapsed since we left."

"I don't know. . . ." Mort didn't sound happy. "In addition to the risk of natural disasters, what about the shooter? He could be there, waiting to finish you off."

"It'd be more dangerous for me to attempt this without her."

"But King Roark—"

"You know as well as I do that Fae exist in the here and now."

"Natasha is not Fae."

Silence, while Mort mulled that over. "I do not wish to lose both of you," he repeated.

"Then do as I ask. Once Dee is well, return us to a time right after she was shot."

"Time travel is still an imprecise trick," Mort warned, his brow wrinkled with worry. "While I can usually place you within a few hours, I don't know about minutes."

"Do the best you can. I'm sure an hour will be fine. Your best is all I can ask."

Dee moaned, stirring restlessly. Smoothing the hair from her brow, this time Cenrick didn't hide his emotion from the mage. He couldn't stop touching her, reassuring himself that she still lived.

"She sleeps peacefully," Mort said. "Let her rest."

Reluctantly, Cenrick forced himself to remove his hand from her hair. Watching her chest rise and fall with her every breath, he hated to take his gaze off her, even for a second. "I'll wait here by her side until she's better."

"As you wish."

As he looked from her to the mage, Cenrick was surprised to see an anguished look on the older man's face. "Mort? What's wrong?"

"Your father is like a brother and you are like a son to me." The simple explanation touched Cenrick's heart. "I couldn't bear to lose either of you."

"You won't. Dee will be with me. We'll get my father out."

Dee healed in record time. If she hadn't known better, she would have thought she'd dreamt the entire shooting episode. But this was Rune, a world full of magic, and Mort was apparently a wizard of great skill.

To her, it seemed she went to sleep one night and when she woke in the morning, the gaping wound in her side had nearly healed.

"How did you do this?" she asked, amazed at the healthy pink skin where before had been a bloody hole. As far as she could tell, there had been no stitches, nothing to hold the damaged parts together to heal.

With a shrug, Mort smiled. "Magic, of course."

The chair beside her bed was empty. "Where is Cenrick?" she asked.

"He refused to leave you and has spent many nights in that chair. I finally forced him to seek his own bed and rest. I promised to wake him when you woke, but he needs his sleep. He'll need all his wits about him to fight this enemy."

"Oh." Oddly disappointed, she shifted in her bed. "Did he say anything about the envelope we retrieved?"

"Yes. He left it with you. Here." Mort handed her the manila envelope.

Pulling out several photos, she began looking through them. "Has Cenrick seen these?"

Mort nodded. "Yes."

"So that's the machine." She tapped one photo with her index finger. "And there's that woman scientist, Natasha Klein. She is behind all this."

"And she's taken King Roark prisoner," Mort said.

Dee's eyes widened. "Does Cenrick—"

"Of course. He'll take suitable action, believe me."

At the next photograph, she froze. "Mick," she said softly. "He's only in this one picture. At least there aren't any showing him strapped into the machine like this poor man."

"Galyeon," Mort informed her. "He's with the Oracle now." *Soulless.* The word hung between them unsaid.

"What do you think Natasha is doing with their souls once she takes them?"

Mort's silver eyes were troubled. "I don't know. I'm thinking she's somehow found a way to extract the magic and use it for herself."

"But she's human, isn't she?"

"Yes."

"Then how is such a thing possible?"

"That my dear"—Mort's expression was grim, and he kissed her cheek—"is for you and Cenrick to find out. When you're well, of course."

"She'd better not harm Cenrick's dad."

"Don't worry. Cenrick won't let them. But he needs you."

Experimentally she raised herself up on her elbows, bracing against pain. Nothing. Not even a twinge. Even when she pushed herself to a full sitting position, she experienced absolutely no discomfort.

"If only normal life could be like this." With a sigh, she tried to smile. "I've never felt so at home. Even when I was." She swung her legs over the side of the bed, still a bit shaky. "I'd like to try standing."

Mort made no move to help her. "Go ahead. You're perfectly capable."

And so she was.

After taking several wobbly steps, she turned to look at the mage. "How long has Cenrick slept?"

The magician shrugged. "A few hours now. Why?"

"If you think he's ready, please take me to him. It's time. I've had enough resting and recuperating. I want to go home."

Nodding, Mort led the way.

Entering his room, Dee saw that Cenrick slept on his back, naked arms flung out. His lower body covered by a sheet. Such a rush of desire struck her when she saw him, she staggered.

"Are you all right?" Mort watched her closely.

She nodded. "Let me wake him."

With trembling fingers, she brushed the hair from his brow, tracing the shape of his jaw.

"Dee?" He opened his eyes, and surprise chased away the sleep. "You're here? I'm not dreaming?"

With a little laugh, she kissed him. "No, I'm really here, all healed and ready for action."

He lifted a brow. Too late, she caught the double meaning in her words, and she blushed.

"Let me see you." He sat up, tenderly running his hands down her sides. Lifting her shirt, he studied her wound, touching the slightly raised area. "You *are* healed!" he exclaimed. Then he pulled her close for a long, deep kiss.

Too late, Dee remembered the mage. What would he think? But when she broke the kiss and raised her head to look for him, she saw that he'd left.

"He's gone," she said.

Cenrick made a sound of need and crushed her to

him. Their lovemaking was slow and languorous, full of the joy of rediscovering each other, careful of her wound.

An hour later, they found Mort in his chamber. Dee could feel her color rising as he studied them, his silver gaze giving nothing away. "Are you ready to return?" he asked.

"Yes." Dee gripped Cenrick's hand. "Hopefully we'll be in time."

Mort spoke a few words, and a tingling started in her body. Holding tight to Cenrick, Dee savored the rush.

The mage's spell worked. Dee and Cenrick materialized in the parking lot sometime after the shooting, twenty feet from where Dee had been shot. Her blood was still a wet puddle on the ground. Cenrick shook his head.

"Yuck," Dee said, eyeing the crimson stain and self-consciously touching her freshly healed side. "I wonder if the gunman's gone."

"Come on, let's check." A stealthy yet thorough search of the lot turned up nothing other than ordinary shoppers returning to their cars. Cenrick wondered aloud, "No one heard anything?"

"He had a silencer," Dee pointed out. She winced as they walked again past her bloodstain. "Double yuck."

Cenrick took her arm. "I thought blood didn't bother police officers. I was guessing you'd be used to it."

"Normally we are. But it's different when it's your own." Dee shuddered.

"Check your watch." Still holding her, Cenrick continued to search the parking lot with his eyes. "Do you remember what time the shooting occurred?"

"Hell, no. I was taken totally by surprise." Lifting her wrist, she peered at its silver dial and frowned. "According to this, it's a bit past eight-thirty. The mall closes at nine. We haven't been gone long at all."

In the distance they heard sirens. Cenrick and Dee exchanged looks. Apparently someone had heard something after all.

"Come on." Pulling him along with her, Dee headed for her car. "Our assailant is gone for sure now. I'd like to get out of here before any of my former coworkers arrive."

They reached her car and started it, but several police cruisers, lights flashing, pulled into the lot. Several more blocked the exits.

"They've sealed off the place," Dee growled. "Standard procedure."

"Now what?"

"We have no choice." She shrugged. "We sit tight and do as we're told."

"Out of the car!" a loud, distorted voice ordered. "Keep your hands above your heads."

"A bullhorn," Dee explained. "Do as he says."

Hands up in the air, they emerged from the car. Two cops approached, one from each side, weapons drawn and pointed at them. One of the cops was Officer Lieber, the one who'd come to Dee's apartment.

"You again?" Lieber said, disgust evident in both his voice and expression. "What're you doing this time, running drugs?"

"Officer Lieber, such talk is uncalled for." This was a different voice, one belonging to an older man. "Put down your weapons, people."

"That's Lieutenant Cowell," Dee informed Cenrick. She gave a small smile. "My boss and"—she looked at Lieber—"his."

Reluctantly, or so it seemed to Cenrick, Lieber lowered his pistol.

"What happened here?" Cowell asked.

Dee shook her head, stone-faced. "I don't know. My friend and I had just finished shopping. We were about to leave when you guys showed up."

"We had reports of a shooting," Cowell informed them.

"A shooting?" Dee gave Cenrick a look of disbelief. "I didn't hear anything."

Cenrick could only pray no one asked him a direct question. Fae were unable to lie.

Lieber glared at them both, his mouth twisted as though he'd swallowed something rotten.

Lieutenant Cowell moved forward, his gaze locked on Dee. "Officer Bishop, with the investigation into your alleged misconduct still ongoing, need I remind you of the advisability of keeping yourself clean? Of answering questions when asked?"

She gave him a suitably chastened look. "No, sir. But honestly, I didn't see anything."

Which was true. Neither of them had seen a thing.

"There's blood over here," a different policeman shouted. "A fair amount of it."

"Look for a body. Or a trail," was Cowell's reply.

A few minutes later, two officers came back. "The trail ends nowhere. And there's no body," one said.

"Find out how old the blood is," Cowell ordered. Lieber took the two patrolmen scurried off to do his bidding.

When they were alone, Lieutenant Cowell frowned at Dee. "Mighty odd coincidence, don't you think— you being here and all?"

"Is it?" Dee was noncommittal. "I'm just leaving the parking lot after some shopping, just like any other civilian might."

Cowell sighed. "Are you armed?"

Dee nodded. "I have a revolver in my glove box. If you look at it, you'll see it hasn't been fired."

The lieutenant didn't move. "Do we have permission to search your vehicle?" he asked.

"Of course," Dee answered. "I've got nothing to hide."

The lieutenant waved another two patrolmen over. Their search, naturally, revealed nothing.

After a thorough sweep of the lot, the first three policemen returned. Nothing had been found other than the car with the shattered window.

"Shots were fired and someone was hit," Lieber reported, sounding frustrated. "But both the perp and the victim are long gone."

"Are you done with me?" Dee asked.

"We have no choice but to let you go." Dee's boss shook his head. "First, though, I'd like a word." He led her away from the group, talking to her in a voice too low for Cenrick to hear.

A moment later they returned, her eyes suspiciously bright. "Come on. We're out of here," she said.

Once they were headed down the highway, with car after car passing them—Dee was driving a law-abiding fifty-five—Cenrick touched her shoulder. "What did he say to you back there?"

Surprisingly, she sniffled and her eyes filled with unshed tears. "He told me he had faith in me. He said he knows I understand right from wrong."

"He doesn't think you did any of this?"

She wiped at her eyes. "He didn't say those words. But that was the impression I got, yes. I can't tell you how much that means to me, to have someone actually believe in me."

"*I* believe in you." He said the words softly, wondering if she'd understand how deeply he meant them. He felt like he'd known her much longer than he actually had.

"Thanks." She smiled at him, tears making silvery tracks down her cheeks. Then, shaking her head, she sniffed and brushed them away. "Thanks for being my friend."

A friend? Though he nodded, pretending a sudden interest in the freeway traffic, her words felt almost like an insult. Is that all she wanted? He wanted to be more than a friend to her. Much more. The revelation stunned him.

No, getting more would be impossible. Her life was here and, once she'd restored her reputation, she'd jump right back into the midst of it. He was here only to do a job. Once he'd stopped the soul-stealers, he had to return to Rune. Unlike his brother, he couldn't stay. He was an heir, and Rune needed either him or his brother. And since Alrick had chosen another destiny, that left him. Wanting a human woman, even one as brave and beautiful as Dee, was completely out of the question. He barely qualified as king material now—his own father doubted him. Marrying a Fae wife, powerful and of good social standing, would be his duty.

CHAPTER ELEVEN

Despite his previous thoughts, despite the fact that he knew he could never have all he wanted, when they returned to her apartment and she invited him to her bed, Cenrick went. And after their blissful lovemaking, he found he couldn't make himself leave her. As Dee drifted off to sleep, wrapped in his arms, he told himself he'd stay with her for an hour just to watch her sleep. When that hour passed, he claimed another. Then another and another, until his own eyes drifted closed and he dozed.

In the morning, sunlight streaming through the blinds woke him. His heart full of an emotion he didn't want to acknowledge, he stared at the slumbering woman in his arms and felt an aching sense of loss. Then, unable to help himself, he kissed her hair, inhaling her sweet, floral fragrance and longing for things he had no right to wish for.

Dee raised her head, a smile curling her lips, and looked at him with a sleepy gaze. "I smell coffee."

He sniffed. "Me too." From the other room, he

could hear the sound of her coffeepot brewing. "How is that possible?"

"Magic!" she said. But the laughter in her voice told him she was teasing. "Actually, I set the coffeemaker to come on automatically. I filled it up last night."

"Hmm." Tightening his arms around her, he nodded. "I could get used to this," he said without thinking.

Immediately she stiffened, telling him his casual statement was a mistake. "Well, don't." Squirming and attempting to roll over, she succeeded only in fueling his already growing arousal.

Her eyes widened as she felt it. "Well, well, well," she said. And as her hand closed around him, he gave himself over to sensation.

They made love again, this time more slowly, the ferocity of his need somewhat abated by their lovemaking the previous night. This time he savored every thrust, withdrawing and teasing her with exquisitely agonizing deliberation. Holding on despite his rapidly disintegrating self-control, he wanted to do this indefinitely, but Dee had other ideas.

"Oh, no you don't," she growled against his mouth, raising her body to meet his thrusts, urging him on until all thoughts of control vanished. And, actions once again savage, they moved together with fury and passion, and when they climaxed, Cenrick believed more than mere animal sexuality fueled them.

"Magic," Dee cried out, her body convulsing around his while he gave her his life's essence.

"Magic," he echoed, and he knew the words were true.

They held each other until their breathing slowed. Finally, Dee shifted in his arms and sighed. "Guess we'd better get up now. We've got to get started trying to figure out how to find Mick, Natasha, and her machine."

Reluctant to move, Cenrick forced himself to release her and pushed back the covers. "You're right, of course."

"So, what do we do now?" She sighed. "Where do we go? Mick's house is burned to the ground. How are we going to find them?"

"Good question." And because he didn't have an answer, he kissed her again—on the cheek this time, making her shiver.

"Cenrick," she protested. "Let's get cleaned up and we'll talk in the kitchen."

Pushing out of his arms, she untangled herself from the sheets, jumped from the bed and disappeared into the bathroom, leaving him to rise and pad after her naked, the scent of her body still on his skin.

While she showered, he watched, amazed he could still be aroused. He thought about joining her, but didn't. When she finished and it was his turn to shower, he left the water on cold.

They went about their morning routines quickly and efficiently, each shooting the other an occasional smile. Only once she'd taken a seat at the kitchen table, pad of paper and steaming mug of coffee in front of her, did he pull out a chair and sit down across from her.

Mug in one hand, she held up the pad with the other. "I'm going to start by making a list," she said.

"Good." He nursed his glass of ice-cold milk. "What types of things are you going to list?"

"Things we need to do. And possible solutions. For example"—she wrote furiously—"we need to find that machine."

"And Natasha."

"Good." She jotted on the paper. "And don't forget Mick."

But when she started the solution column, she had nothing to write. "Start talking." She waved her pen at him. "We'll brainstorm."

"I still need to know how they're luring my people in."

"Right. It must be something only Fae can feel, a magical bait of some kind."

He considered. "But . . . I felt no pull, no lure. Nothing to make me want to go there."

"But you felt something, didn't you?"

"Yes. I felt weak and disoriented." Restless, he shifted in his chair, watching her sip her coffee.

When he fell silent, she rested her chin on her hands and stared at him. "Damn, I wish I could change my aura and appear Fae."

This startled him. "Why?"

"Because they want Fae. If I could look like a decoy, let them believe they'd lured me in, I'd have the advantage of being human. Their machine wouldn't affect me. And I'd have my gun. The metal doesn't cause me any problem, obviously."

He sighed, rejecting the idea. "But you won't pass. Your aura would be a dead giveaway. And . . ." He felt his face heat. I don't want you risking yourself any more than you have to."

"As a cop I risk myself every day," she argued. "That's what I do—or did." She stared hard at him. "Can you use magic to make me look Fae? To change my aura? Is such a thing possible?"

Unfortunately, though he didn't like it, he could only speak truth; she'd asked him a direct question. "Yes. It's possible."

"Then, do it. This is the only plan that makes sense. We'll draw them to us, instead of the other way around. And I'll disguise myself so Natasha and Mick won't recognize me."

He didn't reply, so she pushed herself to her feet. "Look, let me do my job," she complained.

"This isn't your job."

"Yes, it is," she insisted. "Who better? I'm a trained officer of the law. And right now I've not only been accused of being a dirty cop but I'm a suspect in both the arson on Mick's house as well as his supposed death. My former fiancé is soulless, I've been shot at, my apartment has been broken into . . . and every single day those people steal another Fae or two's souls. If my going undercover as Fae will give us a shot at finding this machine and taking these people down, we need to go for it."

What she said made sense. Still, he worried. "You'd be playing right into their hands. They want to hurt you. This way, they'd have you."

She blew out air in a loud huff. "That machine won't affect me like it does you. And, as I've mentioned, I'll be armed. This may be our best chance—our only chance."

He stared at her, torn. He was unable to tell her how much she'd come to matter to him.

Taking his hesitation for dubiousness, she bent down, putting her face on a level with his. "Give me some credit, please. I know what I'm doing, Cenrick. Trust me on this."

He swallowed. Closing his eyes, he tried to hide the fact that all he could think about was kissing her. Damn! He needed reasons, arguments—points he could make to convince her she shouldn't do this, couldn't do this. The problem was, he knew she could.

He shook his head. "What if Mick recognizes you even with your disguise?"

Dee gave him a hopeful look and said, "I have a hunch Mick might be on our side."

He had that same feeling, oddly enough. He hoped it was true.

When he didn't contradict her, she smiled and rubbed her hands together. "Now, are we going to do this or not?"

If he had to capitulate, he wouldn't do it easily. He wanted to make sure they covered every possibility, every angle. "First things first. If I made you appear Fae, where would we go to make sure Natasha and her crew see us?"

"We?" She raised an eyebrow. "I thought we'd already discussed this. You're affected by that machine."

"Well, I'm not letting you go alone. Period. Now, where would we need to go?"

"Easy. I have an idea." He could tell she thought she had him—her smile was triumphant. No doubt she planned to get him to capitulate on this, then talk him out of going along. "I know all the clubs where Mick used to hang out. Where else would he go? Maybe they've been getting the Fae from there."

"Gay clubs?" Cenrick was surprised.

"Hey, Mick and Jack went to straight clubs too. Especially once Peter and I got engaged. Besides, what does it matter? All we need is for them to think I'm Fae—straight or gay—and get me to the machine."

He sighed. "True."

"So you'll do it? You'll make me look Fae?"

He nodded. "Yes. But only once you give me your word you won't go alone. I'm going with you."

"Oh, no you're not."

"I can't let you go alone."

"You have to. Otherwise, that negates the entire benefit. I'd have to watch out for you, which would severely limit my effectiveness. I have to go alone."

He glared at her. She glared right back.

Finally, she gave in. "Okay," she said with a sigh. She clapped her hands. "Let's do it."

Cenrick began the words to the spell, and magic rushed over Dee, making the hair on her arms stand up and goose bumps appear on her skin. He waved his hand and ribbons of silvery glitter trailed after them.

"Wow!" she laughed. "What's that called?"

"Some call it Fae glitter, some faerie dust."

"Faerie dust? Like Tinkerbell used?" She giggled.

He continued the spell, waving his fist, ribbons of

sparkle trailing in a aura around her. Her creamy skin began to glow.

For the first time, she looked uncertain. "What will this . . . glitter do to me?"

"It will magnify your natural attributes, and make them even more so—you will appear more Fae, as we are."

"What about my aura? Externals don't matter, do they?"

He studied her, giving one swift, hard look before glancing back down at his hand and waggling his finger, sending out a shower of lovely sparks. "The changes begin on the exterior. A Fae aura manifests in personal appearance as well."

"Can you be a bit more specific?"

He sighed. "Your lovely brown eyes will appear as liquid pools men can drown in. Your skin"—he trailed a glittering finger along her cheek, making her shiver—"already so pale, will seem to them like the finest ivory."

With a nervous laugh, she tried to pretend she wasn't affected. But he'd seen the shudder that swept through her at his touch, noticed the way her already beautiful eyes darkened with passion.

Desire rushed into him with the force of a hurricane, amplified by the magic. He cleared his throat, looking away, barely remembering to repeat the words to keep the spell going. "You will be . . . stunning," he managed, wondering if she realized that to him she always had been.

"So you're saying I'll be supermodel material? I'll have to fight men off with a stick?" She laughed.

"Basically, yes."

"Then, okay, auras aside, how do Fae move about among us unnoticed? Don't you all have a problem?

"We would if we didn't combat it. It's for that very reason most Fae dim their true appearance when they're among humans. We don't want to attract attention."

"Good Lord." Her hushed whisper made his body stir. "That means . . ." The way she looked at him made him want to kiss her senseless.

"That means what?" His voice came out rusty.

"You're already breathtakingly handsome," she blurted. "You're saying that you—?"

He felt his face color. Unlike his brother, he'd had never been comfortable with his appeal for females. "Yes."

"Let me see. If you're going to make me into a siren, I want to see another Fae in all his glory. I want to see the real you."

Cenrick took a step back, continuing his repetition of the spell. "Dee, I like you," he said at a pause. "We're partners. I don't want to change that. Let's drop it."

But she wouldn't. "Why? What are you afraid of?" she asked.

"It's a well-documented fact that human women are uncontrollably attracted to us when they see us as we truly are."

She snorted. "Fine. Since I'm already attracted to you, what difference will it make?"

"Dee—"

She took a step closer, making his heart stutter. He

was only halfway through the complete spell, and he could barely resist her.

Suddenly, he *wanted* her to see him as he was, to fight the same strong attraction as the one even now coursing through his veins. Without another word, he let his true self shine.

She blinked. "You look the same." Peering at him, she sounded disappointed. "You look . . . the same."

He frowned. "I don't understand. You're supposed to see the true me."

She took a step toward him, head tilted. "Nope, no difference. You look the same. Maybe I already see you as you really are."

"That's not possible."

Something in his expression must have reached her, made her realize his disappointment and dismay. "Hey, don't worry about it. Let's get on with making my aura appear Fae. We've got a job to do." She smiled consolingly.

He sighed. "I'll need to touch you."

Closing her eyes, she nodded.

He touched her shoulder, feather-light. She shivered. His fingers trailed down her arm to her waist, brushed her hip. After skimming to her toes, he placed his hand on top of her head and spoke the rest of the spell.

"All right." Summoning up a strength of will he hadn't known he possessed, he took his hand away. Odd, how bereft that made him feel. "I'm finished. You can open your eyes."

Slowly, cautiously, she did. When she met his gaze, he felt as if he'd been punched in the gut. He growled low in his throat and said, "Even for a Fae, you're exquisite."

"Really?" She grinned up at him. "Okay, now tell me the rest of it. What else is different?"

He blinked, pushing away his raw, animal hunger. "Different? What do you mean?"

"This spell gives me the appearance of a Fae, but does it give me any special powers—like magical ability? I have a mental picture of twitching my nose and my apartment instantly becoming spotless. Or a five course, mouthwatering gourmet meal appearing with the wave of my hand." Her grin slowly faded. "Or better yet, I could use magic to make the charges against me disappear so I can get my job back.

Though he hated to crush her hopes, he had no choice. "Uh, no. Sorry. No magical powers. You just look Fae. Nothing more, nothing less. We've only altered your appearance, not your entire being. You're still human at the core."

"What about my . . . aura?" She stumbled over the unfamiliar concept. "Did you fix that?"

"Yes. Your aura now looks Fae. And remember, don't be disappointed. Your being human is what's going to help us in dealing with these people. Since this machine only works on Fae, you have a built-in immunity."

She conceded the point with a dip of her chin. "Okay, so I now look Fae. I'm armed and a trained law-enforcement officer. I'm ready."

"You're *not* ready." He crossed his arms, knowing she wouldn't like what he had to say.

"What? Of course I am. I've even got spare bullets."

He sighed. "Dee, You might be armed, but you need clothes."

She gaped at him. "Clothes?"

"Yes, magic garments from Rune. No self-respecting Fae woman would wear anything of human make, especially not out to the clubs. They all dress drop-dead sexy."

"Sexy?" She stared. "I can do sexy. But, look, while I love new clothes as much as the next woman, we don't have time. I'm sure I can find something here."

"Time? The clubs don't open for hours."

She checked her watch and sighed. "Fine. Get a Fae dress from Rune."

He stared at her, considering. "I have to be careful using magic. Though, something like this shouldn't be a problem," he muttered.

"What do you mean, you have to be careful?"

"Incautious magic use in a nonmagical world like yours can cause disturbances in the weather. Remember those tornadoes and that massive brush fire down by Austin last summer? That was because of magic." He grinned at her. "Now, here goes nothing." Snapping his fingers, he muttered a couple more words, and a shimmering dress appeared over his arm. Outside, a sudden clap of thunder could be heard.

"Look at that dress," Dee breathed, moving closer. She clearly loved it. The color of amber, the gown was made from some diaphanous material that flowed and moved as if with life of its own. It was a perfect match for her eyes.

"Here you are." Cenrick held it out to her.

She reached out for it, then recoiled. "I could

have sworn the material—or whatever it is—
reached for me!"

He shrugged. "It probably did. Put it on."

After another small hesitation, she snatched the
dress from him. "Turn your back," she ordered.

"But I've seen—"

"Cenrick!"

Giving up, he did as she requested.

"Okay," she said after a moment. "You can look
now."

Slowly, he turned to face her. The enchanted material clung to her lovingly, each fold caressing her with
every breath she took.

Desire consumed him, burned through his body in
waves. He'd thought he'd be able to do this, to look
at Dee Bishop, enhanced with Fae magic, wearing a
bespelled dress, and control himself. He'd been
wrong.

Despite the color, the diaphanous material was
sheer. So sheer, she might have been wearing a veil.
The dress was see-through, and worse, the spell that
gave the material its beauty was a spell of a sensual
nature. He could no more resist the lure than he
could stop his heart from beating.

He took a step toward her . . . and she vanished.

CHAPTER TWELVE

Everything changed. One moment she'd been standing in front of Cenrick, clad in the most sensuous dress she'd ever seen, and the next . . . she was formless. Weightless, buoyant, insubstantial, surfing invisible currents of air. Magical. As though she were truly Fae.

Beside her, a shape materialized, looming—a huge hawk, riding the air beside her. Tinth. As Dee thought the name, the hawk screeched. In the majestic bird's eyes she saw . . . recognition?

What was happening to her? The dress, wrapped tight around her, caressed her body. Had the garment been ensorcelled? Dee reached out, using her hand, her mind, trying to find Cenrick. Instead, she touched . . . the Oracle.

"You have come." The hooded figure moved closer. When she did, the swirling air currents calmed.

Dee nodded. "I was pulled, or sent."

"Do you know what you are?"

Dee wasn't sure at first what the Oracle meant. Then, looking deep within herself, she saw that she had not been diminished by recent events. In fact, the hardships she'd faced in her life had made her greater. Despite the investigation, the loss of her job, her fiancé, and her best friend, she remained strong, aware, and ready to fight. She was *Dee Bishop.* "I don't give up easily," she said. "Never have, never will."

At her words, the Oracle laughed. What Dee could see of the face within the shadows of the hood looked surprisingly beautiful and young.

"You're—"

"Shhh." The Oracle held up a hand. Then, scarlet eyes glowing, she touched Dee's face. The touch was gentle, soothing. It brought tears to Dee's eyes.

"You have always been worthy. But first you must find yourself."

Though she still didn't understand, tears filled Dee's eyes and spilled out onto her cheeks. She asked, "Will you help?"

The Oracle shook her head. *"You two will help each other. Remember, two halves are required."* Once again, the Oracle's voice sounded stern. *"Remind Cenrick of this. If he tries to remember, he will understand."*

"I—," Dee began, but no one was there. The Oracle had vanished.

Suddenly the air was swirling and she was flying, falling, her dress streaming out behind her. Tinth screeched, and also disappeared. With a crash, Dee felt the ground suddenly beneath her. She crashed down beside Cenrick once more, clad in that magical gown.

"Dee?" He rushed over to her, his dark gaze concerned. "What happened? Where did you go? Are you all right?"

She opened her mouth to speak, but before she could, the dress reacted, reached out to shimmer around Cenrick, caressing his arm.

"What the—?"

"The dress is enchanted," she reminded him, oddly breathless. "It took me to see the Oracle, to a place that wasn't solid. Tinth was there as well."

Now the vibrant garment was wrapped around both her and Cenrick, pulling them so close she could feel the beat of his heart.

"The Oracle?" he asked, then kissed her, a long, lingering kiss that made her knees go weak. "What did she want?"

"I think she summoned me." Trying to concentrate, Dee repeated the Oracle's words. "She said you would understand."

"Two halves are required," he mused, while the dress did it's best to meld them together.

"What does that mean? She said you would remember."

"Alrick and I are twins," he told her, passion darkening his eyes to black. "Dress, cease." Miraculously, the gown obeyed, becoming an ordinary dress again.

Cenrick stepped back, his chest rising and falling as he tried to regain his equilibrium. Dee took a moment to do the same. More than anything, she wanted to rip off the Fae garment. She wanted her jeans and tennis shoes. She wanted everything to be normal again.

"Two halves are required," Cenrick repeated, staring off into the distance. "I think I might know. Alrick and I are twins, as you know. Growing up, it was often said we were formed from the same soul. The Oracle must want me to seek Alrick's help."

He held out his hand. "I think it's time we paid my brother a visit. Are you ready?"

Looking down at her now see-through dress, Dee shook her head. "No way am I wearing this to meet your brother. I'm changing first. Give me a minute." And dashing off into her bedroom, she grabbed her jeans and a T-shirt and headed to the bathroom to change.

When she returned to the living room, Cenrick held out his hand. "My brother lives in the Texas Hill Country with his human wife."

"I remember you telling me that," Dee replied, sliding her fingers through his. "I love the Hill Country. I'm ready to go."

"We'll use magic to travel."

Dee stared at him. "What about the weather? You mentioned problems."

"Well, there were problems. Still are sometimes. But mostly that was before Mort discovered magical currents. They even exist in your nonmagical world. As long as I tap into them, your world's natural energy won't be disturbed." He began the spell.

Again, energy flared around them. Dee knew a moment of disorientation, gray and black mingling with all the colors of the rainbow. She closed her eyes.

When she opened them again, she and Cenrick stood under the intense Texas sun, burning so bright she had to shade her eyes. Noon. The sun was directly overhead.

But . . . the sparse landscape and stunted trees told her they were not in the Texas Hill Country.

"This isn't—," she began.

"No, it's not." Grim-faced, Cenrick shaded his eyes with his hand and scanned their surroundings. "By the Plains of Lothar, I don't know where we are."

"You don't?" She too shaded her eyes against the glare. "What happened?"

"I don't know." He grimaced. "To ride the magical currents, I took us to Rune and back. We should have ended up near No-Name Ranch—where my brother lives. Unless we crossed the veil at a different place . . . Locations can be hard to pinpoint, unless one knows the exact coordinates." He sounded like a scientist or mathematician.

"Magic has rules?" she asked.

Somehow, his somber expression reassured her. "Of course. Remember when I told you how the weather used to change?"

She nodded.

"When my brother first came to your world, every time anyone used magic, some natural disaster would occur. Tornados, floods, fires. It was terrible—and limiting. When he and his wife, Carly, defeated an evil warlord from the future, Mort and the Oracle worked together to find a way to fix that particular problem."

"And that's when Mort discovered these magical currents?"

"Right. Now, as long as we're careful and don't abuse our power, we Fae can now use magic here without worry."

Above them, several black buzzards circled.

Dee swallowed. "But you don't know where we are? We're lost?"

"Lost?" He gave a swift shake of his head. "No, we're not lost. I'm sure I can find the way to Alrick's."

Dee almost laughed. Apparently, even Fae men hated to ask for directions. Squinting, she wished she'd brought her Ray-Bans. Wherever they'd landed, they were in a desert wilderness. The dry ground had cracks and splits, and in the distance she saw red earth cliffs that were crumbling to dust. All around were tall spiny cactus reaching for the sun with clawlike appendages. And worse, the buzzards that had been circling above had been joined by several more, making a large flock of birds, black and ominous, their ominous silhouettes stark against the cloudless sky.

"Look." She pointed up.

Cenrick followed the direction she indicated. "Not good."

"Nope." She kept her one hand linked with his. "What are we going to do?"

"I'm going to try again." With one final squeeze of her fingers, he began his spell once more.

As earlier, she felt the tingling down to her toes. The desert landscape vanished, the gray and black and multicolored rainbow swirled, and a second later they stood on the side of a winding road. A warm wind blew, sending enormous clouds scudding across a bright blue sky. Tree-covered hills surrounded them.

"This is more like it," she said. This was the Texas Hill Country, so named because of the rolling tree-covered hills. It was one of the most beautiful parts of her home state.

Flashing her a quick smile, Cenrick pointed to a large wooden sign over the metal gate. "Look. We're here. This is where my brother and his wife live."

"The No-Name Ranch," she read. "Interesting name."

"Carly named it. She was living here alone, a widow, when Alrick met her. He'd been given the assignment of guarding her, as the child she carries is important to the future of the world."

Dee nodded, wondering at herself. These days, she greeted even the oddest statements like that with casual aplomb. Of course Cenrick's brother knew the future—he was Fae, after all.

Above them, a bird screeched. It was close by, and despite herself Dee jumped. When she looked up, instead of the buzzard she'd expected, she saw Tinth. Again, she could have sworn she saw recognition when the hawk looked at her.

"Tinth." Cenrick sounded amused. "Chased the buzzards away. Mort must have sent his pet to keep an eye on us."

Hearing her name, the huge hawk landed on a fence post, preening herself. Seeing its open mouth, Dee could have sworn the bird was laughing.

"Tinth, go tell Alrick we're here," Cenrick commanded. Immediately the hawk flew off.

"She's trained?" Despite herself, Dee was impressed.

"Not trained." Still holding her hand, Cenrick opened the ranch's well-oiled gate. "Just extremely intelligent. She does what she wants."

Dee thought she probably should tug her fingers free, but holding his hand felt just right.

As they walked up the dirt drive toward the freshly painted, one-story ranch house, Dee couldn't help but admire the place. She'd always secretly longed for a ranch, or at least some acreage of her own. She'd wanted a place to raise horses and dogs and . . . someday kids. She felt a pang. Odd how now, when she pictured kids, they all had Cenrick's beautiful eyes and finely hewn features.

What was wrong with her? Blushing, she was glad Fae powers didn't include mind reading.

Before they reached the porch steps, the front door opened. A broad-shouldered man with long, dark hair stepped out. Despite knowing Cenrick had a twin brother, Dee couldn't help but stare. Realizing she had her mouth open, she closed it with a snap.

"I know." Seeing Dee's expression, the pretty redheaded woman who'd emerged after Alrick laughed. "It's unbelievable enough that there's one of them. Two is really, really impossible."

Startled, Dee felt her own mouth curve in an answering smile. She stepped forward, holding out her hand. "Dee Bishop."

The redhead eyed Dee's hand, then grinned and

shook her head. "We're not so formal here." She grabbed Dee close and hugged her. "Welcome. I'm Carly, Alrick's wife."

And, judging from her the size of her rounded belly, soon to be a mother. Dee felt a pang of envy. Pushing it away, she smiled back. "Wow. Cenrick said you were pregnant, but he didn't tell me you were so close to delivering. When's the baby due?"

Carly grinned. "Any day now. He's past due, actually." She shook her head. "I'm getting tired of all this waddling."

"Congratulations."

"I'm relieved Cenrick has found someone," Carly continued. "I was getting worried about him. You two looked so in love, walking up here holding hands."

"Oh." Dee swallowed, shooting Cenrick a glance. Talking earnestly to his brother, at least he hadn't heard his sister-in-law's remark. How much more awkward could things get? "We're not, I mean—"

Carly blushed. "Oh! I'm sorry. I assumed, and I shouldn't have."

"Assumed what?" Cenrick swooped in between them, grabbing Carly up for a quick hug. "You're looking well. Positively vibrant. Being married to my brother must agree with you."

"Either that or pregnancy does." Alrick laughed. "She's always been beautiful." He kissed his wife on the tip of her nose, making her laugh. Turning, he came closer, studying Dee intently. When he smiled, she felt like he'd socked her in the stomach, his smile was so much like Cenrick's.

"You really are identical twins," she said, knowing her comment was lame but not caring.

"We are." Alrick hugged her. "You'll be fine," he told her, sotto voce. "He'll take good care of you."

Before she could ask what he meant, Alrick turned back to Cenrick, grinning broadly. "Welcome, little brother." His voice sounded so eerily similar that Dee couldn't help but stare in disbelief.

"Little brother?" She looked from one to the other. "I thought you two were twins?"

"We are." Cenrick clapped Alrick's shoulder. "But he was born first, by a matter of minutes. He never lets me forget it."

Dee laughed and Carly joined her. For just a moment, Dee let herself bask in the warm feeling of friendship and family, something she'd never had and always wanted. Odd, how meeting these two made her feel as if she'd known them for years.

Taking in their rumpled appearance, Alrick's grin faded. "What brings you here?"

"I have bad news." Cenrick clapped his shoulder. "And I need your counsel."

Alrick cocked his shaggy head. "Tell me."

"Let's go inside," Carly interrupted. "We can talk better there." Even without hearing specific words, Dee caught the implication. Safer, Carly meant. As though someone might be watching.

Dee scanned to horizon, seeing horses and fences and trees but nothing else. Still, who was she to question? After all, Cenrick had proved the Fae and Rune. Who knew what else might exist?

Shuddering, she realized she didn't actually want to know.

As they filed past, Carly held the door open, smiling slightly as Cenrick touched her swollen belly. Inside the house, a black-and-white puppy emerged from the kitchen. He peered at them sleepily, his fur mussed. Plumed little tail wagging, he sniffed at Dee's feet, then Cenrick's, before turning a circle and going to sleep.

"Meet Jasper." Carly smiled. "He looks just like Kayo, my other dog," she explained for Dee's benefit.

"Is he Kayo's pup?" Cenrick rumpled the dog's fur. The pup opened one eye, regarded him lazily, then went back to sleep.

Alrick nodded. "Most likely. We found him on our front porch a couple of mornings ago. Now"—he cracked his knuckles—"don't keep me in suspense. What's happened?"

Inside, the farmhouse felt even more homey, with a good solid feeling of permanence and family. From the homespun rugs to the lovingly polished antique furniture, the ranch house spoke of comfort. Dee looked around, the knot in her stomach fading as she took in the soothing surroundings. She could easily imagine bringing up a child in a place like this. Of course, that's exactly what Carly would be doing.

"Cenrick . . ." Alrick threatened.

Carly immediately chided him, "None of that." Settling them all down with tall glasses of lemonade, the woman took the chair next to Dee.

"They have our father," Cenrick finally said.

"What do you mean?" Like Cenrick had when the

mage told him, Alrick went still enough to pass for stone. Yet his gaze burned with fury. "Who has father, and why? What's going on?"

Cenrick revealed what had happened so far.

"Is our father in immediate danger?" Alrick jumped to his feet and glared at his brother.

Cenrick explained what the mage hoped to do with time.

"Then why have you not done this?" Alrick roared. "Why are you here with me?"

Cenrick stood toe to toe with his brother, facing him down. "Because the Oracle said two halves were needed."

"Alrick, settle down." Carly touched her husband's arm, her voice soothing. "Cenrick, tell us the Oracle's words again."

Cenrick did.

Silence fell while Alrick pondered. Eventually he took his seat. Cenrick did too.

Glancing across the table, Carly smiled. Dee returned the expression, grateful, mouthing her thanks and forcing herself to remain motionless and wait. In her years as a police officer, she'd learned to listen carefully. Sometimes a fresh outlook could help.

At last, she found she could bear the silence no longer. She touched Cenrick's shoulder. "I'd like to hear what Carly thinks about the situation as well," she suggested.

Cenrick glanced at his brother, as though seeking approval. Alrick laughed. "Believe me, you will," he said dryly. "Nothing stops her when she gets going."

"Hey!" Carly protested, making a face. "Not fair."

"We want all the help we can get." Cenrick remained serious, his gaze intent. "Give me your thoughts on this. Both of you."

"Of course." Alrick leaned forward. "As for me, I'm most intrigued by the fact that Dee's touch appears to negate the power of that . . . thing on you, Cenrick."

"Yes," Carly agreed. "That's significant."

"We don't know why," Dee put in. "Especially since I'm not Fae. I don't have any magic of my own."

"Not Fae?" Alrick's brows rose as he looked from her to his brother. "I could have sworn you were. Everything about you, but especially your aura—"

"I changed her. Temporarily." Cenrick explained the spell and his reasons for using it. When he'd finished, Alrick nodded.

"That seems a good plan." Alrick included Dee in his approving smile. "You're trained in law enforcement. And if this spell or machine only works on Fae, then you won't be susceptible. Most important, at least to me, you can protect my brother while rescuing our father."

Cenrick made a rude noise. "What's most important is stopping this for good. You haven't seen what happens to those Fae who've been . . . erased."

"They don't heal?" Alrick asked.

"No."

"It's awful," Dee put in, going on to describe Peter and the other mindless Fae.

Carly and Alrick exchanged a long look. "You're engaged to be married to this Peter?"

Dee looked down at her ringless hands. "I was. Not

201

any longer. I lost both my fiancé and my best friend, and my job. I've had a lot of changes in a short period of time."

"Once we have stopped these people, I will make certain Dee gets her job back." Cenrick sounded fierce. "And her fiancé as well."

"Don't bother." Dee lifted her chin. "Peter wasn't right for me. I realized that shortly after he dumped me. We were comfortable with each other, but not in love."

"And your job?"

Her shrug felt a little too forced. But the sharp stab of pain she usually felt about losing her job was absent.

Cenrick's smile warmed her all the way to her toes. Dee couldn't look away from him. This beautiful man had come to mean so much to her in such a short period of time.

Of course *she didn't want Peter. She wanted Cenrick.*

Good lord. She closed her eyes. How had this happened? She swayed. She was in love with Cenrick.

"Dee?" Carly sounded concerned. "Are you all right?"

"Fine." Clearing her throat, she forced herself to look at the other woman and focus on the topic at hand. "We've got to find them."

"I agree. Father must be saved and the evildoers must be stopped." Alrick looked grim, every inch the warrior. Dee guessed he was itching to go with his brother and fight the nameless threat, but one glance at his pregnant wife and his expression softened.

"What about the others?" Carly echoed Dee's thoughts. "Do you think their minds can ever be restored?"

"The Oracle has promised to try." Cenrick looked his brother full in the face. "We still need to discuss the Oracle's prophecy."

Shaking his head, Alrick made a noise of disgust.

"Two halves are required?" Carly looked from one man to the other. "And you seriously believe she's speaking of you two?"

"Come on, it's possible," Cenrick said. "We're twins after all."

"I know, but that seems too easy." Alrick's frown showed what he thought. "Remember, the Oracle's prophecies have never been direct. Or simple."

Cenrick shrugged. "Still . . ."

Carly interrupted, looking from Cenrick to Dee, her eyes bright. "Guys, usually when someone speaks like that, they're talking about fated lovers. Have you even stopped to consider—"

"Carly," Alrick warned. "No meddling."

Grinning, the woman waggled her finger at them. "Fine. Maybe Dee will figure it out on her own."

Dee flushed, unable to keep from glancing at Cenrick. Seeing this, Alrick laughed.

"Brother, maybe you should investigate the connection between you and Dee. After all—"

"I'm an orphan." Dee spoke before Cenrick could. "And human, while he's Fae. As a prince, I'm sure he has a bloodline that goes back before time immemorial, while my heritage is unknown."

Slowly, Carly shook her head. "Alrick and I are

soul mates, or so we believe. And I am human while he also is a great prince of Rune." She playfully swatted her husband on the arm.

Face still burning, Dee looked everywhere but at Cenrick. Did none of them realize he was far, far above her? He would be king of Rune one day. Not soul mates at all, they were just partners together for one assignment, one mission, before they went their separate ways.

Cenrick cleared his throat. "What if she meant you and I?" He stared at his brother, a muscle working in his jaw. Twin spots of color decorated his cheekbones, which Dee felt certain matched her own. "If I need your help, will you give it?"

"First, I don't think even you believe she meant you and I." Alrick seemed unperturbed. "We are two vastly different souls, and you know it. Second, you are well aware I cannot leave Carly. You know the danger. The babe will be born any day, and not even for Father will I risk losing this child. You know how important he is."

"Yes." But despite his words, Cenrick's tone said he didn't like this. A knife twisted in Dee's heart. "But if the Oracle didn't mean you and I, twin brothers born of the same mother, or Dee and myself, which is clearly impossible, what did she mean?"

Clearly impossible. Dee bit her lip, trying not to sniffle.

Alrick shook his head. "Maybe you should ask the Oracle herself," he suggested. Unfolding his long legs, he clasped his arm around Cenrick's shoulders.

"I'm afraid you're on your own for this one, little brother."

This was getting them exactly nowhere. Feigning nonchalance, Dee began jiggling her leg, aching from the effort of pretending not to care. She caught Cenrick watching and pushed to her feet. "I think we've been here long enough. We're getting nowhere. If we want to rescue your father, we've really got to get going."

Cenrick stood also, taking Dee's arm but still intent on his brother. "Take care, then—," he began.

"Wait!" Disengaging herself from her husband's arms, Carly drew Dee aside. "I want to talk to Dee. Alone."

She pulled Dee into a back bedroom that had been made into a nursery. "My son's room," she said, while Dee took in the crib and brightly painted walls.

"It's beautiful," Dee told her. Then, unable to contain her curiosity, she asked, "What did you want to discuss with me?"

"The Oracle's words. Despite my husband not wanting me to meddle, I've seen the way you look at Cenrick when he's not watching."

Dee blushed, but she said nothing.

With a broad smile, Carly squeezed Dee's shoulder. "It's okay—I feel the same way about Alrick. Anyway, I think it's possible you and he are the 'two halves of the same soul' the Oracle mentioned."

"Soul mates?" Restless, Dee shook her head, the ache in her heart growing sharper. "I don't know about that." She lifted her chin. "Cenrick certainly doesn't feel that way."

Carly rolled her eyes. "Men can be fools. But listen, sometimes, when two who were meant to be are brought together, great magic can result."

"How do you know this? You're human, like me."

"I've been around the Fae and I'm married to Alrick." Carly grinned. "Mort told me his people's history. One of their most long-held beliefs is this: If you can find the one who is the other half of your soul, you are capable of great things."

Every word she spoke made Dee feel worse. "Cenrick and I are not soul mates."

"Really?" Carly cocked her head. "Then what about the other Fae man? Is he your soul mate? Didn't you say you were engaged?"

"Peter?" Dee recoiled, wondering why the thought now horrified her. "No! He and I aren't soul mates either. I know we were going to marry, but—"

"It's okay." Carly patted her shoulder. "Think about it, why don't you? Even I can see there is more between you and Cenrick than you realize."

Dee started to protest, then closed her mouth. Staring at the other woman, she let her doubt and fear show in her eyes. "So many changes," she whispered to herself. "I just don't know."

"Come on." Carly led Dee back to the other room. "Our menfolk await."

Alrick held out his arms and Carly went directly to him. They hugged as though they'd been apart for hours rather than a few minutes.

Feeling awkward, Dee watched, jumping when Cenrick recaptured her hand.

Finally, the other two turned to face them. Arms around each other, they said their good-byes. Dee echoed them, startled to realize her throat was tight.

As they walked side by side to the end of the long, dusty drive, each lost in their own thoughts, they waved at the couple watching them from the front porch.

"I'll miss them," Cenrick said. "I wish he could have come with me. We fight well together."

"I thought you said you were a scholar," she replied.

"I am, but scholars can be warriors, too. We simply have different strengths." His incredulous tone told her this was something he had just begun to learn.

CHAPTER THIRTEEN

Back in her living room, Dee gave in to her exhaustion and dropped onto the couch. She kicked off her shoes and leaned back, trying to forget Carly's words and the longing they caused in her heart.

Soul mates. As if.

"This is so messed up," she said. "What are we going to do now?"

The cushion dipped as Cenrick sat beside her. "We'll go back to our original plan, sending you into the clubs to lure them out."

She glanced at the clock. "It's nearly three A.M. I thought we would come back close to the time we left."

"With all that happened, us going to the wrong place and all, no way was I going to try and control time."

"It's way too late to go to clubs now. They will all be closing." Leaning back, she had to admit she was exhausted, both physically and emotionally.

"We'll do it tomorrow."

"Do you still think that will work?"

"It has to."

Silently, she agreed. Images of Peter and the other soulless Fae milling about aimlessly, tortured husks of their former selves, tormented her. "I hate to think of Peter like that."

"Your fiancé." His voice sounded flat.

"*Former* fiancé," she corrected. "And Cenrick, even if Peter and I had never been together—well, I wouldn't wish such a thing on my worst enemy."

"I haven't forgotten my promise," Cenrick said. "Once this is over, I'll bring him back to you." His gaze caught hers, held it.

She looked away first. "Tell me you think their souls can be restored," she said.

"The Oracle and Mort have a lot of power. If anyone can find a way, they can." Leaning close, he massaged her neck. "Now, relax. We can do nothing further without rest."

Part of her longed to do as he said, to let her body sag, bonelessly against him. But the rest of her, still disturbed by what Carly had said, was restless, unsettled.

"I keep thinking about the Oracle's words. She said two halves were needed. And you yourself said she's never wrong."

Cenrick continued to knead her sore muscles. "Yes. And if she meant Alrick needed to help me—well, she had to know he couldn't. He has to stay with Carly for the birth of their child. He has his own destiny to ensure."

"But they're his people, too," Dee remarked.

"And he's done his part to save them already. This

209

is my task." His voice became sharp. "I *will* find a way to help them."

"No, *we* will find a way to help them." Then, try as she might, she couldn't keep other words from tumbling out. "Why are you so certain the Oracle doesn't mean us? After all, my touch seems to protect you from Natasha."

Still touching her, he hesitated the briefest instant before resuming his massage of her shoulders. "We are far too different."

She nodded, glad he couldn't see her face. She felt like she might be sick. "Human and Fae, purebred and mutt . . ."

"More like warrior and scholar," he finished, his voice as flat as hers had been.

Startled, she shifted to look up at him. "What do you mean?"

"Dee . . ." At the raw need in his voice, she felt her stomach lurch. His gaze, full of heat and desire, transfixed her. "I know it's temporary, but what we have . . ."

"Cenrick, I—"

With a growl, he covered her mouth with his and all her objections faded. She was lost.

Oh, *Cenrick*. Soul halves or not, she wanted him.

The feel of his muscular body, the heady fragrance of his skin and the way he kissed her, made her head swim. Swim? Hell, she was drowning.

Apparently he felt the same. As if helpless with desire, he pushed his swollen body against her. They shed their clothes, bodies always touching, and when he entered her, she felt a rush of joy.

Home, she thought, before all coherent thought fled. *Home.*

Later, as they lay holding each other, she looked up to find him watching her.

"What is it about you?" he asked, his voice husky. "How do you do this to me?"

Smiling, she kissed his chest, watching his eyes darken. "I don't know, but you do the same thing to me."

"I want you again." His lazy tone made her shiver. "But I think we'd better sleep." He swept the hair from her forehead, then placed a kiss on the tip of her nose. "Tomorrow's going to be a big day."

The clock showed noon when she woke with Cenrick's arms wrapped around her. Dee opened her eyes to find him again watching her, desire darkening his eyes to black.

Laughing, she stretched languidly against him. He growled low in his throat, letting her feel his readiness, and they made love once more, this time with fierce urgency.

Later, having showered and dressed, Dee made pancakes for breakfast. Cenrick had never tried them, and he ate with obvious enjoyment. Dee sipped her coffee while Cenrick had milk.

"I'd like to take *some* sort of action," Cenrick grumbled, pacing the small kitchen. His movements reminded her of a caged leopard, waiting for the right moment to strike.

Crossing to the living room window, Dee twitched back the curtain. Instantly she saw the unmarked

211

cruiser, conspicuously parked in the same place as before. "They're still watching us," she announced.

"What can they do if we drive through Mick's neighborhood?"

"Nothing, though they'll think I'm going to gloat over the results of my crime."

He stared. "And . . . do you care?"

The question took her aback. Returning to the kitchen, she refilled her coffee mug and added creamer and artificial sweetener. "Not really," she decided, surprised to find she meant it.

"Then let's go by Mick's. I want to see if the house really is a total loss."

"All right. We've got all afternoon, since I can't hit the clubs until at least eight or nine tonight." She looked down at herself and grimaced. "I haven't been clubbing in so long. What am I going to wear?"

He flashed a grin. "You have something, remember?"

"No, I'm *not* wearing that enchanted dress," she said, though she grinned back. "You know, maybe our tail would enjoy me going shopping. And while we're out, I think we'll stop at Theodore's and buy something." Her grin widened. "Something really sexy and daring. Like you say a Fae woman would wear."

For the first time, Cenrick let himself think about what Dee would be doing at the club tonight. The thought of other men looking at her, knowing they'd be thinking the same amorous thoughts as he, made

212

his chest tight. Thank the Goddess he'd decided to go with her.

"Come on." Oblivious to his conflicting thoughts, she set her mug down. "Are you ready to go?"

He nodded, wondering what was wrong with him. Since when did he feel proprietary toward a human woman—toward *any* woman, for that matter?

She drove to a place less than a mile away. The shop was small and tucked into one end of a strip shopping center, the neon purple sign over the door proclaiming this was THEODORE'S. From inside the car they could see numerous outfits—short skirts, crop tops, and halters—on display in the windows. All of them were slinky or sparkly and left little to the imagination.

"See what I mean?" Dee laughed at his stunned expression and pointed. "I'll get something like one of those glittery skirt sets."

Even though her air-conditioning was turned up full blast, Cenrick felt heat rising. "Dee—," he began.

"You wait here," she instructed, pulling into a parking spot in front of the store. "I'll leave the car running. This won't take long. Five minutes max."

Now *that* would be magic.

"I've never met a woman who could shop that quickly," he said. Her grin made his the tightness in his chest worse.

"Then you don't know me. I hate to shop unless it's online. I'm going to dash in there and buy the first sexy outfit I see."

A quick glance at the window made Cenrick wince. "Do they have any other kind?"

She laughed. "No. Sexy fashion is what this store is known for."

With a lighthearted wave, she took off. Watching her stroll across the sidewalk, he saw an older man do a double take. Another man nearly fell, tripping over the curb while craning his neck to get a better look at her.

Once she disappeared inside Theodore's, he released his breath, preparing for a long wait. But, true to her word, five minutes later Dee emerged, a large purple shopping bag in hand, and headed toward the car.

A passing pickup full of young men slowed for a better look, honking the horn and hooting out the windows. Dee ignored them. Even the two cops in the unmarked cruiser rolled down their windows for a better look.

Fae enchantment, Cenrick reminded himself.

"Got it!" Tossing the bag in back, Dee grinned triumphantly. "I bought you something to wear too."

He shot a dubious look at the store. "They sell clothing for men?"

"Sure. Now all I have to do is decide which wig I want to wear tonight and I'm good to go."

As she backed from her space and headed toward the exit, their tail did the same. "Are you ready to give those guys something to talk about?" she asked.

He eyed the cops. "You want to lose them?"

"Sort of." The laughter sparkling in her eyes made him want to kiss her. "But I have *every right* to drive by Mick's, so I won't."

As Cenrick had feared, Mick's house had been reduced to rubble. Only a few charred timbers on piles of brick and ash remained.

Dee slowed the car to a crawl, even going so far as to wave at their pursuers. Trying to keep a discreet distance, they dropped back. Neither officer returned the wave.

"Poor Mick," Dee said, her voice full of sorrow. "He loved that house."

"Poor Mick?" Craning his neck for one last look before they turned the corner of the block, Cenrick shook his head. "Whatever happened there, he brought upon himself."

She bit her lip but didn't contradict him.

Once back at her place, she again waved at the police cruiser, shaking her head as she climbed the stairs.

"Now what?"

Depositing her shopping bag on the sofa, she eyed the shredded cushions and grimaced. "I'd go shopping for a new couch and pillows, but I'm not sure how much longer I'll have a job."

Cenrick headed to the kitchen and began making them both cheese sandwiches. When he'd loaded up two plates, he returned to find her in front of her computer.

"Check this out." She pointed at the screen. "Natasha Klein no longer works for NASA."

He read the short piece, which detailed how the brilliant scientist had become an independent consultant, moving to the South Worth area and setting up shop.

"I wonder how Mick met her?" Dee mused. "Top-level scientists and cops don't exactly mix."

"That's one question only Mick can tell us."

"If he's able to speak." Grim-faced, she clicked off the screen, closing her Internet program. "I'm wondering if she's making him one of the soulless too."

"I doubt it." He shook his head. "I wondered, but . . . she's using him for something. He wouldn't be of much use to her if she zapped his mind."

Dee nodded. "All right, let's go with that theory. What do you think she's using him for?"

"What does Mick have that no one else does?" In a second, he answered his own question. "He's Fae."

"And he's gay, so he wouldn't be hitting on her," Dee laughed.

"True, but his being Fae is probably more important. I'm thinking Mick's the one who led her to the Fae. *He* had to have conceived of the idea for stealing Fae magic, and therefore their souls."

Dee crossed her arms. "Assuming that's correct, we're still left with learning why. Why would Mick do such a thing?"

Pondering, both of them fell silent. In the end, neither could come up with a plausible motive.

Handing her a sandwich, Cenrick went back for two cans of cola. They ate quickly and silently, both watching the clock, each hoping the plan would work. If it didn't, Cenrick didn't know what else they could do.

When they'd finished eating, Dee searched a bit longer on the Internet, then powered off her computer and stretched. "I'm going to go get ready," she said. The clock read seven. Cenrick nodded, watching her walk down the hall toward her room.

A moment later, she emerged and tossed him a bag. "Here. Get ready."

Eyeing the bag dubiously, he waited until she'd gone before opening it to see what she'd bought him. Inside, he found fitted slacks made of some stretchy material that looked like leather, and a silk shirt in a bright-colored paisley pattern.

He stared in disbelief. No way in Hades was he wearing this. Instead, he snapped his fingers, muttered a quick spell and retrieved some of his own clothing from Rune. Dressed, he sat on the edge of the couch to wait.

"Hey, it fits perfectly. What do you think?"

Cenrick looked up. His mouth went dry and he had to remind his heart to keep beating.

"What the . . . ?" He couldn't find words. The shiny black miniskirt, made of the same material as the slacks she'd bought him, barely grazed the top of her thighs. Her legs, appearing endlessly long, were encased in high, stiletto-heeled boots made of the same material. Her blouse—if one could call it that—also black, appeared to be made of several wispy strips of silky material held together by silver chains. And her wig was the crowning touch—long, raven-colored curls tumbling from her shoulders to her waist. Merely looking at her made his temperature rise.

"You look . . ."

"I look like a hooker, don't I?" Her grin told him this was exactly what she wanted. "With this outfit and the magic you put on me, those goons will be like putty in my hands."

"I was going to say you look fantastic."

"Really?" Her eyes narrowed. "You look great, too, but why aren't you wearing the stuff I bought you?"

"Because"—he crossed his arms—"I'm not Mick."

To his disbelief, she laughed. "Hey, it was worth a shot. Since you insist on coming with me, I figured the more you blended in, the better."

"Sorry."

"All right." She lifted a shoulder and, back to business, rubbed her hands together. "Let me get my car keys and we'll go." About to walk off, she stopped. "I wish there was a way I could get a wire."

"A what?"

"A wire is like a hidden microphone, which would capture what is said and relay it back to you. Cops use them all the time in undercover work."

"Can't you get one?"

"No. Not a single guy in the IT department would outfit me now. I'm on suspension, remember?" Bitterness sharpened her voice. "But I've got something almost as good. Here, catch." She tossed something at him.

Out of reflex, he caught it. "What's this?"

"A cell phone, encased in vinyl so you can carry it." Coming closer, she brought with her the heady scent of her perfume. "Look, you can even punch the keys through the plastic."

"Do you have one?"

"Sure. The one I'm giving you is one of those pre-paid phones. I bought it to give as a gift to someone once, and didn't. Since I have my regular cell, I've never used it. I turned it on and it still works. I even programmed my cell number in it for you."

He turned the vibrant blue object over in his hand. "Why do you want me to have this?"

Her gaze was unblinking. "So I can call you if I need you, or vice versa. It's a way of us keeping track of each other."

"I see." He dropped the phone into his pocket. "We won't lose track of each other. I have no plans to leave your side. Are you ready?"

She stared at him for half a heartbeat before finally nodding. "Now, you promise me you won't do anything rash, like threaten some poor guy in there?"

"If you're in danger—"

"Trust me to handle things. I'll be fine." She held up her cell phone. "And I've got this. You've got to let them talk to me, remember? Otherwise, this won't work."

"No matter what, you're not leaving with anyone, understand? We stay together."

"You worry too much. We're just dangling the bait in front of them. They're not in charge. We'll be doing this by my terms."

He sighed. "Then let's go." Slipping on his gloves, he let her lead the way to the car.

The drive seemed to take forever. Cenrick greatly preferred the Fae method of travel: a quick spell and you were there.

Finally, they exited the freeway. Driving down a four-lane road packed with cars, Dee located an empty spot near the strip of nightclubs and parallel parked.

"Showtime." Inhaling sharply, she made a final check of her watch. "You ready?"

Cenrick nodded.

Sliding out of the car, she smoothed down her shirt, allowing him to take her arm. "Remember, you promised."

"I know." He nodded. Then he said, "You look beautiful." And he meant it.

"Fae beautiful?"

"Very Fae." And very Dee. He wondered why his chest felt so tight. Stupid. Really stupid.

"Good." She smiled up at him. "You look fantastic too. But then, you always do."

They strolled up the sidewalk, joining a crowd of fancy-dressed people who were laughing and talking. Turning onto a closed-off, brick-paved street, Dee pointed several doors down. "That's where we'll try first."

Music boomed from every doorway they passed. Cigarette and cigar smoke mingled with the odors of alcohol and various male and female colognes. The beginnings of a headache pounded behind Cenrick's temple.

The line moved quickly. A burly bouncer guarded the last doorway. Dee paid the cover fee and held out the back of her hand to have it stamped. Cenrick did the same. Beyond the door, the noise and smells were even worse.

"Hey,!" Dee leaned close, having to shout to make him hear her. "I'm going to go work the room. You do the same."

"No." He grabbed her arm. "We work together."

"You're going to blow the entire plan." She yanked her arm free. "Now, go on."

He grimaced and turned away.

A tall, slender man stepped into his path. "Hey there, handsome." He clearly had eyes for Cenrick. "You must be new here." Studying the man's aura, Cenrick realized he was Fae.

From the behind the man, Dee mouthed something. It looked like, "Talk to him."

Cenrick fumed as she sauntered away, but she looked so gorgeous and confident and oh-so-very Fae in her short skirt and high heels that he couldn't hold on to his anger long.

Still smiling expectantly, the slender Fae waited. Cenrick made small talk with him, trying to appear interested in case this guy was somehow related to Mick and Natasha's scheme, while at the same time he tried to keep an eye out for Dee. But he lost sight of her in the crush of people. The other Fae continued to chatter, oblivious to Cenrick's discomfort.

"Excuse me," Cenrick finally said, pushing past and ignoring the stunned look on the Fae's face. And shouldering through the crowd, he searched for Dee.

It seemed an eternity before he located her again, standing at the bar with a tall, good-looking man on each side. She had two drinks in front of her, gifts from each of her suitors. Though he hated to break up her cozy tête a tête, enough time had passed for the enemy to make his move if he was going to here.

Strolling up behind her, Cenrick slipped his arm around Dee's shoulder and kissed her neck. "Sorry I'm late, honey," he drawled, giving both men a warning look. "Want to introduce me to your new friends?"

She glared at him. "I—"

Both men instantly moved off.

When they were gone, Dee said, "Let's go." She tucked her arm in his. "Even though you broke your promise, I think we got what we came for." He started to speak, but abandoned the idea as they skirted the crowded dance floor.

Once outside, the noise level dropped dramatically. "What'd you get?" he asked.

"Later." She gripped his hand hard. "Wait until we get to the car."

Silently, they hurried through the throng waiting to get into the club. Dee pressed the remote, unlocking her car doors.

"Bingo." Sliding into the driver's seat, she flashed a triumphant grin. "We got a bite."

He watched as she turned the key in the ignition, backed out of the parking spot. "When? We weren't separated that long." He shouldn't be surprised. He knew he shouldn't be surprised.

"While you talked to your admirer." The corners of her mouth curved into a smile. "As soon as I got away from you, they surrounded me. This Fae look really works."

About to tell her that her appeal was due more to her own beauty than the spell, Cenrick hesitated. He just took a moment to admire her beauty.

"Guess what else?" she asked. "I saw one of the goons from Mick's house there. He was scouting the crowd."

"One of Natasha's bodyguards?"

"Yep. And even better, he was with Natasha. I saw her holding court up near the stage."

"Natasha?" He hadn't seen her at all. "Don't you think that's a bit of a coincidence?"

Her grin widened. "Maybe. But it helps I knew that's Mick's favorite night spot. Almost all of his running buddies go there."

Dazed by the turn of events, Cenrick nodded. Something was off, even if he couldn't quite put his finger on it. "Did she see you?"

"I made sure she didn't. I also looked for Mick, but he wasn't there. I'm worried about him even more now," she added.

Cenrick was, too, though he didn't believe in his cousin's innocence to the same degree. Not anymore. "You said they took the bait. When?"

"You know those guys you interrupted at the bar? One of them started reciting Shakespeare, if you can believe it. I had to pretend to find it fascinating. He was quoting *A Midsummer Night's Dream,* I believe." She chuckled.

"It's a Fae favorite." Cenrick shook his head, surprised by the insightful approach. "And a good move on his part. Most real Fae would find such a recital fascinating." He paused, considering his next words. "But that man wasn't Fae, Dee. He had no aura. The only way he would know such a strategy is if someone Fae told him." He didn't say the rest, though he knew she must have caught on. *Someone like Mick.*

"Yeah, well. He gave me this." She handed over a card. "Fae Frolic. It's advertising a big party."

223

While she drove, Cenrick read the rest of the card aloud. "'More than a party, the Frolic is a place where Fae living among mortals can get together and cut loose,'" he said. He felt a spell woven into the paper—a beguiling spell strong enough to enchant a weaker Faerie.

When he told her about this, Dee nodded. She said, "Good thing I'm not Fae. This was a good plan we had."

Once more, Cenrick studied the card. "There's no location," he realized.

Dee nodded. "I caught that too. When I asked, the guy said it changed every week. He said he'd call me."

"You gave him your number?"

"Of course." Smiling smugly, she took back the card. "We've got them—hook, line, and sinker. All we've got to do now is wait for the call."

CHAPTER FOURTEEN

The next morning, the ringing phone dragged Dee out of a sound sleep. Beside her, Cenrick sat up. Heart pounding, she reached for the receiver. Caller ID showed an unknown number.

"Hello?" She couldn't clear the sleep from her voice.

"Turn on the television." She didn't recognize the young, male voice. "Channel eight."

"Who is this?" she asked. But the click meant the caller had already hung up.

Dropping the phone into the cradle, she grabbed the remote and turned on the TV. An official department photo of her filled the screen.

". . . suspected in the disappearance and possible murder of her partner, Mick Morsi. The body, which has not yet been officially identified, was clad in a South Worth Police Department uniform and is believed to be that of Officer Morsi. A formal investigation is under way."

Body?

The station cut to a commercial. The jingle for a laundry detergent began playing merrily.

Stunned, Dee fumbled with the remote, finally succeeding in turning the television off. She and Cenrick stared at each other.

"What the—?"

"That body better not be Mick," she cried, throwing back the covers. "So help me, if they've murdered him, I'll—" She choked on the rest of her words.

Cenrick grabbed her, pulled her close. "Listen to me. That body is not Mick."

"How do you know?" She attempted to push him away, though only half-heartedly. "They're setting me up for his murder."

"No, they're not. Dee, it can't be Mick. If they're setting you up for a murder, they're using someone else's body."

Swiping at her eyes, she gaped at him. "What do you mean?"

"Even if they succeeded in killing a Fae, which is not an easy task, I can't believe they'd ever intentionally leave a Fae body for the authorities to autopsy. The anomalies in our blood and bone structure would set off too many alarms."

She blinked, digesting this. "Then how'd he pass the mandatory police physicals?"

"Most likely he used his own doctor for blood work."

Dee nodded slowly. "He did. I used him, too." She took a deep breath. "So, if that's not him . . . then where is Mick? You know what they're trying to do. How can he stand back and let this happen?"

"I don't know. If he's not working with them . . . Perhaps Mick's already been taken."

She stared. "Taken? As in, soulless?"

He nodded. "That would explain his conspicuous absence."

"Can't you ask the Oracle?"

"I would think she would tell us." But after a moment he amended, "Maybe not. She might believe that if I knew, the knowledge would impair my judgment."

"So . . . you don't know any of this for certain." Dee lifted her chin.

"Of course not. But he does appear to be out of the picture. Maybe he just has other, more pressing concerns. Maybe he's just out of town and these guys are taking advantage of that."

She shot him a sideways glance to let him know she didn't buy that theory any more than he did. "He's 'out of town' because they're trying to make it look like I've killed him," she said, her voice grim. Staring at the card she'd placed on the dresser, she shook her head. "All we can do now is hope that guy from last night calls. And soon." Cenrick glanced from her to the phone. "I—"

The doorbell rang.

"Now what?" She dragged a hand through her mussed hair and climbed out of bed, Cenrick right behind her. A quick look through the peephole showed the morning had gone from bad to worse.

"Internal Affairs," she said. "What now? At least I know I'm not under arrest. They'd send regular uniforms instead of these guys."

227

"I'll stay out of sight." Cenrick stepped into the bedroom.

Once he was gone, Dee opened the door. "Riddick and his sidekick, I see. What do you want this time?"

Their eyes widened as they took in her short pajamas. She bit back a curse word. With all the uproar, she'd managed to forget about the Fae spell Cenrick had placed on her, as well as what she was—or wasn't—wearing.

She looked up at Riddick, catching him staring at her chest with an intense look. A quick glance at the younger guy told her he too was besotted, smiling a dopey smile. Great. She directed her attention back to Officer Riddick, since he seemed the tougher of the two.

"How can I help you?" she asked, keeping her voice polite and businesslike, and doing her best to pretend she wasn't wearing pajamas. At least they were shorts rather than some filmy nightie.

Riddick swallowed. Heat blazed in his eyes, which swept over her. "I never realized you were so"—he moved his hand in an hourglass shape—"hot."

Hot? Crap. That did it. "Come on in, take a seat on the couch. Give me a minute to change and I'll be right back."

"Please don't." The younger officer spoke up. His freckled face wore a completely infatuated look. "You're absolutely lovely the way you are. Please don't deprive us."

"Uh . . ." Dee looked at Riddick, her expression

228

meant to convey he needed to do something about his partner.

Riddick shook his head. "He's right. Please, don't change. It's not often we get to see someone as beautiful as you."

Muttering a particularly unladylike word, Dee spun on her heel. "You two can wait in the living room. I'll be right back."

Damn, this pretend-Fae spell worked too well. Oddly enough, she hadn't noticed anything like it in the club last night. But they hadn't been there long.

Whatever. As it was, she needed to find out what I.A. wanted and get rid of them. Between her lack of attire and Cenrick's magic spell, she'd have to be careful.

"We just need a minute of your time," Riddick called out, his gaze burning holes in her back.

"And you've got it," she called over her shoulder. "But first I've got to put on a robe."

Ignoring more protests, she ran for her room and her thick, terry-cloth bathrobe.

"Here." Whispering, Cenrick handed it to her from his hiding place inside the closet. "How long do you think this will take?"

"Not long." She hoped.

"Get rid of them. We've got more important things to do," he hissed.

"I know," she whispered back. "But this is imperative. My career is on the line. I need to find out how seriously they take these new trumped-up charges. And if they know whose body that is. Wait here."

Slipping into her robe and belting it tightly around her waist, she tugged the collar closed and dashed back down the hall, slowing to a casual walk as she reached the corner.

"All right, I'm ready," she said. Entering the room, she plastered a smile on her face. Amazing, how much safer she felt now that she was covered up.

Both men's gazes could have burned through steel. Riddick in particularly appeared predatory, like a hungry lion about to pounce. Both men stood waiting.

Okay. Swallowing, she tried to remember her manners. "Please, have a seat. Would you like a glass of water or anything?" Still smiling, she took a seat on the edge of the chair and crossed her legs, smoothing her robe carefully.

Officer Riddick sat near her on the sofa. His partner, still staring, declined.

"We'd like to ask you a few questions if you don't mind." Riddick's voice sounded huskier than usual. Evidently he realized this, since he cleared his throat. If she was careful, she could use this magical beauty thing to her advantage. Now that she was covered up.

"Of course I don't." She gave them her sweetest smile.

"We found a body."

She nodded. "I saw that on the news."

"Wearing your partner's uniform."

This time, she said nothing.

"Though he had no fingerprints—they were cut off—we were able to identify him through dental records."

Dee held her breath, waiting.

230

"The body was not Mick Morsi's."

Releasing her breath, she didn't try to hide her relief. "That's good. Do you know who it was?"

"Yes." Riddick's look became even more predatory. "The body belonged to a friend of his. Jack Singleterry."

"Jack?" Dee's throat closed. She blinked away tears. "How? Why?"

"That's what we'd like to know." Riddick leaned forward, so close his nose almost touched hers. "We were hoping you could tell us."

Rearing back, she pushed herself to her feet. For one awful second there, she'd thought Riddick might try to kiss her. She wondered if Cenrick could remove the spell and put it back on her when she needed to use it.

"Do you know anything about Mr. Singleterry's death?" the younger officer asked, his tone gentle. "Any idea what happened to him?"

"Absolutely not." Despite her attempt to sound cool and calm, her voice shook. "Jack was a very dear friend of Mick's—and mine as well."

Riddick fell silent, still watching, as though he hoped she'd drop a clue at any moment. His partner, hanging on to her every word, wore a dazed, dreamy look on his freckled face.

Giving herself a mental shake, she looked from one cop to the other. She wanted time alone to grieve. "Is there anything else?" Dismissal rang in her voice.

"Nope. If you don't have anything to voluntarily tell us . . ." Unfolding himself from the sofa, Riddick walked over to his partner, snapping his fingers in front of the younger man's face. "Let's go, Kenny."

They let themselves out. Dee locked the door behind them.

"Jack." She spoke his name in a hushed whisper, wishing for tears and feeling only an awful, blinding rage. Walking into the room, Cenrick caught sight of her face and stopped. "What's wrong? What happened?"

"The body they found? It was Jack. They killed Jack."

He gathered her in his arms. "We'll get them, Dee," he promised. "We will."

She felt cold, like ice, even though fury still burned inside her. "Yes, we will," she agreed. "We'll get them and we'll make them pay." Untying the bathrobe, she let it fall to the floor, then lifted her face to his for a kiss.

"Make me feel alive," she told him.

And he did.

Though she'd given them her number, Natasha's people didn't call that night, or the next. Growing weary of waiting and impatient to take action, Dee deliberated going back out to the clubs.

As she was about to bring up the subject with Cenrick for a third time, the phone finally rang. And, when caller ID showed an unidentified caller, her heart began to race. "Here we go," she mouthed to Cenrick, crossing her fingers before picking up the handset. "Hello?"

"Are you Dee?" The purposely distorted voice was unrecognizable. "Dee Smith?"

Dee Smith was a pet name Mick used to call her. Since they never knew their real names as children, they'd often made up false ones.

"Yes. Who is this? What do you want?"

"Never mind who I am."

"Is this about the"—she glanced at the card—"party?"

All she heard was the sound of breathing. The caller sounded as though he wore a mask or something over his face.

"Party?" He chuckled, though it sounded more like wheezing. "Not really. Mick asked me to call you."

Mick? Her heart stopped. Did Mick know what had happened to Jack? Instead of asking this, she said the first thing that came to mind. "Why doesn't Mick call me himself?"

There was a long pause and then, "He isn't able."

"Where is he? Is he all right?" As if this person would tell her.

"Mick is close. He's hiding out in Dallien."

In Dallien? A tried-and-true South Worth native, Mick always made fun of that little town. What better place to hide?

"Jack's dead," the man continued. "And Mick's afraid he's next. He needs your help. He wants to see you."

She grabbed a pen. "Where?"

"Lower Dweenville. At a club called Flight Risk. The place looks like it's closed, but it's not. Go inside and he'll be waiting in the back room."

"I'll be there."

"Good. And come alone. He wants to talk to you without the Fae prince."

The Fae prince? Why wouldn't Mick have said Cenrick's name? Was this a trap? "Without who?"

The caller grunted, the sound menacing. "Cenrick of Rune. Enough games."

Fine. She acquiesced. They were calling the shots.

"When?" she asked.

"Tonight." He chuckled, the sound sending chills down her spine. "And you'd better come alone, or Mick won't see you."

"Of course," she agreed. Replacing the receiver, she looked up to find Cenrick watching her, waiting for an explanation. She relayed the caller's words.

"You're *not* going alone," he said immediately. "That'd be playing right into their hands."

"Maybe. But if this is a set-up, it makes no sense. It has to be real."

Pacing, Cenrick frowned. "I don't know. Natasha's henchman still may call about the party. They don't know the Fae woman in the club and Dee Bishop the policewoman are one and the same. Unless they found out."

"How would they find out? Who would have told them?"

"Mick? It's possible he connected the dots, told them you're not Fae."

"I want to believe Mick got in over his head and wants out. When Jack was killed . . ." She swallowed. "I just can't believe he would kill Jack. No way."

Cenrick stopped his pacing long enough to cup

her chin in his hands and give her a quick, hard kiss. "Either way, I don't like it. You're not going alone."

"Oh, yes I am." She glared at him, refusing to allow his kiss to distract her. "The question is, whether I let you accompany me or not."

He folded his arms. "Just try and lose me."

The police had stopped watching her house. Most likely, they'd been unable to justify the expense without being able to charge her with a crime. The Dweenville Avenue club scene had its fringe areas, places where it wasn't safe to walk at night, alleys where hapless men had been beaten, knifed, and killed. Dallien cops tried to patrol it, but the area seemed to move as though liquid, shifting from one alley to the next at the whim of the dark-souled types who stalked it. Flight Risk was on one such street.

They parked directly under a streetlight.

"The place looks abandoned." Cenrick seemed to sense the inherent risk—or maybe he picked up on Dee's almost palpable nervousness.

She took in the club's boarded-up windows and shook her head. "He said it would." Her attempt at nonchalance failed miserably.

Watching her, Cenrick's eyes were calm. "Do you want to leave? Regroup?"

"Leave? Hell, no. Not if there's a chance Mick is alive and well here. If he really does want to talk to me, I want to hear what he has to say. Especially since he's about the only one besides Natasha who can tell us what's really going on."

"'Us,'" he mused. "They told you to come alone, remember?"

"I know. That's why I'm getting out of this car and going up there by myself. You wait a little bit, then sneak around to the back. I don't think they want to hurt me."

"Really?" His brows rose. "Then what *do* you think they want?"

"I'm not sure." She wasn't worried. "You know, there's a very small possibility that Mick really is here and needs my help."

"But you don't believe that, do you?"

"Hell no." She gave him her best confident smile. "I wasn't born yesterday." Patting her shoulder harness, she adjusted her jacket. "And I'm betting they won't expect me to come armed, especially since Lieutenant Cowell took my service revolver. Only Mick knows I have my own gun."

She got out of the car and began walking toward the front of the deserted club. Though she forced herself not to look back at her car and give away Cenrick, she couldn't keep from continually glancing left to right, ready for any other assailant.

As she'd expected, the front door swung open before she even knocked. Entering, she sidestepped the burly man who attempted to grab her.

"Hands off," she snarled. "Take me to Mick."

After a moment of startled silence, he laughed. "I can't believe you fell for that. Mick's not here."

She pulled her gun, leveling it at him. "Then I'm leaving. Don't try and stop me."

If anything, her comment made him laugh harder. "Go ahead. We don't want you anyway."

Stunned, she stared. "What?" He pointed to the door. "We didn't want you, fool. We wanted that big Fae prince you've been with."

"You told me not to bring him."

"We knew he'd insist on coming. And, if things have gone according to plan, we've got him now. You're too late."

Before he'd even finished, Dee started running, heading for the door. A trap? And they hadn't wanted her, they'd wanted Cenrick. She'd played right into their hands.

They let her go. No one followed. Outside, she sprinted for the corner, heading for her car. Still where she'd parked it, the streetlight shone off the white paint. When she reached it, she knew before she even yanked on her door handle that she'd messed up royally. The car was empty. Cenrick was gone.

She spun, heading around the back of the building. If he'd followed their plan, he should have gone there. Whoever or whatever had grabbed him couldn't have gone far; there hadn't been enough time.

But the back alley was deserted, the back door to the building locked. She pounded on it anyway. No one answered.

From the front, Dee heard a screech of tires. Her car! Damn it! She had a terrible premonition that they were stealing her car and leaving her no way to pursue. They were getting away.

Sprinting back around to the front of the building, she wasn't at all surprised to find her parking spot empty. And Cenrick—where was he? Where could he have gone? He'd agreed to sneak around to the back where she would come out.

Fishing her cell phone from her pocket, she punched speed dial for the phone she'd given him. It rang and rang. Then the automated recording come on, saying the party had not yet set up its mailbox.

No answer. Cenrick hadn't answered the phone she'd given him—or someone had turned it off.

CHAPTER FIFTEEN

Cenrick stirred, trying to stand, then fell to his knees instead. The creeping weakness had taken over his limbs gradually, so gradually he didn't notice at first. Just like at Mick's house, Cenrick thought right before losing his futile struggle to stay upright.

He did a face-plant, right on the ground. Only by turning his head did he keep his nose from being broken. Once prone he couldn't move, could barely summon up enough energy to inhale and exhale. It was exactly like he'd seen actors do a hundred times on one of his beloved cop shows. Except this seriously hurt.

Dee! He groaned, knowing she couldn't hear him. How were they doing this to him? The machine he'd seen in the photos seemed way too large to transport around.

Unless they'd moved it to this club or developed a mobile version. If that were the case, every Fae everywhere—including those currently blithely unaware in Rune—was in serious trouble. Even their prince, the one who'd been charged with saving them, had been bested. He'd lost, and so would his people, unless Dee was able to help him.

Dee! That was his last coherent thought before everything went black.

Day, night . . . time had no meaning. When awareness returned to him, he was in a darkened room and weak, like a newborn dragon. Whoever had captured him hadn't bothered to tie him up. No doubt his captors knew what they'd already done was more effective than any chains.

Too feeble to do more than breathe, he tried to summon enough strength to even raise his head—and failed.

Where was he? In the deserted club? Or had they moved him to some other place, somewhere unreachable? And where was his father? And Dee?

He groaned. Dee. He had to get a message to Dee. But how?

He must have passed out again. The next thing he knew, he'd been placed upright, strapped into some kind of chair. A bright, blue-tinged light shone in his face, blinding him. His stomach dipped and clenched. For a moment he thought he might be sick.

"How are you?" a woman asked in a cultured, faintly accented voice. "Feeling a bit weak?"

He didn't deign to answer. This must be the infamous Natasha, scientist and Mick's alleged girlfriend. The creator of the machine that stole souls.

"So, you're a Fae prince?" She moved closer, leaning into his field of vision. Her long blond hair was pulled back in a ponytail. She was in her mid-thirties, and her dusky skin and almond-shaped eyes gave her an exotic beauty. This was ruined only by the cruel twist of her full mouth.

Confused, he tried to summon up enough energy to question her. He couldn't seem to string words together to form a coherent sentence. So he attempted to frame his question in one word. "Father."

She narrowed her eyes. "I still have him. He's weak. One more treatment and I won't need to keep him around any longer." Her laugh sounded like rusty nails. "What a homecoming *that* will be. The ruler of Rune, returning a mindless zombie."

Ignoring this, Cenrick summoned his strength for another query. "How?"

She smiled, flashing her perfect white teeth. "How'd I do it? Is that what you want to know?"

He tried to nod and failed. Watching him closely, she saw the tiny tremor of movement. Her smile widened. "I've been wanting to bask in my triumph, but Mick pooped out on me. Since you asked and you're a captive audience, I'll tell you."

Maybe he could stall for time. "Start . . ." He licked his cracked lips and tried again. "Start at the beginning."

Eyeing him, she touched his face. "You're the most beautiful one yet, you know. You want the entire story? Fine. We have time. I knew Mick's friend Jack from our work—we met at one of those all-day scientific seminars. I was bored, he needed someone to talk to. When he got drunk, he started babbling about the Fae and magic and the man he loved. Despite my disbelief, I let him ramble. He spilled the entire sordid story—how he had contracted AIDS, how his disease was progressing faster than either he or his partner Mick wanted."

Of their own will, Cenrick's eyes drifted closed, the bright light creating dancing spots on his retinas. If she kept zapping him so strongly with her machine, he wouldn't be awake long enough to hear her story.

"I knew then I didn't have too long to live. I wanted to believe." Tapping her foot impatiently, she stopped talking. "Look at me, Cenrick of Rune."

Though he honestly attempted to force his eyes open, he couldn't. Mouth dry, he tried to speak instead. "Turn. Down. Machine."

She laughed. "Too much for you, eh big boy?" Her heels clicked on the tile floor as she crossed the room.

A moment later, he felt a bit of his strength returning. Now he could at least look at her again.

"Better?"

He nodded.

"Good. Because I want you to learn about your downfall before I take your magic. Your father's should be the final cap that will heal me."

Now that the power level had gone done, Cenrick could think again. He wanted to ask another question. He cleared his throat. "Where are we?"

"My house." With a grin, she fingered his hair. "But no one knows where I live, not even Mick. Don't hope for help."

"Why? Why are you doing this?"

She patted his hand. "I'll get to that in a minute. Now, where was I? Ah yes, with Jack in that Indiana conference center. When he started talking about faeries and alternate realities, I thought he'd lost his mind. But Jack was—is—a well-respected scientist. NASA—where I worked, you know—used him frequently as a consultant. So when he told me about magic, and how Mick was working on a machine to make Jack a Fae, I knew I owed it to myself to at least check it out. Especially since I had nothing to lose."

Make Jack a Fae? Cenrick wasn't sure he'd heard correctly. Experimentally, he attempted to move. He was able to raise his head a little. Not enough. But something.

She must have noticed the hope that flared in his eyes, or the tiny movement of his chin. A moment later shaking her head she readjusted the dial, immediately removing his recently returned strength. In the space of a heartbeat, he was reduced to Jell-O again, a quivering, mindless lump.

He couldn't help it—he groaned. When he did, she chuckled.

"Sorry," she said, sounding anything but. "Now, where was I? Ah, yes. Mick wanted to make Jack a Fae, knowing this would cure him. Meanwhile, Jack's slowly dying, and Mick's getting more and more frustrated with his lack of success. It's too bad Jack up and died. I haven't had the heart to tell Mick yet."

A sound escaped Cenrick. Could he still talk? He took a deep breath, deciding he could at least try. "You. Made." Deep breath. Again. "Machine. To. Take. Fae. Souls."

Delighted, she nodded. "Is that what your people are calling it? Stealing their souls? I love it!"

Peering at her, he wished he had all his faculties. The odd thing about Natasha was she didn't seem to realize her own evil, or to consider the impact her machine had on an entire race.

Clearing his throat, he attempted to gesture with one hand. He couldn't, but he could still speak. "What—do—you—plan—to—do—when—healed?"

With a frown, she looked around the sterile laboratory set up in her garage. "I guess it can't hurt to tell you. I mean, what are you going to do? Once I've taken your magic, I'll send you back to Rune just like the others. Only this time"—she moved closer, stroking his arm—"I'll go with you."

"Why?"

"To heal me." Lifting a hand to brush her hair back, she laughed—an awful sound. "I have breast cancer. It's metastasized into my brain and lungs. With your soul and your father's, I'll have enough magic inside to kill it. And I'll be strong, too. None in Rune or on Earth will be able to best me."

Rune? What was she planning? And what had she done with his father?

"Where is King Roark?" he demanded, using the last of his strength.

"You're a scholar, according to him," she taunted. "Figure it out."

She gave one more twist of the dial and terrible energy coursed through him. Everything went gray, then black.

* * *

244

When next he woke, head throbbing, he was alone, still strapped into the machine, still feeling his soul being dragged from him slowly, grudgingly. Worse, he was still helpless. Still powerless to stop Natasha from using him as the vehicle to gain access to his people and his home. Only one thing stood between this evil woman and her plan. Dee.

Was Dee all right? Had she escaped the trap unscathed? He had no way of knowing.

Unless . . . concentrating, he managed to move his hand up to feel his left front pocket. A lump of hard plastic told him he still had his cell phone, the one Dee had given him in case of emergency. Natasha must not have believed a Fae would carry such a device. Lucky for him.

Gritting his teeth, he got his fingers into his pocket, slowly pulled the phone out by the stubby antenna. Now, to focus. Concentrating was difficult with everything so blurry. The phone face was small, the metal under the plastic cover seemed menacing. Speed dial, Dee had said. Remembering to punch the ON button, he went through the sequence she'd shown him.

Dee called a taxi and headed home. Once there, she paced and paced, trying to think. They had Cenrick and were no doubt beginning the process of making him soulless. She had to find him. But how?

A sound stopped her frantic pacing. Her cell phone.

Groping in her coat pocket, Dee located the thing and pressed TALK. "Hello?"

Breathing. Heavy breathing.

Good Lord. A prank caller, in the middle of the night, on her cell?

About to end the call, Dee caught sight of the caller's phone number. It belonged to that prepaid cell phone.

"Cenrick?"

The caller made a faint sound.

"Cenrick, is that you?"

"Yes." This time, the single word came across loud and clear, though the voice was so strained she knew speaking had been a major effort.

"Where are you?"

"House," he mumbled. "Her house. Garage."

Her house? "Whose?"

Silence.

"Cenrick? Are you there? Speak to me."

But she heard nothing. He'd either passed out or given up.

Her house? Natasha. Dee couldn't remember her last name.

Moving quickly, she grabbed the folder she'd made earlier. Here was the print-out from her first search. Natasha Klein. Great.

Quickly, she turned on her computer and signed on to her internet provider. Bringing up TAD—short for Torrent County Appraisal District—she clicked on Search Properties by Name. Thank God for being a cop. A second later, she had an address.

Natasha had apparently purchased a home in Teller. She might think no one knew where she lived, but even villainesses had to pay taxes. Dee jotted down the street name and house number. Getting there would take twenty minutes, maybe less. She could only hope she wasn't too late.

Grabbing a pair of jeans and a T-shirt, she snatched her car keys off the dresser and headed outside.

The machine slowly ripped away his soul. Fighting silently Cenrick resisted, with every nerve ending and cell that made up his body. But still, the machine droned on, the lights flickered and dimmed, and Natasha paid him periodic, gleeful visits to check on the progress.

Each time she came by, she gloated. He clung to consciousness through sheer force of will. Though he didn't understand why, she seemed to think a prince's soul would be more powerful than any other. He was so mind-fuzzled, he wasn't sure if that would prove true or not.

Thirsty, he also burned and shivered. The room felt freezing, at subzero temperature, as though soul-stealing wasn't always done in the midst of the fiery flames of Hell.

A light came on, flooding the darkness with over-bright wattage. Through blurry eyes he tried to watch as Natasha crossed the room once more, her high heels tapping sharply on the concrete. Glancing at him, she checked the machinery, twisted a knob, entered some numbers into a laptop computer, then sat back and smiled with satisfaction. Ready to gloat again. He wondered if he had enough of himself left for his hatred of her to blaze through in his eyes.

From the overbright smile she gave, he rather doubted it.

"Almost done." Her cheery voice grated on his nerves. "Soon, very soon, you'll be like all the others. I promise you won't feel a thing."

Glaring at her with all the rage he could summon, he licked his cracked lips and tried to form words. "What . . . will . . . you . . . do . . . with . . . me?"

Coming close enough for his nostrils to flare at the acrid scent of her perfume, she leaned in and brushed hair away from his forehead. "Why, I'll be taking you home, beautiful Cenrick. To Rune. You and I will travel there together. I can't wait to pay that Oracle a visit."

Rune. A shudder went through him. This reminded him: She wanted to go to Rune to destroy his people, his home. He couldn't let that happen.

Couldn't. Let. Tired. So exhausted. His eyes drifted closed. No! He couldn't let her win.

But then, he was so weak, so feeble. How could he stop her? No hope left.

Dee.

Again he closed his eyes, for only a moment, just for a second to gather his strength. But time passed oddly when he was in this state, and when he opened them again, the room was dark and Natasha was gone.

Dee drove like a madwoman, for once disobeying the speed limit signs, glad of the super-duper radar detector Peter had long ago given her. Highway 377 was deserted this time of night, and she made it to Teller in fifteen minutes.

It took five more to locate the street. Even if she hadn't jotted down the house number, she would have had no difficulty finding Natasha's house; the eerie glow, exactly like the one at Mick's, would have clued her in. ╸

As she had when the machine had been at Mick's, Dee parked several houses away, on the opposite side of the street. There were only two streetlights here, placed at each end of the curved road. The middle remained dark, except for the glowing house.

Glad of the relative darkness, Dee checked her revolver, clicked off the safety and holstered it, grabbed her flashlight, and headed down the sidewalk.

Reaching the side of the house, Dee slipped around the side, locating the fence gate. Either Natasha was careless or supremely overconfident, for the gate wasn't locked. Dee could only hope her luck would hold.

Once in the backyard, she drew her gun and proceeded toward the back door. Halfway there, she realized the low humming sound she heard came from the garage. The only way in was through the house or front garage door. She opted for the house.

Jimmying the back door lock with a credit card was simple—Natasha hadn't bothered to upgrade her security. Dee slipped into the silent house.

The glow emanated from the garage. Moving silently, Dee went through the laundry room, knowing there would be a door there. She turned the knob, stepping into the garage.

And came face-to-face with Natasha. Beyond her, she saw the machine, and Cenrick, unconscious.

Both women froze.

"You," Natasha said, the word dripping with venom.

"Don't move or I'll shoot." Dee smiled grimly. "And I promise you, I'm an excellent shot."

"The final piece," Natasha said, staring at the now unholstered gun with shock frozen in her colorless eyes. "How is this possible? You're Fae. You shouldn't be able to hold a gun."

"Am I?"

"Yes." The other woman's voice rang with certainty. "You are Fae. I can tell."

"How? You're human. How do you know I'm Fae?"

"Thanks to your friend Mick and his brilliant though misguided plan, I have my machine." Natasha spread her thin arms. "I've taken on Fae powers. I can see your aura. You can't hide what you are, not from me." Her gaze sharpened, full of icy rage. "Now tell me how you are able to hold that gun."

Ignoring her request, Dee forced a laugh as she edged closer to Cenrick. He'd been aware long enough to see her enter the room, but now he'd dropped his chin back on his chest.

"Turn off the machine."

Flexing her bony fingers like claws, Natasha stared. "No."

Dee raised her weapon. "Do it, or I'll shoot."

Though pale, Natasha stood her ground.

"I mean what I say," Dee told her. "Turn it off right now or I'll shoot you and do it myself."

"Even as I'm filled with power, the machine should weaken you, destroy you. Just like all the others." Fury rang in Natasha's voice. "How can you be powerful enough to withstand it?"

Ignoring the question, Dee started counting aloud. "If I get to five, kiss those Jimmy Choo shoes you're wearing good-bye."

The blond woman didn't move. "Any moment, you will succumb to my creation. Then I'll have you, and you'll be the final Fae to give me her magic—at least here in the human world."

"You don't listen." Dee shot her in the foot.

Natasha shrieked as blood spread across the floor. "Metal bullets. I'm Fae now . . . I . . ."

"I can kill you with one final shot, human or Fae," Dee said coldly. "Now, turn off the machine."

With a snarl of rage, Natasha lurched forward and punched a command in the keyboard of her laptop.

Immediately, the sickly yellow glow vanished. The machine's whirring hum subsided to a low drone, before becoming quiet.

"It is off."

"Good." Keeping her weapon on the other woman, Dee went for Cenrick. "Don't move or I'll shoot to kill."

Nodding, the other woman fumbled for a towel, wrapping it around her foot and trying to keep the blood from spreading.

One eye on Natasha, Dee fumbled with Cenrick's restraints, trying to free him one-handed. He didn't stir, though the rise and fall of his chest told her he still lived. She could only hope she wasn't too late.

As her hand brushed his chest, tugged at the buckle, he opened his eyes. "Touch. Me." His raspy voice tore at her heart. But at least he could speak. The machine hadn't yet robbed him of his mind.

"Touch me."

Then she remembered. Her touch gave him strength, dispelling the awful effects of the evil machine.

"Cenrick." She laid her hand alongside his beloved face. He felt so cold, bloodless. "Come back to me."

Her foot successfully wrapped, Natasha laughed. "He's too far gone for you to help now. Even if you free him, I've already taken most of his soul. I can feel his magic and power filling me, more powerful by far than all the others I've taken. I have him now. He cannot regain what I own."

"I don't believe you." Weapon still trained on the other woman, Dee kept her hand on Cenrick's icy skin, praying warmth would return to him. His heart beat steady and sure. As she touched him, the skin warmed, became a healthy pink, then his normal tan. Dee swore she could feel his blood heating under her hand.

"He will come back to me." The look she gave Natasha carried a promise. "Then we will deal with you."

"You know . . ." The other woman sounded thoughtful. "I was wrong about you. They said you were important, that I should take you out first." Natasha's ice blue eyes were hard. "But I didn't believe them. He's a prince, descended from a long line of the powerful. You"—she looked Dee up and down contemptuously—"are nothing."

"Do you want me to take out your other foot?" Dee retorted.

The blonde laughed. "I have Fae powers now. I heal fast." Then, with a snarl, Natasha rushed.

Dee had no choice. As a police officer trained to act instinctively, Dee squeezed off a shot, aiming for the woman's shoulder. She didn't want to kill Natasha, only wound her. She planned to make certain the woman stood trial in Rune—assuming the Fae bothered with such things.

The bullet stopped Natasha in her tracks. She catapulted back with a bloodcurdling scream. Clapping her hand to her shoulder, she stared in stunned disbelief at the blood spreading on her shirt. She lurched to her feet, weaving unsteadily. Her narrow gaze found Dee.

"You'll pay for this," she vowed. She lifted her hand. "I can summon magic to destroy you."

"Can you?" Cenrick's voice suddenly rang out, much stronger. "Even magic has rules. Be careful what you do, Natasha. The wrongful use of power can destroy the untrained."

Her thin finger wobbling, the blonde looked from Dee to the Fae prince. "Like I should believe you?" And she sang out two words.

A bolt of energy lashed from her, knocking the gun from Dee's hand. Dee screamed, shaking her fingers. Though she saw no smoke, her hand felt on fire.

Natasha lurched over to the weapon, grabbing it

up with her bare hand. "Metal still does not yet harm me," she crowed. And keeping the gun on Dee and Cenrick, she moved in the other direction. Toward her laptop.

The controls of her machine. She meant to turn it up full blast, to take Cenrick's soul once and for all.

Dee started to pull away from Cenrick, to go after her, but Cenrick moved, his hand coming up and gripping her wrist. "Don't," he said.

"I've got to stop her."

"No. She's got a gun. Stay with me." His fingers tightened and the burning sensation in her hand faded. "I need your strength, your protection. She doesn't know the machine can't harm me now that you're here."

At the keyboard, Natasha typed in a command. She sneered. "Don't move or I'll shoot. Though it would be a shame to waste your souls."

The lights dimmed. The machine growled. The glow flashed on, and the noise became a low thrum growing louder and more insistent as the light intensified.

"We've got to stop her," Dee said.

"How?"

"Can't you use magic? Cast a spell, bring her down or knock the gun from her hand like she did mine?"

He cast a dubious glance at the machine. "I can try." Still gripping Dee's wrist, he murmured words in his native language. A spell.

Dee waited for the lightning bolt, a glow, something. Instead, Natasha, the room, the machine—all vanished. They stood back in the Fae field of flowers.

And as she took this in, Cenrick crumpled to the ground.

Something had gone monumentally wrong. Instead of taking Natasha out, or getting the weapon from her, his magic had somehow sent them to Rune. And weakened, casting that spell had used up the last of his strength, the last of his magic. She could only pray that selfless act hadn't finished him. That her touch could, as he believed, save him.

CHAPTER SIXTEEN

Dropping to her knees, Dee felt Cenrick's neck, frantically searching for a pulse. Nothing.

Oh God, no. He couldn't be dead. Not now.

"Cenrick?" He gave no answer, so she cried, "Breathe, damn you! If you want to live, breathe."

With an awful shudder, he did as she asked. He inhaled, dragging air into his lungs. Then he blew the breath back out, which ended in a gut-wrenching raspy cough.

Alive. At least he was alive.

This time she located a heartbeat, weak and erratic. His chest began to rise and fall, reassuring her he breathed.

"Come back to me," she urged. "Cenrick, please. Look at me." She could only pray that when he opened his eyes, he would not be soulless. Natasha could not have won, not so easily. Dee refused to believe this.

A shadow fell across them, blocking out the sun.

"What has happened?"

Dee glanced up. The silver-haired Mort stood ten feet away, staring down at Cenrick. "Mort. Thank goodness. We need your help. Please, can you heal him?" she asked.

The mage shook his head. His image wavered—something was wrong. He looked different. Insubstantial. "I cannot. What has begun to take him has grabbed hold, and his soul is damaged. Only the other half of it can restore him."

Alrick, his brother? She wanted to weep. "Or her?"

"Touch him," Mort replied.

She laid her hand alongside Cenrick's cheek. "I am!"

"Only you can help him," Mort continued. "If you want him to return to himself, to full life, *you* must bring him back. Touch him. Touch him with all of you."

Crying openly, Dee curled on the ground next to Cenrick. His huge, comatose body didn't react. She placed her cheek across his chest, listening as his heart struggled to beat.

The mage shimmered, then solidified as he came closer. "You must cover him with your essence. Quickly." Then Mort's form faded back to smoke, as though he was barely there. Was he only a figment of her imagination?

But Dee didn't have time to concern herself with that. She wanted Cenrick back. She wanted her partner, her friend; she wanted . . .

"The other half of your soul." The words echoing in the silent meadow, the mage disappeared in a puff of mist.

257

The other half of her soul? Cenrick? That wasn't possible—though part of her couldn't help yearning that it be the truth. She wasn't Fae. Even if she believed in this soul-mate stuff, she would think the soul would only split into two of the same species. She was human. Cenrick was not.

Still, if Mort thought this could help him . . . if she was his only hope. . . . She crawled atop Cenrick, covering him with her body, willing him to respond.

Once she was prone, face-to-face with him, chest to his chest, exhaustion seized her. Dizzy, she inhaled Cenrick's beloved scent—beloved?—and let her eyes drift closed. And holding him close, Dee slept.

The early morning breeze tickled Cenrick's nose. A hint of sunlight danced behind his eyelids. He stretched, yawning.

He'd had the worst dream. A machine, and Natasha and his soul—he opened his eyes, inhaling Dee's light floral scent. Dee! She slept tucked into the curve of his arm, the shadows under her eyes telling him of her exhaustion.

A bird screeched in the sky above. He started, glancing around. Though he could have sworn he and Dee had fallen asleep on her couch, they weren't in her living room. Instead, they were lying on the cold, hard ground, in a meadow of dead and dying flowers.

In Rune. Land of the Fae. His home.

He sat up, nudging Dee awake. Memory came flooding back. It hadn't been a dream. He'd been locked into a battle with the soul-stealing machine.

Dee had rescued him. He'd used the last of his energy to send them to Rune.

"Cenrick?" Dee came instantly awake. "Are you all right?"

He nodded and she kissed him. When she did, he tasted the salt of tears.

"Are you crying?"

"Yes." She sniffled. "I thought you were gone, lost forever. One of the soulless."

He kissed her back, swift and hard. "Almost, I think. But you, you brought me back."

"Yes."

"Where are we?"

"The last spell, the one you tried to use on Natasha, sent us to Rune."

"Home . . ." Standing, he helped her to her feet and looked out over the land. "Dee, something's not right."

"What do you mean?"

"Look around. Rune is not the same."

After a moment, she gasped as she saw what he meant. A thick fog hung in the air like a shroud. The riotous carpet of flowers had vanished. Even the grass had lost its emerald luster. Everything seemed dull . . . and fading.

"What's happened?" Dee turned a slow circle. "Are we even in Rune? Remember what happened that one time? Maybe we got sent somewhere else."

"This is Rune." His voice was firm. "I know my home." He tugged at her arm. "We've got to get to the palace in a hurry. I've got to find out what's going on."

Together, they ran.

"Look." Skidding to a halt, Cenrick groaned. "Look at the palace."

The palace. Dee gaped up at the gray monstrosity looming above them. "What's happened to it? It doesn't look the same."

Cenrick couldn't believe his eyes. The crystal palace now appeared to be made of dull, cloudy glass. Instead of the glittering structure full of magic and light, the structure could have come straight out of some grainy, black-and-white Dracula movie from the forties.

Dee shook her head. "Are you *sure* we're in Rune?" she asked again. Heart pounding, he didn't answer, just kept urging her along.

They hurried up the steps. The huge, ornately carved, double glass doors were open, as though the place had been abandoned in a hurry. Abandoned? Nearly running, Cenrick made a sound of dismay as he entered the great room. Inside, the colorlessness was even worse. He shivered. All this dirty gray brought a chill. *Like the chill brought on by Natasha and her machine.*

Their footsteps echoed painfully in their ears as they hurried down one long, twisting hallway after another. The farther into the palace they traveled, the colder the air. Cenrick couldn't get warm, and Dee couldn't seem to stop shivering. She wrapped her arms around herself and shook.

"Is it winter here?" she asked.

"No. This coldness isn't normal. Something terrible has happened. The palace is deserted. No one's here." Cenrick turned a slow circle. "But where in the name of the Goddess are they?"

Dee only shook her head.

They continued on. In each hall, doors had been flung open, some cracked. Inside, rooms were in various states of disarray. "Either the Fae became completely untidy, or everyone had fled in a mass panic," she said. "It looks like each tossed a few possessions into a bag and fled. But why?"

"Why, exactly." Grim, Cenrick clutched her hand. "This looks like they expected a natural disaster of epic proportions."

Finally, they stopped in front of one single closed door. Dee's shivers had communicated to him, and Cenrick clenched his teeth to keep them from chattering.

"This looks familiar. Is this—?"

"Mort's room." Cenrick cleared his throat. "I hope he's here."

Raising his fist to knock, he froze as the door swung slowly open. "Enter," a voice boomed from within. Inside, a fire blazed.

"Warmth!" Dee's sigh of relief was audible. She squeezed Cenrick's hand, tugging him into the room and the blessed, wonderful heat.

When he stopped, she tugged her hand free and continued on toward the hearth, stretching her arms out to the fire.

"Mort?" The room appeared empty. Cenrick saw no sign of the mage. "He's gone."

"But we heard him." Dee looked around. "That's what happened when we first arrived here and you were so ill. I saw and heard him, but he vanished like a wisp of smoke."

"I don't like this."

"Me, either. But this room feels the best." Keeping her back to the fire, Dee took in the chamber. "The entire castle is gray, but not in here. Whatever creeping malady had affected the rest of this place, it hasn't made it into here."

She was right. Rather than the overwhelmingly depressing shades of gray that permeated the entire local atmosphere, Mort's sleeping chamber and workspace glowed with a vibrancy of fabrics and colors. In addition to the roaring fire in the hearth, the room was also lit by hundreds of fragrant candles.

In short, like normal.

Movement in the shadows caught Cenrick's eye. A hooded figure stepped forward. His appearance might have been menacing had his robe not been made of a rich purple material like silk. However, since this room and his clothing were the first hints of color they'd seen since arriving, the man simply appeared to glow with vitality.

"Mort?"

The man lowered his hood. "Not Mort. It is I."

"Father?" Cenrick's heart sank. His father's appearance had him even more worried. "What are you doing here, alone in this room? Where's Mort? For that matter, where is everyone else? What's happened here?"

Never taking his eyes from Dee, the older man shook his head. "The palace is empty," he said simply, as though that was explanation enough.

"Empty?" Cenrick's sharp tone belied his panic. "How is this possible? Where's Mort?"

"He has gone."

"He was here when we first arrived," Dee put in. "He spoke to us."

"When was this?" Lowering his hood, King Roark swept his piercing blue eyes over them. He swept back his mane of curly white hair and smoothed his flowing beard.

"Just now." Dee lifted her chin, looking at Cenrick for confirmation. "I think."

"Impossible. He has been gone several days."

"Gone where?" Cenrick stepped forward, drawing his sire's attention.

"To consult the Oracle." The king turned the full force of his piercing blue gaze on his son. "Since you left, things have steadily worsened. More and more Fae have returned to Rune as husks, stripped of their souls. We could no longer keep such a thing hidden. The people have panicked."

"Left?" Cenrick asked. Such a concept was incomprehensible. "They've abandoned their homes?"

"Yes. For the first time in many millennia, the Fae have deserted Rune." The king's bleak tone matched his son's.

"Where have they gone?"

King Roark sighed. "Some have gone to the forest of Zanbar, but most traveled across the Plains of Lothar to hide in the mountains of Kilian."

"What about the damaged ones?"

"Mort has taken the latest batch to the Oracle." Again the king's bright gaze found Dee. "Now who is this? I sense great power in her. I thought I knew all of my subjects, but I don't recognize you. Son, are you going to introduce us?"

Cenrick sighed. "Father, she's not Fae. This is Dee Bishop, a human woman. Dee, allow me to present my father, King Roark of Rune."

Dee's expression nearly made him laugh. Cenrick could tell she didn't know the proper protocol for meeting a king. Should she bow? Curtsy?

Finally, she settled for dipping her head in a gesture of recognition. She gave a visible jump when the older man took her hand and kissed the back of it.

Again, the king's bright gaze showed his approval. "Exquisite, my son. Your taste equals your brother's. But do not lie to me. I know Fae power when I see it."

Quickly, Cenrick explained what he'd done, but his father argued.

"No. No spell could work so well on a human, not here. Not in Rune. She's Fae."

Dee and Cenrick exchanged a glance. Finally, Dee shrugged. "If believing that makes you happy, then I'm glad."

"But this is not a social call." Cenrick went on to detail as concisely as he could what had happened to bring them here. When he'd finished, the king appeared to have aged twenty years.

He said, "I had hoped you'd come with better news."

Heart heavy, Cenrick turned to Dee. "We must go back to the Oracle. Perhaps together, she and Mort can come up with an answer."

She nodded in agreement.

"Father?" Cenrick touched the older man's sleeve. "Will you come with us?"

"Nay." Pride and another more sorrowful emotion flared in King Roark's eyes. Replacing his hood, he shook his head. "I will not leave my home. As long as one Fae remains, the magic will not entirely desert Rune."

Cenrick clapped his father on the shoulder. "I swear to you, I will find a way to stop this."

"I know you will, son. But you'd better hurry. If you take too much longer, I'm afraid it will be too late for us all." He stepped back into the shadows.

Cenrick held out his hand. Without hesitation, Dee took it. He began speaking the words to send them to the Oracle.

When they appeared at the edge of the Oracle's mountain, they saw the gray lifelessness had reached the boundaries of the fields, even here, though the mountain itself still retained the normal hues of sepia and earth.

And the number of hollow-eyed people milling about had quadrupled. Or—he made a hasty reestimation—worse. There were now so many that the Oracle could not contain them within her caves.

Above, a shadow. A screech. And with a swoop of massive wings, a hawk flew over them, landing on an outcropping of rocks.

"Tinth."

The bird cried out in reply. Taking off, Tinth flew low, leading them toward the Oracle's cave.

"At least Mort sent his pet hawk," Cenrick told Dee. "And he does not bid us hurry. I know not to fear for him when the bird leads us so slowly."

Hand in hand, he and Dee silently climbed. When finally they gained the summit, Cenrick helped her make the last few feet, pulling her into his arms.

"Thank you," she said softly. Her heart-shaped face was cloaked in shadows and gold, courtesy of their flickering torches.

Never had he found a woman so precious, so lovely. He told her so, and she smiled a wan smile. "Maybe it's time you remove the spell that makes me appear Fae."

Shaking his head, he leaned forward and kissed her. "Not yet. And your beauty has nothing to do with the spell."

She sighed. "Let's go."

Tinth called out agreement.

No one, neither the Oracle nor the mage, nor any hollow-eyed soulless Fae, came out to greet them. Every few feet, more torches flickered along the stone walls, their flames sending shadows but beating back the encroaching grayness from above.

Holding tightly to Dee's hand, Cenrick led the way up the steps and into the Oracle's cave. At the entrance, Dee hesitated.

"Even here something is different," she mused.

Cenrick sensed it too. Sniffing the air, he realized it was no longer heavy with the spicy fragrance of the Oracle's incense.

"There is no perfumed scent like before," Dee said,

and her words confirmed his fear. "Only the damp smell of cold earth and stagnant water upon stone."

"There's something else," he told her. "The silence—there are no wind chimes tinkling, as they were the last time we came." He tugged her forward. "Come on. At least the torches still burn to light our way. Let's find the Oracle and Mort and learn what's happened."

Traveling the narrow passageways, finally they came to the great central cave. All was ominously silent, save the steady drip of water from some internal stream. Still no one came to meet them. Only Tinth, circling above, reassured him that not all was lost.

Dee squeezed his hand. "I know I've only been here once, but this feels . . . wrong."

"I know." He'd begun to get used to her intuitive understanding of all things magical. "But I trust the hawk. She would not lead us down here if we were in danger."

Still, when they reached the inscribed, double stone doors, he hesitated.

"What's wrong?" Dee asked.

"One does not usually enter the Oracle's home un-invited." Heart heavy, he pulled the handle.

The heavy stone groaned and the door began to swing slowly open. The huge room was only dimly lit. No smoke burned from the numerous incense braziers, and only a few of the hundred plus candles were lit. Even the hearth fire, though burning, seemed dispir-ited, the weak flames giving little light and even less heat. It felt as if the grayness had made its way here.

"You have come." At the head of the room, on the seldom used dais, the Oracle waited, hooded and cloaked as usual. The red of her burning eyes even seemed duller. At her side, clothed in black, sat the Mage of Rune. His hawk flew to him, and perched on the back of his chair.

"Come closer." The Oracle's voice carried across the distance.

The Oracle sounded so . . . old. And tired. Exchanging a glance with Dee, Cenrick led the way.

"About time you got here, boy." Mort stood as they approached the dais, holding out his arms in welcome.

Cenrick hugged him. "What has happened? I've been to Rune and the palace is—"

"I know, I know." Mort waved him to silence. "Things have gone to hell in a handbasket. Everything's bad. We've got to fix it. But first, what brings you here?"

Again, Cenrick told the story of his capture and Natasha's claim of power.

While the Oracle remained silent, the mage appeared most interested in Cenrick's physical reaction to her machine.

"So this thing, whatever it is, takes all your strength." Mort stroked his beard. "And then, somehow, this human woman absorbs your magic into herself?"

"That's what she said. I barely made it out of there with my soul intact," Cenrick admitted, glad he still held fast to Dee's hand.

"But your theory was correct? For some reason, as long as Dee touched you, the effect was negated?"

"Yes."

Mort turned his attention on Dee. "You look different. Your aura—it's as if you were Fae rather than human."

Dee nodded and stepped forward. "He put Fae glitter on me so Natasha's associates wouldn't realize I was human. We meant to trick them into trying to capture me, believing I was Fae, so we could find their machine and destroy it."

"What happened?"

"They took Cenrick instead."

"Yet . . ." The mage still studied her. "This is more than a spell. You truly appear to be Fae."

Cenrick spoke up: "That's what father said."

Mort nodded, his gaze still on Dee. "But you were unaffected by this machine?" He watched her closely. "You felt no pull, no weakening of your strength?"

"No. But then, I'm human, not Fae." Her grip on Cenrick's fingers tightened. "No matter what you people think you see. Of course, I never got close to the machine . . ."

Mort shook his head sadly, suddenly reflective. "I can't believe one errant Fae has brought such a thing upon our people."

Cenrick had no choice but to agree. "Mick. We haven't been able to locate him either."

The Oracle spoke for the first time since bidding them enter. "Talmick is here." Her voice sounded weary and forlorn.

Cenrick stared. For the length of his lifetime, his father's lifetime, and for many centuries before that, the Oracle had been all-powerful. Now she sounded defeated, beaten.

"Talmick?" Dee asked, not recognizing the name.

"Talmick is Mick's real name." Cenrick squeezed Dee's hand then turned his attention back to the Oracle. "What do you mean Mick's here?"

"They all make their way home, once everything has been taken from them."

His stomach dropped. They were too late, at least for Mick.

With a strangled cry, Dee sagged against him. Then, visibly collecting herself, she squared her shoulders and looked the Oracle directly in the face. "You mean he's—."

"One of the soulless now." The Oracle's eyes flared. "And still more come. Daily, sometimes hourly."

"Aye." Mort shook his head. "Soon every Fae who lives in the human world will be affected."

"And worse . . ." The Oracle's voice regained a touch of its old assurance. "Rune itself is now in danger. This Natasha has crossed the veil. She is here. And she has brought her machine."

CHAPTER SEVENTEEN

"Here?" Cenrick, Dee, and Mort all exclaimed at once. "How?"

The Oracle's eyes glowed scarlet as she focused on Cenrick. "You led her here."

A great weariness seized him. "I? I tried to use my magic against her. Instead, the magic sent us here."

"Unfortunately, that showed her the way. Your weakened magic used the last of your strength to bring you home, but it also showed her the way into Rune."

Shocked, Cenrick glanced at Dee. Her amber eyes were narrowed, though he saw no accusation in her face.

Still, that did not negate the fact that he had failed his people. Momentously. Not only had he been unsuccessful in destroying Natasha and her evil machine but he'd unintentionally brought her to the very place he'd wanted to protect. Hell of a scholar he'd turned out to be.

"Wouldn't she need a lot of magic to follow Cenrick? I know she has some, but in the end she's still human." A voice of reason, Dee nearly made him smile with her comment. Nearly.

"She has 'a lot of magic,'" the Oracle responded. "She has become a powerful sorceress in her own right."

"But how?" Dee persisted. "How is this possible?" She seemed unwilling to accept.

"Sometimes magic has a will of its own," Cenrick answered. "She has somehow gathered all the magic from those Fae she ruined, and taken it into herself, though she knows not how to use it. She resonates with their power. If she was truly Fae, she would already be known and greatly feared."

"Or revered." Mort's mournful sigh echoed Cenrick's weariness. "Unfortunately, she is evil."

Dee shook her head. "I still don't understand. Are you telling me the magic brought her here, just like it did us?"

The Oracle's eyes grew brighter. "Oftentimes, magic has a will of its own."

"I don't understand," Dee repeated.

"Even we Fae do not always comprehend that which guides us. This is why scholars"—the Oracle glanced at Cenrick—"are so highly prized."

Cenrick grimaced. "As are our mages and sorceresses. Learning how to control magic is a difficult art."

"Regardless, Tinth has seen her. She and her machine are here."

Dee nodded. "But this doesn't explain how she was able to bring that machine of hers, made of metal, across. I mean, if my gun never crosses with me . . ." She trailed off.

From her perch on the back of Mort's chair, Tinth screeched again. The sound echoed through the stone room.

Mort indicated the huge bird. "My hawk is afraid."

"So should we all be." The Oracle rose, her robes billowing out around her like white smoke. "This battle will begin sooner than you think. But now, come with me. I'll take you to see Talmick."

"Mick . . ." Dee stumbled, looking at Cenrick with sorrowful eyes.

He took her hand, his chest tight, and spoke for her. "Peter is still here, too?"

"Yes." Mort replied. "They all are."

Dee made no comment.

Cenrick squeezed her hand, offering her silent comfort. He wondered why she didn't respond at all to the mention of her former intended. Had perhaps he been wrong? Perhaps Dee didn't pine for Peter after all. Every step of the way, her concern had been more for Mick. The aching in his chest lightened at that thought.

As before, the Oracle led them deep into the earth. "The Pool of Dreamers dries more each passing day," she warned, a great sorrow in her voice. "The soulless ones drink the water, using it to sustain their empty lives. The magic of the earth has stopped replenishing it."

"Why?" Cenrick asked. "The pool has always refilled itself."

"I know not, though I think it has something to do

with the absence of magic. In these caves, I alone still retain my power, my soul. But though I try, that alone is not enough to sustain the hungry earth. I have not enough to give her, so the water turns brackish and dries."

"Can we help?" Dee wanted to know. "Is there something Cenrick or the mage can do to help restore the pool?"

Stiff-shouldered, the Oracle continued leading the way and did not answer.

Beside Cenrick, Dee subsided into silence. One look at her pinched, miserable expression, and Cenrick decided perhaps her thoughts were with her former fiancé. He vowed that, once Natasha and her evil machine were vanquished, he personally would heal Peter and lead the man to Dee's side. If the man did not love her, he at least owed Dee an explanation. Closure. While living in the human world, he'd heard a lot about this closure, and the value human females placed on it. Still, he could not help but wonder how Peter could be such a fool.

When they finally reached the large chamber in the earth, Cenrick saw what the Oracle meant. The once immense pool had withered to little more than a pond. The water seemed brackish, as though all magic had fled.

Here, like outside, the damaged Fae were numerous. They crowded the rock walls, filling crevices while they slept and reclined. Many wandered, moving through the others of their kind like wraiths.

"How many are there now?" Shock was a knife in Cenrick's chest.

"Well over a thousand," Mort answered. "And there are many thousands more living among humans, who may yet be called. Of course, with our enemy in Rune . . ."

Dee stood on her tiptoes, scanning the crowd.

"Are you looking for Peter?" Cenrick asked, the awful weight on his chest doubling.

"No. Mick," she informed him, turning to the Oracle. "Where is he?"

"Look, and you will find Talmick." The Oracle swept her arm, indicating the vast crowd milling in the cave. "But Cenrick, don't look too closely at their faces, for you will see many others you have known since you were a child." Such sorrow rang in her voice that Cenrick's throat tightened.

"There!" Dee gasped, yanking her hand from his and making her way unerringly across the cavern to a small knot of Fae.

Cenrick followed close behind, helping her move the somnolent and unresponsive others. He saw one man he recognized, and a woman: people who had taught him magic in his youth. In between these stood his cousin Talmick, slack-jawed and hollow-eyed.

"Mick." Crying openly now, Dee gathered the slender man close. Completely unresponsive, he seemed unaware of anything save what he might see inside his own head.

"I've failed him." Dee turned her face to Cenrick's, showing him the fury and the despair in her eyes. "They took his soul, and we let it happen."

"They have harmed more than he," the Oracle reminded them. Stern-voiced, she stepped between

Cenrick and Dee, gently disentangling Mick from Dee and sending him shuffling off in the opposite direction. Tears streaming down her face, Dee watched him go.

"Come with me." The Oracle turned to go, Mort close behind. Unresisting, Dee let Cenrick take her arm. He led her from the chamber behind the others, and back out into the passage. All silent, they climbed until they stood once more in the great hollow cave of the Oracle.

"Do you see what needs to be done?" Mort asked. He touched Cenrick's shoulder, his gaze full of both worry and hope.

Cradling a too-silent Dee, Cenrick nodded. "But I need more than magic."

"You already have more than magic." The Oracle turned to face them, eyes blazing. Full and strong, her voice once again rang with power. "*Much* more than magic, if you will but use it." And in the still, quiet air, the sound of wind chimes began. A moment later, the scent of Oracle's heady incense, so notably absent before, filled the cave.

"Magic accompanies with your return. Together, if you and Dee will but see the way, you can call forth even more."

The hair on Cenrick's arms rose as he stared, at the Oracle, and he knew, though he did not yet understand, the great Fae seer spoke true.

Even more? Where? How?

Dee sagged against him. Despite the fact that the Oracle and Mort watched, Cenrick gathered her and held her close, letting her cry silently.

Finally, she straightened. Swiping at her face, she looked at the Oracle. "There is one thing I need to know."

"You may ask," the Oracle replied.

"Once we've located this . . . monstrosity and stopped it, is there any chance you will be able to restore these poor lost Fae their souls?"

The Oracle's gaze flared bright red, like glowing blood welling from two fresh wounds, before she turned to look at the slack-jawed Fae shuffling aimlessly about. "That is my fondest hope," she replied. "I will do all that is within my power."

Tinth screeched, spreading her immense wings. Mort spoke soothingly to the huge bird, and she settled back without a ruffled feather.

"Tell us where we might find Natasha." Keeping his arm around Dee, Cenrick faced Mort and the Oracle.

The two exchanged a look. "She is at the palace, preparing to rule the city."

Horrified, Cenrick froze. "My father is there. Alone."

Dee gripped his arm. "We've got to go. Now."

They turned to leave.

"Wait!" The Oracle's command stopped them. "You have not listened to us before, so we shall tell you once more. Sometimes, two halves of the same soul must combine their strength. It is one of those times when such power is needed."

"More than magic," Mort intoned. "Such a joining will bring forth other power."

Cenrick frowned. "Alrick is not here."

"Alrick?" Frowning, the mage shook his head. "What's Alrick got to do with this?"

"Two halves of the same soul." Cenrick waved his hand. "People are always saying twins such as Alrick and I share a single soul. But he is—"

"No." The Oracle interrupted, turning away as if disgusted. "I've already told Dee that is not what we meant." She waved Cenrick forward. "Go to the palace. See if you can stop her. But I can promise you this: If you do not combine the power of the two halves, this Natasha will win." And she clapped her hands.

Suddenly Cenrick and Dee stood again in the meadow, amongst the dead and dying flowers. The gray outline of the castle shone dimly through the thickening fog. But now it was glowing.

Sickly yellow light filled the drab sky like an obscene bonfire.

"That's how Mick's house looked." Dee sounded as exhausted as Cenrick felt. And as furious.

"Yes. She's there," Cenrick agreed, letting his own rage show. "She and that damnable machine."

They moved forward, walking carefully.

He looked at her, noting the fierce light shining in her eyes, and he reiterated, "I still don't understand how she did it. How did she get that metal across the veil? Such a thing is practically impossible."

Dee patted her empty holster. "I don't know, but I sure wish I could have brought my pistol. It would have come in handy right about now."

Cenrick thought of where they'd been when they

crossed the veil, and grimaced. "I hope she doesn't have it."

Dee's mouth worked. "Me, too."

A moment later, confidence in her voice, Dee clutched his hand and said, "Well, don't fear. She is dangerous, but we will destroy her and her creation. And as long as you don't let go of me, you'll be protected from it. Remember that."

He nodded.

Together, they dashed up the steps. Inside the palace the glow was a phosphoresent shimmering on gray dead walls and floors. "This way," Cenrick said. Footsteps echoing, he led Dee down a hallway, following the intensity of the light. "I think it's brightest in the throne room."

As they approached, the light grew almost blinding. The double doors flung themselves open without assistance, and the light blazing beyond was brighter than searchlights. Full of seductive malevolence, it beckoned, called, as though it recognized them.

Dee looked up at Cenrick, fear in her eyes. With a fierce smile, he kissed her, hard. "Ready?"

She nodded. "Don't let go of my hand." And together, they stepped inside.

As Dee and Cenrick entered the room, the glow intensified as though in triumph. A raised dais occupied the far end of the room. There, on the throne, Natasha waited, the glow surrounding her like a nimbus of evil.

"I've been expecting you," she said, her voice echoing. "I've become stronger, thanks to you. And I've developed other weapons." Her foot appeared perfectly healed.

Behind her, the machine hummed. Ready. Waiting. Without Dee's touch to prevent it, the thing's power would have incapacitated Cenrick immediately. Would have . . .

He had to pretend! Dee squeezed his hand. Natasha had no idea that Dee's touch could protect him.

Understanding immediately, Cenrick dropped to his knees, moaning. Dee kept hold of his hand.

Natasha glanced at Dee, smug satisfaction in her smile. "And now you. Though you claim to be human, I can see the truth. My machine will steal your soul as well."

Dee stared. Natasha apparently still believed her to be Fae. Why did everyone believe that? Well, it didn't matter. If she could use it to her benefit . . . Mimicking Cenrick, she dropped to her knees beside him, all the while never letting go of his hand. Cenrick was her lifeline. Her strength, protection, and safety. As she was his. Together, they would have the element of surprise, which would enable them to best this blond woman. She hoped.

Natasha's laugh echoed through the cavernous room. "You shall be the second, and the third." Snapping her fingers, she gestured and two men came forward, supporting a limp body between them. Dee saw a flash of fear in Cenrick's eyes, though he kept them downcast so the blond woman wouldn't.

"My father," he protested, making his voice weak.

"Yes. King Roark." She chuckled. "Three centuries

of power reside inside this man." She licked her lips. "I can't wait until it fills me." Her expression positively orgasmic, she stroked the unconscious monarch's cheek. "I will be so powerful then, none will stop me. Then I will take on your mage and your Oracle."

Again Natasha focused on the king, lovingly caressing his white hair. While her attention was diverted, Cenrick crawled forward, dragging Dee with him. They managed to advance a good ten feet without drawing the woman's attention. When she looked at them again, he dropped his head, pretending an attempt to struggle to his feet.

"Stop," he choked out. "Take me instead of him. Leave my father alone."

The machine hummed while Natasha considered. Eyes narrow, she studied Dee and Cenrick. Then she shook her head. "All in good time, my beautiful ones. All in good time." Again she laughed, the sound striking Dee as evil incarnate.

Motioning to her bodyguards, Natasha supervised them strapping the king in the machine. While she did this, Cenrick and Dee continued to scoot forward, inch by inch.

Once she had the king secured in her monstrous invention, Natasha faced Cenrick and Dee again, her expression full of anticipation. "I'm going to enjoy making you watch while I steal your father's soul."

Cenrick moaned again, trying to sound weak. He clearly was convincing, because it made Natasha chuckle. As soon as she turned her head, he moved forward another couple of feet.

He froze when she swung around to face them, though; and with one more quick look, she crossed the room. She'd set up her laptop on a table—another modern item that shouldn't have been able to pass through the veil. She lifted the lid.

The instant Natasha began typing, Cenrick leaned close to Dee. "Ready?"

Dee nodded, her muscles tightening as she prepared to leap to her feet. Beside her, she felt Cenrick do the same. Natasha continued typing, occasionally glancing from her computer to her machine. The glow intensified as she upped the power. King Roark groaned, a loud tortured sound.

"One . . . two . . . three—go!" Together they rushed Natasha full out. Surprise and shock reflected in her face when she realized neither was incapacitated by her machine. Savagely, she twisted a dial. The machine grew louder, the glow brighter. King Roark screamed, a bloodcurdling sound of such agony, it chilled the blood.

"Enough!" Cenrick roared. He pointed a finger at Natasha, muttering a spell. Flame blazed from his hand, directly at her—but with a sneer she deflected it. Unafraid, she stood her ground, her face alight with unholy glee.

He tried another spell, this time a blaze of pure energy. This time, instead of deflecting it, Natasha absorbed the magic into her body. She seemed to swell with power, and her shadow grew so long she seemed to tower above them. Meanwhile, the hum and glow from the machine intensified, reaching a fevered pitch.

The king moaned, struggling against his restraints. Dee saw he would not last long if they did not rescue him. But to do so, they'd have to destroy Natasha.

The two bodyguards rushed forward, their solid bodies full of intent. A simple wave of Cenrick's hand, and they scattered like muscular bowling pins, and did not move again.

"Have a care with my pets!" Natasha's warning swept over them like a cold northern wind. Face lit by sickly green and yellows, Natasha raised her hand, pointing at Cenrick.

Dee felt the build up of magic even before Natasha began speaking, and when the woman did utter her spell, using a language so arcane that even Cenrick looked surprised, the unintelligible syllables boomed through the room.

Cenrick's knees buckled. Even if Dee's touch could shield him from the machine, she apparently could not protect against such powerful magic. Natasha continued to advance, her grim concentration intense.

"That's enough!" Dee shouted, moving forward. Cenrick's hand was still in hers. Natasha ignored her.

With her free hand, Dee lashed out. The blow was a good right hook, under the chin, and it knocked Natasha to the floor. When she fell, the woman's elbow caught the edge of the table and her laptop tumbled after her. The edge of the plastic casing hit the stone, shattered. The screen went blank. Instantly, the machine went silent, dead, and the ominous green glow winked out, leaving the room in partial darkness, with only the remaining light from the flickering torches.

"No!" Natasha screamed, her face contorted as she pushed herself up on her elbows. "You cannot win. I'm powerful, I'm—"

Cenrick pushed to his feet. Directing all of his and Dee's combined energy at the evil woman, he shouted the words of a spell into the awful silence.

"No!" With a spastic contortion, Natasha writhed on the floor. "What is happening to me?" Bubbling, steaming, smoking, the skin appeared to be melting from her bones. And Dee and Cenrick watched in horror as she dissolved into a puddle of liquid before dissipating in a poof of steam.

"She melted," Cenrick said.

"Ding, dong, the witch is dead." Dee stared in morbid fascination.

Behind them, the machine squawked. Natasha's laptop bleeped, then made an awful grinding sound. Something inside the frame began to smoke.

"Father!" Cenrick suddenly recalled. He and Dee rushed to the still humming machine. With her assistance, he pulled his father's limp form from the restraints. Just in time. With a horrible screech and howl, the framework folded in upon itself, the implosion emitting a shower of glowing sparks and whirling smoke. The green glow dissipated.

Dragging King Roark across the room to safety, Cenrick faced the mechanical monster and spoke another spell. The machine puffed smoke and ashes. There was a flash, echoes of the sickly glow, and then nothing. The machine was entirely gone.

"Magic and machines have never mixed well," Cenrick said. "We have returned to normal."

The instant the machine vanished, color flooded the room, returned in a rush of vibrant warmth. King Roark opened his eyes. "What—?" He groaned. "My head."

Cenrick explained what had happened. When he'd finished, his father pushed himself to his feet.

"Shaky, but standing," he said. "Don't worry about me. You must go to the Oracle. Let her know what has happened. And find Mort. If ever there was a time when what has been done to our people can be undone, this will be the time."

Without waiting for a response, the king clapped his hand and Cenrick and Dee went.

CHAPTER EIGHTEEN

This time when they arrived at the base of the stone steps, the Oracle was waiting. "There has been a subtle shift in the fabric of existence," she said, her scarlet eyes glowing from within the shadows of her hood. "What has happened?"

Cenrick told her quickly of destroying Natasha and Natasha's machine. "My father has said this is the time to try and heal the others."

"Heal them? If you have freed all the captured souls, their inherent magic should bring them home to their rightful bodies. Come." She turned and hurried off, motioning for them to follow. "We shall move among the soulless and touch them."

"Touch them?" Cenrick echoed as they followed.

"By so doing, we may awaken them."

When they reached the first cave, at first glance nothing appeared to have changed. Still the soulless Fae milled aimlessly, nothing behind their eyes. But . . .

"Watch." The Oracle reached out and grabbed the arm of a tall, slender man.

"Who?" He started, shaking his head as though to dislodge water in his ears. "What? Where am I?" Cognizance flooded him. "Who are you?"

Murmuring soothing words, a promise of a later explanation, the Oracle turned away from him, motioning Cenrick and Dee closer. "Move among them, touch all you can. If they ask to understand, promise that they shall later. But all must be awakened before too much time has passed.

Cenrick and Dee did as she asked, going among the crowd and reaching out, grabbing an elbow here, brushing against a hand there. Each Fae they came in contact with started awake, awareness flooding the eyes that before had been blank. And while helping awaken them, Dee continually searched for the one she most wanted returned to normal: Mick.

In the middle of the milling crowd, half aware and still soulless, they found Peter. When Dee touched his cheek, he clutched at her hand, his expression bewildered.

"Dee? Am I back in Rune? What are you doing here? For that matter, what am *I* doing here?"

Shaking her head, she cupped his familiar face in her hands and kissed him lightly on the mouth, conscious of finally being able to say good-bye to this part of her past. "I'm sorry, Pete. I'm looking for Mick. Someone else will answer your questions later." And she let him go, attempting to brush past.

He caught at her arm. "Dee? Don't go. We were

engaged. I loved you. I need you now. You can find Mick later. Help me."

His demand made no sense. "Peter, you were correct to break up with me when you did. We weren't right for each other. Now let me go. I've got to find Mick."

"Mick?" His mouth twisted as he tightened his grip on her arm. "Don't you realize Mick's the one who sold you out? He tricked all of us, bringing us to that witch and her contraption to steal our souls." He spat, "Mick's *nothing* to me."

Dee tugged on her arm, trying to disengage herself. "Whatever he's done, Mick's my family. He's all I have. I've got to find him. Now let me go."

Peter started to argue, then closed his mouth, looking at something over her shoulder. Suddenly Cenrick was at her side. "Do you need help?" he asked, his voice low and menacing, his gaze on Peter.

Peter let go of her arm, watching as Cenrick took Dee's hand. "So that's how it is," he said. "You certainly didn't waste any time replacing me." Dee ignored him.

Grimly, she scanned the crowd for the one beloved face she couldn't find. "Cenrick, I can't locate Mick," she said. "Help me find him."

They searched the crowd by the pool, lightly touching each Fae they passed to awaken them, but found no sign of Mick.

On the other side of the pool they found Mort, who was doing his own part. The mage told them he'd seen Mick, along with Galyeon, outside the main cave. The two had already been awakened. Dee hurried outside, Cenrick alongside.

They finally spotted Mick wandering alone. He too looked bewildered. Dee's heart clenched with fear as she saw him stumbling along the edge of the cliffs near the steps.

"Mick!" she cried. She hurried over, gently steering him away from the dangerous precipice. "I've been looking for you."

"Dee?" His elegant face crumpled. "I thought she had you." He looked beyond Dee, seeing Cenrick standing behind her. "And you as well, my prince. Oh, what I've done. I am so sorry. More sorry than I can say."

Dee held out her arms and, after a brief hesitation, Mick walked into them. She hugged his slender body, holding him close. "No matter what you've done, you're the brother of my heart."

At her words, Mick pulled away, his face full of shame. "I don't deserve to live. Not only have I dishonored my badge, but I almost destroyed the Fae."

"What did you do, exactly?" Dee asked. "I'm not sure I understand your role in this."

He hung his head. "When Natasha first built her machine, she needed Fae to test it on. Then, neither of us knew what it would do. Even knowing this, I led my friends to her like sheep to slaughter." He peered up at Dee through his long lashes. "Peter was in this first group."

Swallowing hard, she nodded. "I see."

Mick raised his head and met her gaze. "Understand this, Dee. Peter wasn't right for you. He was living a lie. He couldn't live with his homosexuality, so he was using you as a cover to hide behind. I love—loved—both of you too much to let you get married. In the end, it would have caused too much pain."

"But you, Mick. You say you loved me, but you lied to me all these years." Her voice broke. "How can you claim to love me so much yet keep so much hidden? Especially since you knew how badly I always wanted a family."

A trace of regret crossed his handsome features. "You had me, Dee. Brother of your heart."

"And you lied and set me up, as I'm now finding out." Dee couldn't keep the bitterness from her tone. "All along, I thought you were my family. I had no idea what you'd done."

He sighed. "Are you any happier now, knowing the truth?"

She was about to answer when Cenrick stopped her with a touch on the arm. "It's my turn," he said, his voice icy. "Natasha told me why you did these things, but I want to hear it from your own mouth. Why, Talmick of Rune? What could make you do this?"

"For Jack." Mick grimaced. "Everything I did, I did for him." He sighed, glancing around again, his expression both wary and eager. "I wanted to make him Fae, so he would live. Natasha promised he'd be first, and the Fae power would heal him. Have you seen him? How is he? He's been very sick."

Dee winced. Somehow, Cenrick's hand on her

shoulder gave her strength. "He's gone, Mick. Jack's gone."

"Gone?"

Throat clogged with emotion, Dee struggled to answer. Before she did, Mick read the truth in her expression. "He's dead?"

All she could do was nod.

"Jack . . ." Mick's voice made her heart break. "Natasha told me he was getting better, that the magic her machine stole was healing him." He swallowed, fighting back tears. "Did he die from . . . ?"

"No, *she* killed him." Dee swallowed, hating what she had to say next but knowing she had to say it. "Natasha lied to you. She wasn't giving Jack any magic. She was keeping it all for herself."

His blank look said he didn't understand. "But why? Why would she do such a thing?"

"For power," Cenrick answered. "She was trying to make herself Fae, to destroy us all."

As he absorbed this information, Mick's face hardened. "It's my fault. She got the whole idea from me. I only wanted to make Jack Fae." His look became earnest, beseeched them to understand. "He was HIV positive, and dying. If he became Fae, the disease couldn't touch him. He would live forever." He broke down, weeping, and turned away, out of Dee's arms. She let him go.

Cenrick came up behind her and put his hand on her shoulder, offering silent comfort. God help her, she took it. And unable to bear watching Mick suffer so, she reached out to him too, meaning to offer him support.

He spun away from her touch. "No!" His gaze, full of anguish and the awful knowledge of what he'd begun, flicked to her face. "Help all the others. I must find a way to atone for my grievous sin."

"My father awaits you," Cenrick told him. "Go to the king. He and the mage will mete out your punishment."

"I must straighten things out for Dee first." Grim-faced, he crossed to her and took her hand. "Natasha was behind those that ruined your reputation in the department. She knew how close we were, and feared you would interfere. She wanted to destroy your credibility."

Stunned, Dee could only stare. "You let her do this? Knowing my job is all I have?"

"I was half out of my mind." He shook his head. "That's not an excuse, I know. But I will get your reputation restored, no matter what."

"They tried to frame me for your murder," Dee snapped. Still shocked, she began reciting. "Police brutality, taking protection money, and more. Internal Affairs has been out to my place a couple of times now. On top of that, someone tried to shoot me."

His chagrinned expression turned to shock. "I swear I had no knowledge of that."

"Did you send the photos?" She crossed her arms.

He looked blank. "What photos?"

Dee told him of the phone call, and the envelope full of photographs.

"I don't know about that, either. Maybe Peter sent those."

Cenrick interrupted; clearly impatient. "Go to my

father and talk to him. Explain how you must right so many wrongs, and I'm certain he will let you return temporarily to the human world. As long as you give your oath to return quickly and face your punishment."

Dejected, Mick nodded. Then, kissing Dee lightly on the cheek, he looked up at Cenrick. "My Prince, I would ask one favor."

"What?"

"Tell her the truth of what she is, will you?"

Cenrick frowned. "Who?"

"Dee. She deserves to know what she is." His mournful expression bespoke knowledge of yet another sin he'd committed. "I should have told her long ago, but I didn't want to lose her. As long as I was all she had, I knew she'd never desert me. Again, I am sorry, Dee."

Then, before she could react, he snapped his fingers and vanished.

Puzzled, Dee looked at Cenrick. "What did he mean?"

"I'm not exactly sure. But if anyone can tell us, the Oracle or the mage can. Let's go find them." He tugged on her hand.

She resisted. "First let's finish helping all these Fae. We can't rest until everyone has been restored." Then they would have their answer. Whether or not they liked it.

The faces blurred as they worked. Fae after Fae, male and female both, started awake as they were touched, looking at Dee and Cenrick with confusion and shock. Yet they were aware, were themselves once more, and Cenrick knew they would return to the palace and the city as soon as they were able.

Several hours later, the two of them staggered into the Oracle's cave, exhausted. A few minutes later, Mort and the Oracle followed, equally drained.

"They are all back to normal." The joy in Mort's voice made Dee smile.

Beside her, Cenrick exhaled. "Now we can rest."

"Do not think to rest so soon." The Oracle glided into the room, her white robes once again shimmering. "King Roark has need of his son. He has rested and is calling for you."

Immediately, Cenrick pushed himself up. "Send me."

Dee struggled to her feet and grabbed his arm. "I'll go with you."

He nodded, covering her hand with his.

"Leave the woman here." The Oracle's voice was solemn. "Let her rest. We can care for her. Go alone to your father. He has things he must discuss with you in private." The Oracle's glowing scarlet gaze met Dee's, warning her not to object.

Cenrick started to protest. But Dee, who saw something else in the Oracle's gaze, silenced him with a squeeze of her hand. "She's right. I'll be fine here. Hurry back." And pulling herself free, Dee stepped away from Cenrick. Immediately, the Oracle clapped her hands and Cenrick vanished.

"Thank you," the Oracle said. She drifted closer. "The time has come for Cenrick to take his rightful place in Rune. His father will name him heir, I believe."

"I believe this as well," Mort spoke up. Smiling,

the mage crossed to Dee's other side. "And the Oracle's prophecies are rarely wrong."

"Good." So tired she could barely think, all Dee wanted was a hot bath and a soft bed. And Cenrick, of course.

Then, she remembered Mick's words. *Tell her what she is.* She repeated them aloud to Mort. "Will you tell me?"

"Of course." Mort motioned her to sit. When she was comfortably settled on the hard stone ground, he swirled his robes around him and lowered himself beside her. "You are half-Fae, like Mick. You shared the same Fae mother. Each time she got pregnant, each time she learned she carried a half-human baby, she celebrated. For a time."

Joy and fear warred inside Dee. "You know who my mother is?" Could she meet this woman? Did she want to?

"Was," Mort corrected. "Your mother was a victim of her own appetites. Sometimes, when Fae go to live among humans, they are eager to experience every facet of human existence. Unfortunately for some, this includes drugs and/or alcohol. For others, it's an all-consuming addiction to sex. When those of our kind lose their way, we try to bring them back to Rune for cleansing. But they must want to go. Your mother refused."

"So she left me—and Mick—in an orphanage and forgot about us? Her own children?" Dee could scarcely credit such callousness.

"The drugs claimed her mind." Mort's tone was

gentle. "All she cared about was her next high, her next fix."

Watching him closely, Dee took a deep breath before she asked her next question. "Where is she now? You speak of her as though she's dead."

"She is. She was killed in your world by a horrible fire several years ago."

Dee's heart sank. "Oh." She shook her head. "My mother had no family? No one to retrieve her neglected children?"

"I believe she intended to come back for you. But she was killed before she could return."

"What about my father?"

"No one knows who he is. Just as no one knows who fathered Mick."

Dee looked at Mort in horror as she realized how long he'd known. "So I was left there, in the human world, alone? Is that what you people do to half-Fae, half-humans?" It was bad enough knowing her parents hadn't wanted her. To realize an entire race had abandoned her . . .

"But metal . . . ?"

"Your half-human blood protects you."

Mort's voice was soothing, but Dee would not be soothed. Agitated, she jumped to her feet. "I can't believe this!" Then, to her horror, she started to cry.

Exhaustion and shock were taking their toll on her, and she cried out great, gulping sobs. Dimly conscious of Mort and the Oracle watching, she wrapped her arms around her waist and turned away.

Everything she'd lived for had turned out to be a lie. She was no longer certain she believed in the fairness of the justice system she'd been sworn to uphold. She'd been set up and convicted, all without a trial. She no longer wanted any part of law enforcement.

In addition, she'd been betrayed by her best friend; no, *worse*—her own brother. Mick had known how deeply she'd longed for family, but he'd chosen to keep their relationship a secret. Though she knew she'd forgive Mick someday—he was her brother, after all—right now she felt too raw, too wounded, to even speak to him.

Saying good-bye to Cenrick would be the final straw. She didn't know that she could do it, as fragile and defenseless as she felt.

Though she'd never been a coward, this time she took the coward's way out. When her sorrow had subsided into soft gasps, she wiped at her eyes. "I'd like to go home," she said.

"Would you?" The Oracle's soft voice pierced Dee's fog of pain. "I can send you there."

Dee opened her eyes. "Yes. Back to my own apartment, in my own world."

"Of course." The Oracle looked sad. She held out her hand. "Are you ready?"

"Yes." Straightening, Dee stepped forward.

"Wait!" Mort moved between them, breaking the Oracle's hold on Dee's hand. "Take this." He handed Dee a stone. "If you need us or wish to return, you only need to hold it and think of me."

"I . . ." Dee swallowed. "Thank you. I'd like to go now."

The Oracle took her hand and sent her.

* * *

Back in her familiar apartment, Dee stumbled into the bathroom, turned the shower on hot and shed her clothes. Once she'd scrubbed herself clean, she dried off, wincing at her reddened skin. Then, with her heart aching as much as her body, she crawled beneath the covers of her still-rumpled bed, and slept.

The sound of the ringing phone woke her. Sitting up with a groan, she glanced at the alarm clock. Nearly noon. She'd been asleep for five hours.

"This is Chief Ferguson," a voice said on the other end of the line.

Her heart began to pound. Wide awake, she dragged her hand through her hair and cleared her throat. "Yes, sir?"

He wanted her to come in to the station. Internal Affairs had concluded its investigation. She'd been cleared of all wrongdoing. Both the prostitute and the store owner had recanted their allegations under questioning, and:

"I want to give you back your badge and your gun. Get you back to work."

She agreed to be there in an hour. Hanging up, she knew she'd be handing in her resignation. She'd always felt a bit of an outcast. Now she knew why.

Never had the drive to the police station seemed to take so long. Dee parked her car, fiddled with her purse, checked her appearance in the rearview mirror, and touched up her lipstick.

She hadn't been back since the last time she'd talked to Internal Affairs. Her coworkers, those whom she'd once counted as friends, had by and large turned their backs on her, as if by supporting her they could be tarred with the same brush. She wondered what they thought now that she'd been cleared of all wrongdoing. Then, as she lifted her chin and grasped the handle of the glass door to go in, realized she no longer cared. Those people—those other officers—weren't the reason she'd joined the police force. Nor would they be the reason she left.

As though he'd been watching from his office window, Chief Ferguson met her at the door. "Welcome back," he said. His voice boomed in the suddenly silent squad room. Where before when she'd visited, every officer and clerk found something urgent to do, this time they smiled and nodded. "Glad to have you back," the chief continued.

"Thanks." Dee met his gaze squarely. Oddly enough, though she'd longed for this day, she felt no vindication, no sense of pleasure. True, she'd been cleared of any wrongdoing. An investigation had even been started to learn who'd been trying to frame her, though now that Mick had chosen to remain in Rune, she knew they'd never find out.

Everyone in South Worth now knew she'd done nothing wrong. The newspaper had been given a statement, as had all the media, and the story would run on both the early and late news.

But Dee had discovered she no longer cared.

Mick hadn't tendered a resignation, choosing instead to simply disappear. Dee would do it differently. She carried a typed letter, neatly folded, inside her purse. Once this unfinished part of her former life had been closed, she could look to the future.

Cenrick. Rune. A new family? She briefly closed

her eyes, swallowing. The man she loved—not knowing how he felt about her was torture.

"Follow me." Smiling broadly, the chief led the way into his office, closing the door behind them. Dee waited until he'd taken his seat behind the desk; then she extracted her letter and handed it to him.

"I'm leaving," she said. "No regrets, no hard feelings. But I'm done."

"Dee," he protested, exactly as she'd known he would. "Don't let this incident discourage you. Stuff happens. Always has, always will. We're targets simply because we're cops—you more so, because you're a woman."

She'd thought her heart would pound, that her hands would tremble. Instead, she felt cool, calm, and very, very certain. "I'm doing the right thing. I no longer want to be here."

"It's because of your friend, isn't it?" He made no move to read her letter. "Mick will turn up. Every officer in the state is looking for him."

She simply nodded, knowing Mick would never be found. At least not here.

"Please. Read the letter," she said. With a disappointed frown, he did as she requested.

"You have vacation time coming to you?"

"Yes. I'd like to use that as my notice. I'd like to quit, effective today."

His bushy eyebrows rose. "So soon?"

"The sooner I can put all this behind me, the quicker I can move forward." *And . . . across the veil*?

"You were born to be a cop," he said. He was fishing now.

Dee slowly shook her head. "No. I became a cop for the wrong reasons, though I truly thought I was making a difference. I followed a friend into law enforcement. I didn't go because I had any calling, but because he did."

Ferguson nodded, his gaze thoughtful behind his wire-rimmed glasses. "What will you do?"

"I'm not sure." She shrugged. "Maybe I'll sell shoes."

He laughed at her joke. Her obsession with shoes was well known around the department.

The department. Dee shivered. Once, she'd thought of this as her family. Fellow officers, always there to get her back. She'd been wrong.

Returning to her apartment, she took one last look around at her possessions. Things, that's all they were. There was nothing here that she couldn't live without.

When she was ready, she took out the stone the mage had given her. All she had to do was hold it, he'd said. Hold it and think of him, and he'd come to take her back. Home.

Home? Even thinking of Rune in that context made her shiver with mingled longing and fear. It was time, time to find out where she belonged.

Drawing out the stone, she studied its smooth blue surface. The color felt soothing, the temperature cool, though it was warming in her hand.

She thought of Mort, pictured him appearing in her living room, ready to take her hand and lead her back to Rune. But nothing happened. She tried again.

Sparkles of light swirled on the edges of her vision.

Ahhh, *now* something was happening. The sparkles became blinding. Blinking, she shielded her eyes with her hand.

"Mort? Is that you?"

"No, it's me."

That achingly familiar voice. Cenrick. Dee's heart stuttered.

Once he'd materialized, he stood staring at her, his gaze dark, his expression tortured. Dee let her gaze roam unabashedly, taking in each beloved detail. His chocolate eyes, his raven hair. Cenrick. The other half of her soul.

"You called?" he said, grinning.

"I was expecting Mort," she said stiffly. "He told me if I called him, he would come."

"I had to see you," he said. "I'm sorry, I know I should let you resume your life, but I couldn't stay away."

"Why have you?" She'd expected him to come after her the moment she left, or as soon as he could. He hadn't. But she was glad she had the courage to ask the simple question, though she held herself utterly still, afraid she might shatter.

"I've been waiting for you to come and get me." Her voice caught, faltered.

"I had to help my father. Mort and I worked with him on regaining the memories he'd lost."

"He's all right?" She couldn't contain her happiness. "The way Natasha was talking, I feared he might be dying."

The heat in his gaze scorched her. "He disappeared again. Still in Texas, in Houston. We had to employ

302

ancient magics to learn where we might find him. I researched the spells and helped Mort work the magic." Satisfaction rang in his voice. "In this a scholar was needed, rather than a warrior."

"And you're both," she told him, tentative hope flaring into joy. He hadn't forgotten about her after all. "How is King Roark?"

"He's recovering. And"—he lifted his head, his expression full of pride—"he's announced I'm to be the next king. I've proven my right to lead."

Just like that, the faint flare of hope inside her extinguished. "Congratulations!" So what if her smile felt a bit wobbly? She couldn't let her love for him destroy his life. She guessed she'd better get used to once again being completely alone. After all, she'd had lots of practice.

"Will you come with me to Rune, where you belong?" he asked, shocking her.

Tentatively, she took a step toward him. "Why? Wouldn't it be easier on us both to say good-bye now?"

"Good-bye?" His dark brows rose. "Is that what you think I came here for?"

Biting her lip, she held his gaze. "Isn't it?"

In the space of a heartbeat, he closed the distance between them, covering her mouth with his. His searing kiss sent heat all through her body.

When they broke apart, he touched his nose to hers. "There, Dee Bishop. Do you still doubt the way I feel about you?"

Again hope, that traitorous longing, blossomed. "I—"

"Let me also *tell* you." Satisfaction and love rang in

his deep voice. "You are all I ever want and need, the woman who fills my nights with longing. You are the mate I want to stand beside me as my lover and my friend. I *love* you, Dee Bishop. You, and only you."

He kissed her again, and this time she kissed him back, pouring every bit of her love for him into the kiss. But then she remembered. Cenrick was to be king.

Immediately, she broke the embrace. "Wait! I can't think when we do that. What about the throne?"

The look he gave her was thoroughly male and supremely confident. "Do you have objections to becoming my queen?"

"But I'm—"

"Half Fae. A warrior to my scholar. And my soul mate."

For a moment she couldn't catch her breath.

"I love you," he said.

Dee raised her head, deciding finally to simply follow her heart. "If you're sure . . ."

"I've never been more certain of anything."

She took the plunge—wrapped her arms around him and gazed up into his eyes, letting him see the depths of emotion in hers. "I love you too, Cenrick of Rune. And I will joyfully become your queen."

"And return to your rightful place, where you belong?"

"Yes." Her smile was full of wonder, and love. "Home."

A look of elation crossed his features. Covering her mouth once more with his, he kissed her. "Now that

I've found you," he said, "know that I will never let you go."

At the fierce look of love in his gaze, tears spilled from her eyes, while the awful tightness in her chest eased. "Nor I you," she swore, sealing their bond. "You're mine."

"As you are mine." Pulling her to him, he held her tight, while her tears dampened his shirt and the beat of their hearts spoke of one rhythm, one soul, one love.

"Cry no more, beloved. We've found each other now. We'll never be apart again."

And when he slipped a crystal engagement ring on her finger, all clouds lifted. All the color had returned. The two soul-halves were united and every last scrap of missing magic had now returned to Rune.

KAREN WHIDDON
SOUL MAGIC

The ancient magic of Rune is fading, and legends speak of mortals and fae joining together to renew it. Thus to Thorncliff Keep the fae Alanna goes, to seek him: the mortal whom she left at the altar. Betrothed from childhood, she has always loved Darrick Tadhg. The knight's strong arms and mighty sword still cause her to shiver with desire. But a terrible wrong came between them, a terrible shame that she has no desire to reveal.

No, Darrick will not want Alanna, not now, with her secret, after his life has been darkened by tragedy and when his keep is besieged. He will not want to leave on the journey they must undertake. But Alanna will, for the sake of her life and the sake of her kingdom, and for the sake of their love, convince Darrick of the power of their joined souls—and of Fate, which never meant for them to be apart.

KAREN WHIDDON

LONE STAR

★ MAGIC ★

Broad shoulders and chiseled features set Prince Alrick of Rune apart from all but his twin brother. Both Fae princes are accomplished horsemen, swordsmen and seducers. So in the hope of becoming sole heir, Alrick accepts a quest to another time and another place, to save a Texan beauty whose recent widowing has made it well-nigh impossible to maintain her ranch. And now Carly Roberts is threatened by dark sorcery. Alrick will protect her, he swears, for the sake of his world. Fate brought them together. Fate and…

Lone Star Magic

PRINCE OF ICE

STOBIE PIEL

The power of the Arch Mage has grown strong enough to immobilize the defenders of Amrodel, woodland kingdom. Only one hope remains: a girl, the would-be sorceress Cahira. Upon her shoulders lies the fate of her people.

Cahira's task is to find the prophesied man of "pure light" and arm him with the Dragonfly Sword. She saw him once as a youngster, but Aren is one of her people's ancestral enemies. All Cahira loves lies in the balance, and she and her friends are being sent into the cold north to find a barbaric rogue. North to danger, north to salvation, north to find the...

Prince of Ice
